DOUG MCELWAIN

Edited by
JOHN F. CARR

Created by Jerry E. Pournelle & John F. Carr
War World: Andromeda Flight
A War World Novel

Pequod Press

Printed in the United States of America
First Printing 2021

V 10 9 8 7 6 5 4 3 2 1

ISBN: 978-0-937912-77-5

War World Volumes Edited and Created by John F. Carr and Jerry Pournelle

War World I: The Burning Eye
War World II: Death's Head Rebellion
War World III: Sauron Dominion
War World IV: Invasion!
CoDominium I: Revolt on War World

War World Novels

Blood Feuds
Blood Vengeance

New War World Volumes edited by John F. Carr

WAR WORLD: The Burning Eye (new 2nd edition)
WAR WORLD: Discovery
WAR WORLD: The CoDominium Takeover
WAR WORLD: Jihad!
WAR WORLD: The Patriotic Wars
War World: The Fall of the CoDominium

War World Novels

Falkenberg's Regiment
The Battle of Sauron
The Lidless Eye
Cyborg Revolt
Andromeda Flight

DEDICATION

To Jerry Pournelle
Who created such an interesting universe to explore.

And

John F. Carr
Who asked me to write stories in it.

ACKNOWLEDGEMENTS

I want to thank David Sooby, Darren J. Rout and Andrew E. Love, Jr. for their feedback, ideas, help and editing of the Alderson Drive essay, it is a much better work because of their efforts; Mark E. Moeser for his continuity feedback, the book is better because of his time and effort; Larry King for his feedback on *Long Shot* and his Science Fiction Timeline Site (http://www.chronology.org/) which I have used many times to reference events in my War World stories; John F. Carr for giving me the opportunity to write these stories and encouragement to keep extending and improving on them; Victoria Alexander for her character suggestions; Andy Shipley for his encouragement to write and the belief I could actually learn to do so; and finally to my significant other Joan Kayser, for her support and encouragement throughout the process.

Table of Contents

Chronology

1969	Neil Armstrong sets foot on Earth's moon.
2004	Alderson Drive perfected at Cal Tech.
2020	First Interstellar Colonies founded. Great Exodus period of colonization begins.
2032	Captain Jed Byers of the CDSS *Ranger* discovers a planetary-sized moon of a gas giant and names it Haven.
2038	Sauron is discovered by Avery Landyn, a survey pilot for 3M; the world is rich in radioactive and heavy metals.
2042	3M sells Sauron to wealthy English Separatists from Quebec and former South African expatriates living in Canada and Australia.
2092	Langston Field discovered on Sparta by Jonathon Langston.
2098	Saurons evict the CoDominium Viceroy and declare their independence. They begin to build their own space navy.
2103	Great Patriotic Wars. End of the CoDominium. Exodus of the Fleet.
2110	Coronation of Lysander I of Sparta. Fleet swears loyalty to the Spartan Throne. Marriage of dynasties produces union between Sparta and St. Ekaterina.
2111	Formation Wars begin.
2250	Leonidas I proclaims Empire of Man.
2250-2600	Empire of Man enforces interstellar peace.

2432 First Cyborgs created on Sauron. These "prefect soldiers," will later become known as "Sauron Supermen" or "death-heads."

2567 Maxroy's Purchase plants a colony on New Utah.

2594 Emperor David II dies with no heir. The Imperial Senate acts quickly to crown Alexander IV, a collateral descendant of David II, as Emperor. The ascension is controversial and begins a gradually escalation of struggles and violent revolts. These "succession wars" are the prelude to the Secession Wars.

2598 In the Imperial Parliament, a "Coalition of Succession" forms and begin to demand the right to withdraw from the Empire. This coalition is primarily led by Sauron. A series of skirmishes involving secessionist planets takes place, but the Empire does not suspect the extent of the threat.

2600 Imperial Navy Initial Assessment Report filed on New Utah.

2603 Growth of Sauron supermen. St. Ekaterina attacked and nearly destroyed by the Saurons. Secession Wars begin.

2622 Alexander IV dies unexpectedly. Alexander's eldest son is crowned Lysander V.

2623 The Empire withdraws from frontier worlds to concentrate Fleet resources. The Seventy-seventh Imperial Marine Division is withdrawn from Haven along with all Imperial officials.

2640 Sauron supermen thought to be destroyed along with their home planet. Betelgeuse detonates in a massive supernova explosion. Effective end of the Empire of Man (later known as the First Empire of Man).

Long Shot

ONE

The war with Sauron and the Coalition of Secession is going badly; worse than is publicly known. We continue to take heavy losses. The Realm still has formidable resources but replacement of warships and crews is not keeping up. Last year we had to retreat from the frontier worlds to focus on our Fleet resources. The future is more uncertain than ever. It is time to make contingency plans.

— *Personal Journal of Emperor Lysander V*

2624 A.D., Sparta

CRACK!

The sound of a single rifle shot pierced the crisp mountain air. Three hundred meters away a big bull elk dropped to the ground with a bullet hole through its heart.

"Top drawer, Majesty."

The Emperor rose from his kneeling position. He smiled as he engaged the safety on his vintage New Aberdeen hunting rifle, then pointed it downward toward the ground. The Emperor looked at his guest and responded, "Thank you, Dickie."

His Most Royal and Imperial Highness and Majesty, Lysander V, was elk hunting with His Excellency Sir Mikailov Fuller, Minister of War and His Excellency Sir Richard Trevor, Minister of Science. The Royal Game Preserve was located in a heavily forested area of the Phokian Mountains. Although the Royal Guard was deployed near the Emperor, as ordered they were discreetly out of earshot. It was not a security breach. As a standard precaution both guests only possessed weapons provided to them by the Emperor's Guard. The hunting rifles they held contained electronic governors. That is, the rifles could not fire in the direction of the Emperor or his Guard. As the Emperor's rifle could only be fired by him, it would not respond to anyone else. These precautions ensured that there would be more than enough time for the Guard to react if the unthinkable was attempted.

It was fall on the Serpentine Continent and the elk were in rut. The bulls' bugling sounds were eerie; a deep roar escalating to a high whistle ending with a grunt. The sound cut through the thick forest but the trees masked the direction from whence the sound came. It wasn't a problem for the hunting party. Trackers were out following the animals.

The terrain was difficult for the Emperor's small party but not impossible. It was a clear and cold day. The smell of pine lay heavy in the air. Aspen groves dotted the hillsides, turning them from a deep green color into one of mottled gold. The Emperor and Sir Mikailov each bagged two six-point bulls. Sir Richard bagged nothing. He claimed the exertion caused his aim to be off but in reality, hunting wasn't something he was good at. Back at the Royal Hunting Lodge they had a light dinner, only six courses, though the meat was from the elks the Emperor had shot. A high honor. His guests knew the Emperor was courting them, that he wanted something from them. They just didn't know what.

The Royal Hunting Lodge, known formally as the Lermontov Okhota Domik, had been built just after the fall of the CoDominium over five hundred years before. It was intended to be a remembrance of Earth. The preserve itself was created to be a genetic repository for a part of Earth called the Rocky Mountains.

Earth still hadn't fully recovered from the Great Patriotic War and it would be hundreds or even thousands of years before it did. But someday, some of the Earth-stock plants and animals in this preserve would be used in the remediation process for that blasted world. A few people on Earth had survived that epic spasm of thermonuclear insanity. But none thrived. Death still stalked the land in many forms: the climate was chaotic, man-made plagues were not completely eradicated and radiation poisoned much of the world. A few years before his death, Emperor Alexander IV had hit upon the idea of using Earth as a penal colony with the prisoners preparing that world for remediation. How ironic for Earth to become an Imperial prison planet. The ancestors of CoDominium criminals and political undesirables were sent back to the planet of their forbearers for the same reason their ancestors had been sent to the stars. Needless to say, most didn't survive long.

The Royal Hunting Lodge was built of native stone and pine, at least the above-ground portion of it was. Like an iceberg ninety percent of the lodge was underground. The domik was protected by a powerful Langston Field that could be raised instantly. Further out, surrounding the lodge, laser and missile batteries protected against aircraft and missile attack. Beyond the batteries, troops were stationed with heavy weapons. Protecting the ruler of the Empire of Man required a defense in depth.

After dinner, the three men retired to the Emperor's wood-paneled den. The paneling came from half a dozen different worlds. The book-shelves lining the walls contained real books, not the Tri-V holographic replicas most nobles had in their dens. Many of the books were more than six hundred years old. The wood floor was covered by a large, hand-knotted silk rug from Levant.

The three settled into comfortable leather chairs in front of a roaring fire. The servants poured each man a glass of hundred-year-old sherry from Thurstone. Sherry that was now impossible to obtain since the Empire had blasted the planet back to the stone age in order to liberate it from the Saurons. Then the servants gave each man a cigar made of Corojo tobacco from Tanith. Tobacco that had been specially processed to remove any trace of radioactive contamination. Subtle reminders to the

Emperor's guests of the battles fought and the destruction wrought thus far in the war.

When they were done with their duties the staff quietly retreated, leaving the three men alone to talk. Once the door to the den was closed, the Emperor turned to his two guests. "I imagine you both are wondering why I wanted to meet with you here. The confidentially of this discussion is of the utmost importance to me. This lodge ensures we have privacy. I do not want the subjects of this meeting to leave this room. Do you both understand?"

Both men looked at each other and then answered in the affirmative.

The Emperor continued, "I have been thinking about the war against the Coalition of Secession. You know as well as I do that it is not going well." Then coming more to the point, he added, "We need to set up some hidden colonies far from the Coalition. Redoubts if you will where we can rebuild the Empire if necessary."

Sir Richard was surprised, "Majesty! Surely the war is not that far lost."

Sir Mikailov's response was different, "What precisely are you thinking, Majesty?"

"Have you heard of the Far Frontiers Expeditions?"

"No, Majesty," each replied.

"In the middle of the last century George IV ordered a renewal of outward exploration and conceived the Far Frontiers expeditions. Twelve specially built exploratory vessels were sent out from the marches of the Empire in six different galactic directions; north, south, coreward, rimward, spinward and antispinward. Some of the ships made it a thousand light-years from the borders before returning.

"While the expeditions were off exploring, George died in a hunting accident. Killed by several Weem's beasts while big trophy hunting on Tanith. Very odd. Weem's beasts are usually solitary creatures. These were working together but an investigation found no foul play. His Privy Council had never been keen on the Far Frontiers' project. They classified the expeditions and all of their discoveries an Imperial High Secret. Here are the encryption keys to the Library subsection pertaining to it," he said holding up two datacubes.

"You both can review the expeditions' discoveries in your rooms tonight. I'll need these keys returned tomorrow before we return to the palace." Then he handed each man a datacube.

"Some of their discoveries are truly remarkable. One of them in particular has fascinated me since I first learned of it. Fourteen hundred light-years from here are three habitable planets in two systems, seven light-years and one Jump apart. What makes this so interesting is that the three planets have plants and animals that are biologically related."

"Why…Why, that's unheard of, Majesty."

"Yes, Dickie. And it gets more interesting. Astronomical studies determined the two star systems had never come within five light-years of each other. The expedition performed a genetic drift analysis and determined that the last common ancestors of the specimens they collected were two million years ago. They searched nearby star systems but found no habitable worlds with any related life. There was a promising system nine light-years away but they couldn't find any tramline connections to it and couldn't investigate further.

"The implication is that two million years ago, there was an alien civilization that had technology at least as advanced as we had during the CoDominium era. That is, they were able to cross interstellar distances and had some terraforming technologies. With these capabilities they should have been able to colonize the whole galaxy by now. What happened to the aliens is not known. The expedition speculated that the discovery of the Langston Field was such an unlikely event; it meant the aliens didn't have it. And without the Field they probably destroyed themselves. But that's not important now. The point is we've already explored far beyond the Empire's boundaries and found habitable worlds we can colonize. We can follow without first having to send scoutships to find suitable worlds and drawing attention to what we are doing."

Sir Mikailov didn't care about aliens two million years dead. He cared about the war he was fighting, so he brought the discussion back to the present. "And the ships and resources needed to build these hidden colonies, Majesty?"

"We will need to build the ships of course. And provision them. I think we need to build a new shipyard. This project needs to have the highest level of secrecy. An asteroid belt based yard seems to me to provide more operational security than a planetary based one. We also need a backwater system located far from Sauron. Maybe the Eden System. Arrarat is located there. An agrarian world not much visited these days. The system has got an asteroid belt that hasn't been mined since the CoDominium period."

"Sire, how many of these redoubts do you plan to build?" Sir Mikailov inquired.

"Three should give us enough insurance to mitigate the possibility that we may lose this war."

"Majesty, three redoubts mean three fleets. That will take considerable resources that are badly needed for the war effort."

The tone of the Emperor's voice turned cold and hard as steel, "I consider this part of the war effort, Minister. A critical part." Then after a momentary pause he added more formally, "I have decided. Do I have your support, Sir Mikailov?"

The Minister of War, understanding the significance of his response, replied, "Yes, Majesty. Of course."

"Very well. We need to put a small working group together to make this happen. Who do you gentlemen recommend we put in charge?"

"Highness, if I may," Sir Mikailov said.

"Yes."

"What of the rest of the Privy Council, Majesty? Won't they have concerns?"

"Leave them to me. Now, back to the question, who should lead this project?"

"Majesty, hasn't the Blaine family been a loyal and staunch supporter of the Empire from the very beginning?"

"Are you suggesting Admiral Blaine?"

"Yes, Highness. The Marquis' youngest son. He is one of the best we have. I do believe it will impact the prosecution of the war but, since this is as important as you say, he is the man you want."

TWO

2625 A.D., Sigismund

Lysander hated these morale-boosting reviews. Not so much because they were about esoteric science, though occasionally those were tedious, but because the speaking style of the presenters was so boring. Even so, at times he would find something worthwhile in them.

The Emperor also hated to be away from Sparta. Even though he was three short Jumps from the Capital, it was a time of war. The logistics needed for him to maintain communications with his forces had to be planned with extreme care. But, it was important for him to see firsthand what the brightest technical minds in the Empire came up with to help the war effort. The Emperor knew they couldn't beat the Saurons one-on-one, so they had to beat them some other way. Technical breakthroughs were high on the Emperor's list to do just that. By visiting, he was trying to motivate the Academicians, to show them how important they were.

At least yesterday there was one presentation that offered a game changing weapon. If it could be developed and mass produced. The meson bomb. Something that could pierce a Langston Field and destroy the ship within. But that other bomb, the quark fusion weapon, while theoretically interesting is a step farther out from practicality. At least for now.

This morning's presentation, by that Cosmologist, what was his name? Describing his work about the effect of the Alderson force on the evolution of the universe. He replayed the highlights of the talk in his mind. *Einstein's equations say all matter, energy and stress tensors … whatever those are … have gravity so the Alderson force should have it too. Though it is very, very small. Just as the Alderson force is transmitted across space instantaneously the gravity created by it should be too. That affects the evolution of our cosmos. Such as the rate of its expansion. How will this research help the war effort? Don't these academicians understand what's at stake here?*

He was brought back from his inattentiveness by his Minister of Science. "Majesty?" He waited a moment before addressing the Emperor again. "Majesty? Did you just hear what Senior Academician Hardy said?"

"No, I was thinking about yesterday's presentations."

"Yes, of course, Majesty." Then he addressed the speaker. "Senior Academician Hardy."

"Yes, Minister?"

The Minister, being politically astute, decided to take the blame for having the Senior Academician start his presentation over. It was never good to embarrass the Emperor. "Would you start over, please; I seem to have missed what you were saying."

"Yes, of course, Minister." The astrophysicist paused for a moment to collect his thoughts and then started again. "Majesty, Minister, colleagues and honored guests. We have been deep mining the data collected by the Imperial Alderson force observatories. We have discovered a pattern associated with the red supergiant star Betelgeuse.

"Before I explain the ramifications of the pattern we found, I want to give you some history on Betelgeuse. We now know it started life as a double star system. By about one hundred thousand years ago, Betelgeuse finished expanding into its red supergiant stage. During that expansion, it engulfed its companion. We have determined that the companion was at least the size of Sol. That merger started a chain of events which are only now culminating.

"We believe the pattern we found means that, in fifteen years, Betelgeuse will explode in a supernova. We have never observed such a powerful stellar explosion this close before. We expect it to produce four times ten to the fifteenth as much energy as Sol does each second." He paused again. The astrophysicist looked at his audience and saw many blank looks. "That is an immense amount of energy. And what is most exciting is that it will allow us to study the Alderson force at intensities we've never seen before. The science we can obtain will be priceless. But only if we prepare now."

The Emperor interrupted, "Have you considered what that will do to all of our Alderson tramlines? Won't it scramble all the Alderson paths throughout the galaxy for some period of time? And since the Alderson force propagates instantaneously, won't it affect all of interstellar travel and trade?"

The astrophysicist looked confused for an instant, then said, "I'm sorry, Majesty, we weren't focused on that. But we do believe that the Alderson flux densities will be large enough to create temporary tramlines between the Andromeda galaxy and several points in the Empire of Man. That is, it might be possible for a ship to make a Random Jump there. Think of that, Majesty. A two and a half million light-year Jump. But, of course, the ship could never return."

"*Bah, Academicians,* the Emperor thought. *Doesn't he understand that this could hurt the Empire and the war effort? Our Naval forces need to be forewarned and prepare for this event.* Then the Emperor had an epiphany. *I wonder if we can use this to our advantage. Maybe the Navy and the Empire will just have to endure the consequences for the greater good.*

"How many points, Senior Academician?"

Misreading the Emperor's reaction, he responded enthusiastically, "Not so much points as small regions. Specifically, three reachable ones,

Majesty. All far from their suns. One in the outer regions of the Byers' System beyond the fifth planet; the gas giant named Hel. Two others in regions that are about the same distance from their stars." He then showed a backup visual showing the regions overlaid on Imperial space. Two of the temporary Jump regions were in systems without any habitable worlds.

"You said we could send a ship and not ships, why is that?"

"We would only want to send one ship, otherwise the ships would materialize far away from each other."

"Where would a ship materialize?"

"We have no way of knowing that, Your Majesty. Andromeda is bigger than the Milky Way, so somewhere across its two hundred thousand light-year diameter. Then the Academician got a faraway look in his eyes and mumbled, "Imagine that. Sire."

"And how long does the Alderson force production phase of the supernova last?"

The Academician refocused on his audience. "About a minute and a half, Majesty."

"That short? I thought supernovas outshined all the stars in a galaxy for months."

"They do, Majesty. But that energy comes from the radioactive decay of isotopes created during that first minute and a half. That radioactivity does not produce any Alderson force. In fact, after the initial explosion, the nuclear decay processes absorb the Alderson force. Remember, only fusion reactions produce the Alderson force, not fission or decay."

Minister Fuller winced at Hardy's lecturing tone but the Emperor didn't seem to notice. He seemed to be engrossed in learning more.

"Next questions. I thought Random Jumps were dangerous? That they destroy the spaceship?"

"Your Highness, experience suggests that a ship surviving a Random Jump in spaceworthy condition is twelve percent. It is also estimated that the ship would have less than a point zero zero four percent chance of surviving in a condition to Jump again. But that is for a ship that is not designed for a Random Jump. We think that new structural reinforcements can improve the first number considerably. In fact, some of our simulations suggest a three times improvement in survivability. And by adding a spare Alderson engine room to a ship, we may be able to solve the second problem too."

Emperor Lysander was thinking about the ramifications of this new information. He knew that the redoubts in the Milky Way were still at risk, if the Saurons won the war. It would only be a matter of time before they expanded their dominium and came in contact with them. And that would result in another war. One the Empire might not win. *If this Academician is correct, the Saurons won't be able to follow us to Andromeda. Even if the Saurons somehow made a Random Jump there they would, in all likelihood, materialize far from the Imperial redoubts.*

The Emperor turned to his Minister of Science, lowered his voice and said, "We need to talk about this in private. This information, his presentation and his research are now classified an Imperial High Secret. Everyone in this room is to sign the Oath of the Privy Council. Take care of it."

Not comprehending the reason but only the importance of the matter to the Emperor, his minister simply replied, "I will see to it, Majesty."

2632 A.D., Imperial Navy Yard, Eden System

Fleet Admiral George Sergei Carlton Blaine was still getting used to his new rank. He smiled to himself. The Emperor was very pleased with the progress on the redoubt program. At least, based on his last status report.

"How is the latest project status report for the Emperor coming?"

"Good, Admiral Blaine. We are on schedule to send it to him. But I wish we didn't have to do them so often. This time, I would like to prepare the report differently. I would like to prepare a Tri-V movie with narrative. After all, if a picture is worth a thousand words, a movie is worth what, a million? This should cut down on our admin workload."

"Show me what you've got so far."

"Yes, sir. Watch."

The lights dimmed and an image formed in the middle of the room in the Tri-V tank. It was the Navy shipyard in Eden System's asteroid belt. Several space-based industrial facilities had been constructed in orbit around an asteroid similar to the one known as 16 Psyche in Sol System. The two-hundred-kilometer-wide asteroid was made out of iron, nickel and other metals. Astrogeologists thought it was the core of a long-lost planet. The remnants of a Mars-sized world that had been battered and broken soon after the formation of the Eden System. As the scene zoomed in, three dots in orbit around the asteroid became spheres. All three had zero-gee scaffolding around them. The scale was difficult to make out until only one sphere dominated the Tri-V. Zooming in closer, tiny dots could be seen moving across the sphere, like ants on a huge beach ball. Further increasing the magnification showed that the dots were construction pods covered with remote manipulators called waldos. The waldos were sticking out at all angles from the pod. The pods reminded the Admiral of his antique Swiss Army Knife. One from Earth during the CoDominium era, albeit a big one with all the tools opened.

The scene showed mankind's largest and most complex spaceship being built. It was designed to handle every situation imaginable. If the Andromeda Jump landed it far from any star system or in one without any

Alderson points, it could travel through normal space for up to twenty light-years before re-provisioning. Because this was a one-way mission, triple redundancy and self-repair had been designed into the ship from the beginning.

The Emperor's decision to change the destination for the redoubts had caused a radical redesign of the colonial fleets. Calculations suggested that the Betelgeuse supernova would cause a fleet of individual spaceships to materialize in different star systems all across the Andromeda galaxy, dooming the original plan. What had been many smaller spacecraft had to be combined into just three very large ships. A two-year delay redesigning everything into three spaceships was required. That it was done in two years was short of miraculous. But wars drive innovation more quickly than normal.

At this magnification, the great ring around the middle of the sphere could be easily seen. When the ship wasn't under acceleration, the ring would be rotated to provide artificial gravity for those on board. As the image swung around the great ship, three large circles could be seen on the upper hemisphere of the sphere. These were openings to the hanger decks. Each hanger deck was large enough to hold a frigate, two scoutships, two longboats, an asteroid mining ship, two refueling scoopships and four landing shuttles. The hanger deck ports were open to space. Construction pods, small structures and materiel were being moved continuously in and out. At the far end of the sphere, away from the hanger decks, were three large fusion engines. They would normally exhaust into the Langston Field to provide thrust. However, if all three Field generators failed, they could be used directly for that purpose, albeit at a lower efficiency.

The narrative began. "The complex keel structures of all three ships have been laid down using large-scale additive manufacturing fabricators. Ninety percent of the outer hull plates have been attached to the keels. The keels and hulls are made of the strongest material known: a single crystal titanium alloy. The fusion drives have been installed and connected to the keels. The engines are currently undergoing stress testing. Hydrogen fuel bunker installation is complete. The interior outfitting is scheduled to begin within the month. This is where we expect delays might occur.

The complexity of the installation, integration and testing will challenge our engineering skills. We are currently ahead of schedule by six months. However, we are not proposing any changes to the project schedule as we expect unanticipated problems to eat into this additional reserve.

"Ten thousand frozen sleep tanks, the gene banks and the incubators are being fabricated and will be installed within the next two years. Frozen sperm and eggs for additional humans as well as animals for the incubation tanks, will be loaded on board just prior to departure. The gene banks will include thousands of different plant, fungi and bacteria species. Based on the Empire's experience terraforming New Scotland and New Ireland, enough variety to terraform any suitable lifeless world.

"The largest Langston Field generators ever built are currently being installed on their mountings. As with every spaceship, the mountings are tied directly into the keel. Three separate Alderson Drives, one primary and two backups, will begin installation in eleven months. Weapon systems' mountings have been installed and they too are tied directly into the keel. As with the biological cargo, the weapons magazines will be loaded just prior to departure. The life support, food synthesizer and micro-fabricator subsystems are currently being constructed in the orbital manufacturing plants."

The narrative continued for another thirty minutes, drilling down into more and more detail; deliverables, critical path, risks and other project management metrics.

"Well, what do you think, Admiral?"

"It's a good idea. It should cut down on our admin workload. But until the Emperor approves this new format, prepare the regular report too."

THREE

2635 A.D., Sparta

The Supreme Pontiff of the Ecumenical Catholic Church, Pope John Paul VI, traveled from his residence in New Rome to the Imperial Palace in Old Sparta City to speak personally with the Emperor, Lysander V. The Church, which had been formed six hundred years before with the reintegration of the five major Christian groups, was the official religion of the Empire of Man. All people were free to practice any religion they chose or none at all, but only the Ecumenical Catholic Church was supported by the government, and they had significant political clout.

"Majesty, I would like to discuss with you the representation of the Church on the Andromeda expeditions."

The Emperor was taken back. He unconsciously looked around the room to see who else was there. "Not here, Your Holiness.

While my working office is swept regularly, I want to have this discussion in an even more secure location. Come with me."

The Emperor led the Pope to the far wall of his working office, to a side door which when opened displayed an elevator. The Emperor stepped inside and indicated to the Pope to follow him. Two of the Emperor's guards stepped into the elevator with them. The doors closed and the Pope felt his stomach drop. Then the feeling lessened and the feeling of sideways acceleration built up. Finally, that reversed and there was another period of dropping downward until the box they were in slowed and the doors opened.

"That was quite a ride, Majesty," the Pope said.

"E-ticket, Your Holiness. E-ticket."

The Pope looked at him quizzically.

"Not important, Your Holiness. An ancient saying."

The Emperor led the Pope down a short corridor until they came to a vault door. The Emperor placed his palm on a sensor pad and looked into an eye-scanner. Then he punched a code into a shielded pad. The door slid open. The Emperor ordered his guards to wait outside. While the guards were uncomfortable leaving their Sovereign alone, the Emperor had done it before. The guards knew he had other ways to protect himself, if necessary.

The door closed. In a stern voice, the Emperor addressed the Pope. "Your Holiness, do not ever mention the Andromeda project outside this room ever again. Do I make myself clear?"

The Pope flinched at the Emperor's tone. He was not used to being talked to in that manner by anyone. "Majesty, my apologies. I thought we were in a secure room. I will not make that mistake again."

"Very well, Your Holiness. What did you want to discuss?"

"This war with Sauron is about more than just the creation of a race of supermen and the subjugation of the rest of mankind. It is about the spiritual well-being of the human race too. The soul of the human race is at stake in this war, if you will.

"The Church does not challenge the doctrine of evolution. It is God's way. God has given man dominion over the plants and animals on all the worlds we inhabit. Therefore, He has granted us the right to apply genemod technology to them, if we so choose. We do not have the right to take the place of God in that process for people. The Saurons use their genemod technology to create humans who could never have existed before. That is blasphemy."

The Emperor had always disliked how wordy the Pope was. "Yes, Your Holiness. Wars rarely have only a single cause. What you point out has always been one of the fault lines that caused this war. Again, I would like to know what you want?"

"The Saurons are Godless. We are the warriors of light. To that end I want you to replace one of the Cardinals on the expedition. I want a replacement who has more ... fundamentalist views in these matters."

The Emperor was surprised by the Pope's rationale for his request. It was a non-sequitur transition from broad religious orthodoxy to a personnel decision, but he just said, "Who, Your Holiness?"

"I want to replace Cardinal Gregory with Cardinal Peterson."

The Emperor was not surprised. "I have heard that Cardinal Peterson is resisting some of the changes you want to make to Church doctrine. Does that have anything to do with this?"

"No, of course not, Majesty."

The Emperor didn't believe him but he didn't see this as something important enough to argue over. *Politics are everywhere. At least, he will be in my debt for this.* "Very well, Your Holiness. I approve the substitution."

2639 A.D., INSS Cassiopeia's Daughter, Beyond the orbit of Hel, Byers' System

"Admiral Blaine, we could use samples of the Earth-stock plants and animals from Haven. That planet is one of most extreme environments ever colonized by man. The plants and animals did start out as genemods but over the last six hundred years there has been natural selection."

"Just a minute, Academician Ivanov. We are docking with that small comet to begin processing it for fuel," The Admiral said, pointing to the Tri-V tank in front of him. "I want to see how the Captain handles the maneuver."

A few minutes later, the Admiral activated one of the comm systems, "Nice work, Captain Fainchurch." Then he turned to his visitor. "Okay, Academician Ivanov. What do you want? I agreed to hear your request again because you are our best biologist. At least currently awake. But we have orders to remain here at the predicted Jump point until Betelgeuse explodes. We were not given orders to travel to a habitable planet, even one that is relatively close."

"The earliest estimate for the Betelgeuse supernova is not for two more years. And that estimate has a low probability of happening. The astrophysicists tell me it's more likely to be five years. We can load one of our shuttles into a frigate. The frigate can reach Haven and the shuttle can land and retrieve data samples of their Earth-stock life to add to our gene banks. All within the two-year timeframe. The models I used indicate a ten percent increase in our chances for success if we acquire more samples of Haven's Earth-stock plants and animals."

"I agree that is very significant, but we've also been ordered not to reveal our presence to the locals, Academician."

"We won't, Admiral. We'll land in the backcountry in an area that is minimally inhabited."

"Explain again to me, why you want to do this? From the beginning."

"We're Jumping to another galaxy. Once there we have no recourse. None. No outside help. The Imperial astronomical observatories haven't detected much chlorophyll in the Andromeda light spectra but they have detected quite a lot of selenium. The xenobiologists are convinced that selenium-based plant life is the predominant basis for the food chain there. We can't use that. That means we will need to terraform our new homes. This excursion will give us a broader range of usable Earth life. There was very little Haven life in the Imperial gene banks. Haven's Earth-stock plants and animals may make the difference between life and death for us. As I said, the models give us a ten percent increase in our chances of being able to plant a successful colony." *Come on Admiral. This is our lives we're talking about.*

The Admiral paused and thought for a few minutes. "Very well. Let's look into it more. Call up a visual of the planet in the Tri-V tank. Show inhabited regions in red."

"Done, sir. The largest landmass is called the Western Continent. It contains the Shangri-La Valley."

"I don't think you should land there. We need somewhere more remote. Somewhere without as much industry. What's this island here? In the middle of this Occidental Ocean," he said pointing to a small dot. It looks like it's lightly inhabited."

Referring to the Library entry that popped up with the map Ivanov said, "It's called Cracovia. It's isolated from the rest of Haven. A large island about one million square kilometers in area. About the size of the island of New Alexandra on Sparta. According to our branch of the Imperial Library, it has a broad range of ecosystems: mountains, plains, valleys, lakes, rivers, forests, pastureland and cropland. All the different ecological niches that would be beneficial to sample. And, as you pointed out, there aren't many people there."

"Cities?"

"Nowy Kraków is the largest city and its capital. A few other cities have been built but they are spread out. There are a few ports, too. At least that was the way it was back in 2023 when the last entry to the library was made."

"That was when the 77th Division of the Imperial Marines was pulled out. Wasn't it?"

"Yes, sir. Fifteen years ago," he replied then continued on with his original summary, "Nowy Kraków has a spaceport. Lightly used as of that time."

"What species do you want samples from, Academician?"

"Based on references in their literature, here is the list of what I hope to find, Admiral."

The list was long. Food plants as well as industrial crops such as cotton and hemp came first. Next trees such as willow, oak and redwood were listed. This was followed by food animals such as sheep, goats, chickens and pigs. A footnote indicated the need to sample the microbiomes for each individual plant or animal, too.

"That's a lot of work, Academician. Can such a small team do that in such a short amount of time?"

"Yes, Admiral. Our automated sequencers will allow us to do that with just plant and animal samples. The sequencers are a variation of our food synthesizer. After all, the food synthesizer needs to be able to identify the molecules fed to them before they can convert them into something we can eat. We can use the standard synthesizer installed in the shuttle. We just need to add the backend data processing to make meta-biological sense out of its data. This is well established technology, Admiral."

"What about the diversity within each species?"

The Academician was surprised at the insightfulness of the question. He had thought of the Admiral as a muggle. "That's the limitation to this approach, Admiral. We will be trying to obtain five different samples for each species but we will still be relying on computer models to extrapolate it from those."

"You've seemed to have done your homework, Academician. Magnify Cracovia on the Tri-V." As he said that, the view of the planet zoomed inward. Pointing to the display, the Admiral said, "You need to stay well north of Nowy Kraków, the spaceport and this mountain called Góra Rog. Looks like a volcano." Checking the library window, he continued, "Yes, it is a stratovolcano. Anyway, there seems to be farmland in Cracovia and not too many people. The geography there should give you a wide selection of Earth-stock adapted plants and animals while staying away from the population centers. Do you concur?"

"Yes, Admiral. Then I have your permission?"

"You do with some caveats. Before the shuttle lands, you will recon from orbit to confirm the information we just discussed. You and your team are to learn the local language on your way to Haven." The Admiral paused for a moment looking at the side of the Tri-V. "It seems to be called Polski. Let me be clear: You and your team will make no mention of our mission to anyone you meet. There is a refueling station on Cat's Eye's third moon. It is comprised of fuel bladders in orbit connected by a tether to a deuterium-cracking plant on the surface. They have an active radar array; therefore, you will not go near Ayesha for any reason. Lastly, if you run into trouble, there will be no rescue. We will not send another ship to bail you out. Do you understand these orders? Will you obey them?"

"Yes, sir. I understand and will obey your orders."

FOUR

2640 A.D., Haven

Ivanov was the first to regain consciousness. He was groggy. They had crashed in what, an open field? There were strange trees in front of him. Reddish trees. Recognition hit him. A few more feet and they would have hit that alien forest and would have died. He heard the pilot next to him moan. Smoke began to fill the small cockpit. *I've got to get out of here.* Ivanov found the emergency release and the cockpit glass popped away from the flyer. He reached over and triggered the release on Marine First Lieutenant Conrad's restraining belts. More smoke was starting to swirl around him. Ivanov had had a shot of oxy-nanites just before the mission. Enough to last two months before his body flushed them out, but he didn't know how recent Conrad's shot had been. He grabbed a breathing mask and put it on Conrad as a precaution. Then Ivanov climbed out of the cockpit, turned around, and reached back in for the pilot. In the relatively weak gee field of Haven, he had no trouble lifting the Lieutenant out of the flyer. He slung him over his shoulder and, moved a good distance away from the burning wreckage. Just as he was laying the pilot on the ground, the flyer exploded.

What the…? Then he remembered. The flyer had an automatic self-destruct mechanism to prevent anyone from gaining its secrets. *Damn.*

Conrad opened his eyes. "Who were those guys?"

"You're asking me?"

"Those two fighters came out of nowhere and just blasted us out of the sky. No warning at all."

"What were you able to grab before you had to get away from the flyer?"

"Besides your breathing mask, only what we are wearing. At least that includes our laser handguns in our holsters. But that's it. No emergency kits. Nothing else. Well, nothing but a couple of collection kits for me. We should make a fire and wait for rescue. Did you get an emergency message off?"

"No time. I don't think it would've mattered anyway. With all the radio interference that Cat's Eye is putting out today, I doubt it would have been heard. No, we're on our own. First things first, no fire. And we need to get away from here. Those fighters may come back for us."

Conrad took off his breathing mask. "Thanks for putting this on me but I don't need it. I had my shot last week. We'll keep it, though. We may need it yet. I think I remember seeing a building just before we crashed. Over there beyond that low ridge," he said pointing to the other end of the field. "It looked just like the landscape until we were right on top of it."

"Camouflaged?"

"I don't know."

"Okay, let's head that way but we need some cover. Keep to the edge of the forest."

* * *

Franciszka Soltyk was stirring the big pot on her electric stove. Everything went in the pot to make a kind of *bigos*, what non-Cracovians would call a stew. Leftovers, the marrow from bones, anything edible. Nothing was wasted. They couldn't afford the luxury of wasting food. The contradiction amused her. They had plenty of electricity because of the geothermal direct conversion units in the nearby hot springs, but life at their dacza was still close to the edge. *My and Pitor's dacza*, she thought. The hidden country home they inherited after their parents had been assassinated by Gletscherheim terrorists. A refuge that was well away from the chaos that Cracovia had become.

At times like this, Franciszka would start to reminisce about her days as a little girl in Nowy Kraków. The heady days just after the Empire withdrew its last division of marines from Haven and before everything started falling apart. The days when her father, Brigadier Soltyk, had led the Cracovian Home Guard. Though there was a mystery from that time, too. Her father had been a Major in the Imperial Marines. And then he wasn't. No one would talk about what happened though she knew cousin Lech was involved somehow. She wondered where on Cracovia he was right now. She missed him.

Franciszka was brought out of her daydreaming by a loud explosion. Franciszka grabbed her hunting rifle and opened the door to look outside. It was trueday out, and over the ridgeline she could see a plume of black smoke. *What now?* With Pitor off hunting, it fell to her to go investigate. She put the rifle down long enough to write a note to Pitor. Then she put on her coat, picked up her Go bag, grabbed her rifle again and headed out the door.

* * *

The two pirates landed their fighters well away from the plume of smoke rising from the edge of the field. If there were survivors, they didn't want to be met with gunfire before they could respond. The two bandits, Ian Dalager and Bjorn Heilmann, had once been cargo pilots. Now they were privateers operating under a letter of marque from the Kingdom of Gletscherheim. Under that letter they could pillage any part of Cracovia north of the Nidgy Lato for their king and, of course, themselves. While legal in Gletscherheim, if they were caught by the Cracovians, they would be hanged if not shot outright.

Gletscherheim had been settled during the CoDominium era by exiles of Northern European-Inuit ancestry. People from a not-quite-country called Greenland on Earth. Like Cracovia, Gletscherheim was a volcanic island. About two hundred thousand square kilometers in size but the habitable area was a fifth of that.

The island of Gletscherheim was directly exposed to the thinner air found outside the Shangri-La Valley. That valley was one of the few places on Haven that supported human birthing. Both the Gletscherheimers and the Cracovians were too far away from the Shangri-La Valley to use it. The Cracovians found a way to create birthing centers on their island but they wouldn't let the Gletscherheimers use them. They didn't have any excess capacity.

It was something the Gletscherheimers never forgot or forgave. The colonists of Gletscherheim had to find a way to increase the air pressure so their women could survive childbirth. Just as it had for the Cracovians, volcanism came to the rescue, at least partially.

The Gletscherheim colonists discovered several long underground tubes created by lava flows. Three of the basalt tubes were suitable for their needs. The colonists were able to seal them and use windmills to pump air inside, increasing the air pressure so they could be used as birthing centers. The tubes couldn't accommodate many women but they didn't need to. They were suitable for the population of a small state like Gletscherheim. Over time the birthing centers became centers of wealth and power. That eventually led to wars between them. Wars that lead to a single king ruling them all and the entire island.

Once consolidation was complete, the king eyed his larger, southern neighbor. The driver of its strategic competition with Cracovia was *Lebensraum*, the desire for land that they could colonize. And, of course, a remembrance of past injustices. Cracovia was warmer and bigger, so the Kingdom of Gletscherheim set in motion a long-term plan for its conquest using asymmetric warfare. One that slowly ate away at the pillars of Cracovia society. A plan put on hold once the Imperials rediscovered

Haven. But not one forgotten. When the Imperials withdrew from Haven, the plan was put back in motion.

* * *

Pitor Soltyk was a lot like his father, not only physically, but also in temperament. He was a stocky young man with blond hair who loved nature. This trip, he had fared widely hunting but only had a turkey and a few rabbits to show for it. *Game is getting scarce around here,* he thought. *Or smarter*. Of course, he had trapped the turkey and rabbits with a snare instead of shooting them. Ammunition was too valuable. It was scarce and couldn't easily be replaced. He was still two days away from home when he first spotted the black smoke in the distance. He had an instant of fear. *Was that from the dacza?* He squinted at the landscape and then sighed in relief. *No, that's coming from in front of the ridge that protects it.* The color of the smoke told him it wasn't a forest fire. *It must be from some kind of tech. Something must have crashed. I'll investigate as I pass by it on the way home.*

* * *

Ivanov and Conrad skirted the edge of the forest keeping an eye out for the pirates. Soon, they saw the two fighters land on the far side of the field. Both men ducked into the forest and watched while two men got out and carefully made their way toward the crash site. Once the two pirates were out of sight, Conrad steadied his handgun on some rocks and fired at first one fighter then the other. He wasn't expecting to destroy them this far away but he was hoping to damage them so they couldn't fly. After burning through what he hoped were some vital areas, Conrad turned to Ivanov. "They're going to be angry as hell. We've got to get away from here. Let's move out."

Ivanov and Conrad began moving as quickly as they could in the direction away from the crash site. Conrad had injured his leg in the crash. The further they jogged the more he limped. Finally, the two men took a rest break. Even though he'd had his oxy-nanite shot last week, he was breathing hard from the exertion. They weren't watching their immediate surroundings when they heard, "Hold there! Don't move."

Both men looked. "Conrad," Ivanov said. Then he nodded to their right. "Over there."

A woman with a hunting rifle pointed at them stood up. "Don't move or I'll shoot you."

"Okay, okay."

"Raise your hands."

The two Imperials complied.

"What are you running from?"

Conrad told her what had happened. "Do you know who shot us down? And why?"

"Those were Gletscherheim pirates. They rove over the northern part of Cracovia including this part called Male Lato. We've kept hidden from them but now you've drawn them to us. Damn you all for crashing here."

Ivanov offered, "We're sorry. We can't do anything about the past and we need help. My friend here needs his leg looked after. We lost all of our survival gear in the crash. Please, help us."

Something about his plea touched Franciszka. Although the fact that she hadn't seen another person except Pitor for a T-year and a half affected her decision too. Against her better judgement, she said, "Come with me. I'll bind your injuries and give you one meal. Then it's on your way with both of you. Agreed?"

"Yes, agreed. Thank you."

"What is that thing your friend is holding?"

"It's a breathing mask. He's not used to breathing air this thin but he is acclimating."

Excitedly she asked, "He is from off planet then? And you?"

Lying, Conrad answered, "We were both sentenced to exile here for the rest of our lives."

"What were your crimes? No, never mind. We will talk more about that later. What are your names?"

"Joe Conrad," the marine pilot answered.

"I am Dmitry, Dmitry Ivanov," the biologist replied.

"I'm Franciszka Soltyk." She then gestured with her hand and said, "This way."

FIVE

The pirates were furious. When they returned to their fighters, they could see they were damaged by some sort of energy weapon. The Empire had proscribed that all energy weapons be eliminated from Haven. Publicly, it was their way of trying to bring peace to that world. Coincidently, it also served to better control the population and ensure the people of Haven were loyal to the Empire. Even the knowledge of how to build an energy weapon was illegal to possess. As with much Imperial science and technology, it had been encrypted in the local branch of the Imperial Library, thereby making it unavailable to the locals.

Upon closer inspection, the fighters were too damaged to fly. The King was going to be angry beyond words. Fighter craft were scarce and they knew what the King was like when he was angry. Even though the fighters were not legally the King's possessions, the King thought of them as his military assets. He would torture and kill their families in front of them before he did the same to them. He had done it before to his enemies. And you were his enemy if you lost something as important as a fighter.

They had seen two sets of footprints around the crash site. Unless they could capture those two people and bring them back to the King, they were sea dragon bait. They knew that if they brought him prisoners, the King would have an outlet for his rage. He could hold the prisoners for ransom or torture them. Probably both. He was a brutal psychopath. But if they could acquire the energy weapon that caused the damage, that would be worth more than just absolution from the King. The two pirates knew what they had to do. Grinning to each other they started looking for the spoor of their prey.

* * *

Franciszka was having second thoughts about her decision to befriend these strangers. Their story sounded lame. Even so, she had bound the leg of the one called Conrad. Then she dished up some *bigos* and poured them both some cold water. The two were in a heated discussion about what they should do next. That gave her a chance to look at both of them more closely. Both were tall and had muscular builds. She imagined both Ivanov and Conrad were very strong. Both had a professional air about them. Courtly mannerisms? She wasn't sure. Finally, they turned to her. And in her native Polski language Dmitry asked her to be their guide over the Nidgy Lato range into the Wielki Lato area.

Franciszka was surprised Dmitry knew her language. While flattered, she answered back in Anglic, "No, I am not a guide."

"Franciszka, we need to reach our friends there. Please, reconsider," Conrad asked.

"No. I agreed to feed you one meal then it was on your way. You agreed."

Dmitry looked at her. Really looked at her, for the first time. He saw a young woman, maybe twenty-three or twenty-four. Strands of ash blond hair falling over her face. Her blue eyes were alert, a sharp intelligence dwelling behind them. She was big with strong features. That was all he could tell given her heavy clothing. "Yes, you are right, we did. And we will leave. But what about a trade? We have these laser pistols that can be very useful tools. I do not see anything like that here. You can recharge them with any source of electricity. And you have a source here. Please take us to our friend's camp in the Wielki Lato and we will give you both tools."

Franciszka thought about it for a moment. "I would like to wait for my brother to come back. He can help escort you to your friends."

"When will he be back?" Conrad asked.

"I don't know. He's out hunting. Maybe a week."

"We can't wait that long, Franciszka. And those Gletscherheim pirates may still be around."

"Please," Dmitry asked. Something in his eyes made her heart flutter. Franciszka thought it over: She could leave a message for her brother. And the pay was worth it. Too good? She'd make sure Pitor understood the bargain and followed them as an insurance policy.

* * *

Five T-days trek from the dacza was a village called Zalipie. Franciszka, Dmitry and Joe made their way into the half-burned village very carefully. This was the closest community to Franciszka and her brother's cottage. The village was named after a small town in what long ago had been Poland on Earth; before The Great Patriotic War there.

Franciszka had hoped to find an electrical vehicle in the town to speed their travels but all the vehicles they saw were damaged or had no charge. She wondered if they could find some horses or muskylopes to ride.

She was surprised and sad to find Zalipie abandoned, half destroyed. Her memories of it were of a picturesque, friendly place. One that combined simple charm and modern technology.

She remembered back when she had first seen the town with its streets made of hexagonal pavers. Back then the contrast between the red tile roofs of the houses and the black pavers had made a very quaint scene. Franciszka still imagined she was walking on a honeycomb. That was fitting since beekeeping was one of the main agricultural activities in the region. Back in her youth, Zalipie honey had been exported as far away as the

Shangri-La Valley. With greater maturity Franciszka now saw the pattern had been more than just a practical choice by the people here. There had been an element of marketing to it.

Still, Franciszka marveled at the ingenuity the ancestors of these townspeople had shown. Hundreds of years before they had taken basalt columns that had naturally cooled into six-sided shapes and used an industrial laser to slice them into short pieces. Just like how one would cut a loaf of bread. Then they laid the pieces down on a crushed gravel bed. Fitting the pieces together created a solid and smooth black surface. The basalt would absorb heat during the trueday and release it to melt any snow that fell on it. The melt water then flowed through the joints between the pavers percolating into the ground beneath the surface. Practical and representational at the same time.

Franciszka had stayed in a hostel back then when she was a university student. She had been backpacking through the area studying the nearby Kaminski Geyser Field for a geology class. One of the largest geyser fields on Cracovia. She hadn't realized the violence had spread this far north. Her surprise turned to horror as they began to see skeletons scattered about.

"What happened here?" she wondered aloud.

"From the looks of it there was some kind of fight," Joe said. "Maybe raiders surprised them."

"We knew things were falling apart. That's why we fled to our dacza. But this amount of destruction so close. We didn't know." Franciszka was stunned. She realized how lucky she and her brother had been.

"When the rule of law breaks down, the rule of might takes over. It's not a pretty sight," Joe offered.

"You've seen this before?" Franciszka asked.

Shading the truth, Joe replied, "I was in the Imperial Marines once. Before…well before I came here. I was posted to a brigade assigned to maintain order on Novi Kossovo. A planet the Saurons had taken and ruled for a few years. After the Imperial forces liberated the planet, it took some time to reintroduce Imperial law and order. A brigade wasn't big enough to do that but it was all the Empire could spare.

"The orbital bombardment and ground fighting did almost as much damage to Novi Kossovo as the Saurons. Starvation was widespread. It wasn't possible to ship enough food across interstellar distances to save more than a few of the population. So, the Empire brought in automated factories to make fusion reactors and industrial-scale food synthesizers. The reactors were needed to power the plants."

"Food synthesizers?" Franciszka asked.

"Machinery that can convert any organic matter into food. Garbage, weeds, dead animals, that sort of thing. We also had to set up distribution systems. All that took time. We did it as fast as we could. In the meantime, scenes like this were common. It was every man for himself. Taking by force whatever food, medicine and women were left. There was even some cannibalism," he said with a look of distaste on his face. "Horrible."

"Do you think that's what happened here?" Dmitry asked.

"Cannibalism? The winners would have scoured the town for any food they could find before resorting to that," Joe responded. "The winners may still be around. I think it best for us to be on our way as soon as we can. Let's fill our water bags at the well in the central square and move on. We won't stay the truenight here."

Just as they reached the village's central square, three shots rang out. Two bullets whizzed by Dmitry and Joe and buried themselves in the stucco siding of the unburned building behind them. The third bullet ricocheted off the street's pavers in front of them.

"Cover!" Joe yelled.

All three scattered, diving behind whatever they could find.

Franciszka yelled out, "Where did those shots come from?"

"I think from that church on the other side of the square. I saw a flash from the steeple." Then with some disdain, Joe added his take on the shooter's marksmanship, "Lousy shots."

Dmitry responded, "You'd be happier if they hit us?"

"No, of course not. They are firing at us from long range. Longer than prudent; they should have let us get closer. They probably don't have any military training. And, it tells us they don't have much experience with the weapons they're using. Which themselves aren't very good. Not military.

Probably very old hunting rifles. Those are all good for us."

"Are you suggesting we attack them?" Franciszka asked warily.

"No. We need to retreat. Find a way around this village. We don't want to fight unless we absolutely have to."

Franciszka relaxed a bit at his answer.

Joe continued, "Byers will be setting soon. I'd like to get around this town and set up camp before truenight falls. Franciszka, do you know a way around it?"

"There's an old road about a kilometer back the way we came. I'll show you."

* * *

Zalipie was two truenights behind them now but they still grinned at the memory of teaching those three Cracovian townies a life lesson. Dalager and Heilmann had reconned the town in the middle of truenight. The townspeople hadn't expected that. They thought they were safe because of the cold. Especially in that church. They paid for that mistake with their lives.

"How far behind them are we?" Dalager asked.

"Not more than a day. We would have caught up to them by now if we hadn't spent so much time in Zalipie."

"We both enjoyed that. A little R&R from work," Dalager replied with a grin.

"And, our wives," Heilmann added.

"Where do you think these guys are going?"

"They seem to be hiking around the edges of geothermal areas. But from the map it looks like they're heading roughly for the Nidgy Lato. But there's nothing there. At least on my map."

"What's the Nidgy Lato like?" Dalager asked.

It's a small range of extinct volcanos dividing the north section of Cracovia from the south. That is the Male Lato from the Wielki Lato. As the name Nidgy Lato suggests, it has snow on it all year. Here, look at the map. Cracovia has volcanos that run north-south down the length of the island on its eastern side. Like a spine. The Nidgy Lato is a spur off that spine that extends across the island in an east-west direction. My guess is that it would take them too long to hike around it so they must be going over it."

"Good. That should give us enough time to catch up with them."

* * *

Joe, Dmitry and Franciszka hiked along the rim of a deep canyon, peering at the waterfalls stepping down through the gorge below. The rainbows created by the icy blue water splashing off the rocks were dimmer than Joe and Dmitry were used to. Haven was further away from Byers' Star than Sparta was from Agamemnon. Still, the subtle beauty awed them.

Dmitry was enjoying the hike for another reason. He was walking alongside Franciszka, talking with her. He was so distracted; he wasn't paying attention where he put his feet. The next thing he knew he stepped on a small rock which threw him off balance and caused him to fall toward the canyon. Franciszka reacted quickly. She took a step in his direction, reached out and grabbed his arm. She pulled him to her; steadying him. Dmitry felt her body pressed into his. They looked into each other's eyes for a moment. Then the instant passed and she stepped back onto the trail. Dmitry knew something important had happened between them but didn't know what.

"Thank you, Franciszka. You saved me from ending up at the bottom of the gorge."

"I think you would have done the same for me, Dmitry."

Not knowing what else to say he just responded awkwardly, "Yes, of course. Still, I will try to be less distracted."

It was dimday when they finally stopped to set up camp. Cat's Eye was hanging above them. An enormous orange banded globe with a huge swirling storm that could swallow Haven if it was placed in it. A storm that looked like its namesake and gave the gas giant its name. Two of its moons, Ayesha and Brynhild, were also visible, hanging in the sky, this dimday. They sparkled like a pair of shimmer stones.

Franciszka and Dmitry were sitting around the fire. Joe had already climbed into the sleeping bag Franciszka had given him.

"I can't believe how beautiful Cat's Eye is hanging over us like that. Do you ever get used to it? The beauty of it, I mean."

"I suppose when you grow up on this world, you do tend to take it for granted."

"Franciszka," Dmitry asked, "did you grow up around here?"

"You mean this countryside? No. We would come here sometimes. If we were visiting Cracovia. That's how I learned my outdoor skills. My father was in the Imperial Marines at the time, so I grew up in the Shangri-La Valley mostly. But my fondest memories were when we visited my mother's family in Nowy Kraków."

"What was it like there?"

"It was magical. But you've got to realize my memories are those of a young girl. One of my favorite places was Booksellers' Alley. I … I was a bookworm. I loved curling up with a new book every truenight. And Chopin Hall. My mother would take us to concerts there." Franciszka chattered excitedly. "There was Czartorny Park where we'd play. And St. Jan Pawel's Church." She blushed and then blurted out, "I hoped to be married there one day. But given the way things have fallen apart here, I doubt that little girl's dream will come true."

"It sounds more," he stopped and chose his words carefully. "Nurturing than mine was."

"Tell me about your childhood, Dmitry."

"There's not much to tell. I was born and raised on Sparta. We didn't live in the Capital but outside it. It was too expensive for a commoner family to live in the Capital," he added sadly. "My parents sent me to boarding school when I was ten. My parents meant well. They were trying to prepare me for a challenging future as best they could.

"The land on Sparta was terraformed. Much like this island of yours. But without the natural beauty you have here," he said, nodding toward Cat's Eye. "After boarding school, I went to the Imperial University to study biology. Not the campus at the Capital but the one at Trevorton on New Alexandria. I did well enough to get into a doctoral program there. Basically, I focused all my energies on my studies. I'm afraid I'm a pretty dull boy."

"Oh, I think you're anything but that, Dmitry." And with that she stood up, walked over to her tent, climbed into it and got into her sleeping bag.

* * *

Pitor knew from the tracks that his sister and two men were heading south. Franciszka made it clear that he wanted him to follow her. She was leaving clues: small broken branches, footprints, that sort of thing. He also could read from the traces that two men were following her small party. He figured he was about two days behind Franciszka and one day behind the party pursuing her. Based on the two damaged flyers he had found, her pursuers were likely Gletscherheim pirates. Very dangerous men.

Pitor was sickened and outraged by what he discovered in the church in Zalipie. Why would anyone do those things to someone else? And on Holy ground? Pitor took the time to bury the three bodies. It was the least he could do for those poor souls.

Once the burials were finished, Pitor took off after the monsters that had killed the three townspeople, the pirates who were following his sister and her small party. Pitor knew he needed to overtake them and kill them before they caught up with his sister. What he was going to do about her companions was still an open question.

* * *

The small group had been hiking for several truedays. More and more, Dmitry and Franciszka walked together and ate together. And found things to laugh about together. The group mostly skirted large geothermal areas. Areas that contained geysers, boiling thermal pools and mud pots. Beautiful places that were very dangerous to get close to except when they wanted to camp on warm ground and cook in the boiling pools. Finally, in the distance, they spied snowcapped mountains. The Nidgy Lato range.

Joe used a rope to pull a metal basket with a turkey in it from the boiling pool. "I'm getting tired of turkey and potatoes. It seems that's all we eat."

"It is all we have been eating. Scrambled turkey eggs, hard boiled turkey eggs, roast turkey, boiled turkey, turkey soup. And potatoes. Fried potatoes, boiled potatoes, baked potatoes. Potatoes cooked in so many different ways." Dmitry didn't want to come across as complaining so he ended his response on a positive note. "At least these geothermal pools make it easy to cook everything."

Franciszka offered an explanation. "In this area of Cracovia, the turkeys and potatoes are plentiful. We don't have much time to hunt for other food if you want to get over the Nidgy Lato before heavier snows begin. We need the easy gatherings."

"Tell me something, Franciszka. It looks like most of the plants and animals here are Earth-stock. Why is that?" Dmitry asked.

"I have studied some geology at our Copernican University. It's not an Imperial University but still an excellent educational institution. When the CoDominium exiled my ancestors to this island, it had very little native life on it. Scientists believed it was created by volcanic action from a massive hot spot, or what some call a volcanic plume, that is located under a mid-oceanic ridge. As a result, this land is pinned in place in the middle of the Occidental Ocean. Continental drift has yet to bring other Haven land masses close enough to it for Cracovia to be colonized by native life.

"That is a generalization. There is some native life here. We think dactyls brought wireweed and heartfruit seeds here in their guts. Float sacs and algae arrived over time too. A few other lifeforms. That reddish tree over there makes up extensive forests in the south," she said, pointing. "It's a mainland species that propagates by heavy seed pods. After hundreds of years of study, no one has been able to figure out how those trees got to Cracovia since the island is so far from the other continents. Some researchers believe they may have floated here as part of trees that were washed into the ocean but that's just speculation. So, the land was ripe for terraforming.

"A few native species have been introduced over the last five hundred years. You remember the wild muskylope herd we saw? Those shaggy beasts were imported from the Shangri-La Valley. As was their native fodder. The reddish, shin-high bunchgrass and the coiled screwgrass we trekked through a few T-days ago. Not all species introductions have been as well received. Some idiot brought a valecat here as a pet and it escaped. Since they can procreate without a male, they established a viable population on Cracovia."

"What's a valecat?" Dmitry asked.

"They are very … shy is the word. They hunt vermin mostly at night. Vaguely felinoid in shape. About as large as an Earth-stock cat. Valecats and cats don't coexist well though. The valecats drive the cats out of the areas they colonize. At least we don't have to contend with drillbits. No one was stupid enough to bring those here, even as a pet.

"As to the Earth-stock life here, early in the CoDominium period when genemods were still legal on Earth, our Polish ancestors bribed CoDominium officials to allow them to bring modified plants and animals here. Plants and animals specifically adapted to this world. Once the colony was established, BuReloc sent more transportees. More bribes ensured they had our language and culture. With Cracovia, our ancestors were able to achieve something they had never been able to achieve before; strategic depth for their nation.

"But I got off-topic. Remember Zalipie? The honey bees found there are genemods. They needed to have bigger wings due to the lower air pressure here. They also needed mods to concentrate oxygen better. Then there was their navigation system. And they needed to have their instincts adjusted so that they built heavily insulated nests in order to thrive in the colder temperatures. A lot was done to the bees. They have since undergone natural selection. They collect both nectar and pollen from the alfalfa fields around here. The flavor and sweetness of their honey is indescribable.

"The turkeys and the potatoes are also genemods. They have adapted almost too well. Which is why they are all around here and easy to find."

Dmitry showed visible interest in her comments. Franciszka smiled and asked softly, "You seem unusually interested, Dmitry. Why is that?"

Missing her intent, Dmitry responded. "I'm going to be stuck here for the rest of my life. I want to find out as much as I can about my new home."

Franciszka just looked at him disappointedly and sighed.

* * *

"How far behind them do you think we are?" Dalager asked.

"A few hours. We can overtake them by tomorrow. They are definitely heading for the Nidgy Lato."

"Let me see the map."

"It looks like there are several trails over the range. Each one a little higher than the next. I'm guessing they'll take the lower trail. Why don't we take the middle trail? Pass them up and set an ambush?"

"Where do you think we should do that?"

"It looks like there are two huts along the lower trail. Figure two T-days to hike over the range to the Wielki Lato. Let's set it just before they reach the second hut. We can pass them in the truenight as they sleep. By the time they make it to the next hut we'll be rested. No defensive position available for them. They'll be tired and never see us coming."

* * *

Pitor knew he had to pick up his pace. He knew the pirates were catching up to Franciszka. Pitor was close enough to see the pirates take the middle trail over the Nidgy Lato. He saw the traces that indicated his sister took the lower trail. *Why take the middle trail?* he wondered. *They're going to try and pass them and set an ambush. Two can play that game.* Pitor took the high trail increasing his pace knowing that he had to put everything he had into the final push.

* * *

The huts were warmer than Dmitry had expected. Franciszka explained to him that the huts were heated by geothermal energy. Hot water pumped in from nearby hot springs. Although there was no electricity for the electric lights. And she didn't know why. Joe decided to find out and left the hut.

Even with geothermal heating the hut was cold. Franciszka and Dmitry had been getting closer throughout the trip. Now they were lying next to each other, talking. "Tell me more about Cracovia, Franciszka."

"Where to begin?"

"Are these the highest mountains on the island?"

"No, there is a spine of volcanoes down the eastern side. Much higher. While Haven doesn't rotate very fast, there is some wind. The winds generally move from west to east. Over the water of the Occidental Ocean there is nothing to stop them so they build until they hit Cracovia. As the winds rise over the spine, they drop their moisture. That puts the eastern side of the island in a rain shadow. So, it is much dryer. There's another effect too."

She paused for a moment. Almost too embarrassed to continue. "As the winds make landfall on the western shore, they run into several ancient volcanoes. One of them partially collapsed into the ocean several thousand T-years ago. It is a very important place for us. The caldera is now a box canyon open to the ocean on the western side but remains surrounded by tall cliffs on the other three. As the winds come ashore, they blow up this canyon. This increases the air pressure in the eastern end of it. This is where we built our birthing centers." She paused for a moment before adding quietly, "I'd like to see one of them someday."

Now she was looking directly at him, her face flushed. Dmitry leaned toward her and kissed her. She returned it with a passion that surprised him.

Sometime later Joe returned. He came through the door and without looking said, "Damn it. It looks like someone stole the copper wire between the geothermal conversion units in the hot springs and the hut." He turned and noticed Dmitry and Franciszka sleeping next to each other with a satisfied look on their faces. He just smiled, turned around quietly and climbed into his sleeping bag.

* * *

Dalager and Heilmann settled into their firing positions. The two men had chosen them carefully, or so they thought. The positions were directly uphill from the lower trail and fifty meters apart. On the uphill side of the lower trail, there was little cover to hide behind. On the downhill side there was a shear drop-off. Their positions were difficult to see from below and allowed the two to provide covering fire for each other. They needed to position carefully. After all, their targets had at least one energy weapon. While exposed to the elements, the two pirates were wearing Gletscherheim-made gear, designed for glacier coldness. So, they were comfortable.

Hellman thumbed his short-range comm. "Remember Dalager, leave the woman alive."

"I know, I know. You don't have to remind me. I want her alive too," he said with a lascivious grin.

"But kill the other two. You target the one in front. I'll target the other one. And don't damage the energy weapon. That's going to be our currency to buy our way back into the King's good graces."

* * *

Pitor was panting as he arrived at the overlook. It had taken every physical reserve he had to arrive in time. Below he could see the two Gletscherheim pirates setting up their ambush. Further down the mountain his sister and her two companions were just coming into view on the lowest trail. He saw something that only later he thought about. His sister and one of the men were holding hands like lovers. Then the immediacy of the situation pushed everything else into the background.

Pitor knew he didn't have much time. Other than attacking the pirates from behind and from above he wasn't sure what he could do. Even though he was an expert shot, the pirates were too far away for him to guarantee taking both of them out. Then Pitor noticed a cornice below him and had an idea. He raised his weapon.

* * *

Franciszka was the first to hear it. A loud crack and then a low rumbling sound like a flyer taking off. She looked up and saw the avalanche. A white wall of snow and ice was racing down the mountainside. She relaxed when she realized it was coming down the mountain just ahead of them. *Thank all that's Holy, it just missed us*, she thought. *It will be more difficult to hike over the broken snow to reach the hut but at least it will be a safe passage.*

* * *

Pitor fired three quick shots near the cornice. As he hoped it was unstable, just waiting for the right trigger. The sound of the rifle was just enough to set it off. He heard the loud cracking sound as the snow broke away. Then he watched as it began to race down the slope, accelerating rapidly as it picked up more and more snow.

The roar of the avalanche alerted the two Gletscherheimers to their impending doom. Pitor saw the two pirates turn around just before the avalanche hit them. On seeing the approaching wall of death one of them froze in place. The other had slightly more presence of mind and tried to run. Neither had a chance in hell of getting away.

Pitor was too far away to see their faces but he imagined the surprise and fear on them. Then they were gone. Now part of an accelerating mass of snow and ice heading for a five hundred meter drop-off. Knowing what they had done to those Zalipie townspeople, Pitor felt no remorse. Instead, he felt it was a righteous killing.

* * *

Joe and Dmitry had left the hut to give Franciszka and Pitor a chance to talk privately. Both were overjoyed to see each other but neither was happy.

"Franciszka, are you insane?" Pitor said trying hard not to raise his voice. "You don't really believe his story, do you? That he has 'friends' he has to reach. What is really going on with him and Joe?"

With tears in her eyes, she responded. "Pitor, Pitor, I've been so lonely. I love you but I need more in my life than just a brother. He…he loves me too. I know he's not telling me the whole truth. I don't know why but he is a good man. Just like you. I know he has a good reason."

"So, you want me to help you guide Dmitry and Joe to those map coordinates in the Wielki Lato? From the map there's nothing there. In fact, it's almost as far into nowhere as you can get." Then he had a thought. *What are they hiding from, I wonder?* "Okay, I'll help you but we both need to be on our guard. Agreed?"

* * *

The small party made sure that they were making plenty of noise as they approached the location of the shuttle. They didn't want to be shot by the guards. As soon as Franciszka saw the small ship she blurted out, "That's a spaceship? That's what you've been hiding from us? You're not exiles at all are you? Just what is going on? Why are you here?"

"Franny," he said using his pet name for her. "I can't tell you. I'm under orders not to say a word. I'll be shot if I disobey and you will be too. I need you to trust me. Please, all I can say is that I'm…we…are on a mission of great importance to the Empire. I need to leave for a short time. We can take you back to your dacza, if you want. But beyond that I can't guarantee transportation. At least not yet. I'll keep my promise and give you our laser weapons. I promise you I will be back. We will raise our child together," he said putting his hand on her growing belly.

Dmitry reached for a small chain around his neck, opened the clasp and took it off. He held it up to Franciszka. At the end of it was a small diamond. "Here, Franny. I want you to have this. It's the most precious thing I own."

"What is it?"

"It is an artificial diamond. I told you my parents were killed in a flyer accident. This was made from the carbon in their bodies. Their genetic codes and life histories have been encoded as information in its crystalline structure. With the proper Tri-V reader … well I can visit them, after a fashion."

"Is that how the Empire remembers its dead?" She asked, not sure whether she was horrified or honored for him sharing something so macabre yet so personal with her. Or both. Like most Cracovians, Franciszka was very religious, believing in God, and Heaven and the sacraments. She was used to visiting cemeteries, not carrying one around with her.

"Some do. There are many different ways to honor those who have passed. This one…well, this one is more personal for me. I always carry them with me. I want you to hold it for me. As my promise that I will return for you. Will you do that? Will you wait for me?"

"Oh, Dmitry," she said with tears welling up in her eyes. "Yes. Of course." Then Franciszka reached for the chain around her neck. At the end of it was a small gold cross. "This…this was my mother's. She was wearing it the day…the day she was killed. I want you to wear it until you return. Will you promise me you will do that?"

Solemnly, Dmitry answered. "I promise, Franny."

After Joe and Dmitry were debriefed, they were brought up to speed on the expedition's progress. Pursuant to its orders, the frigate had been in an orbit that kept it on the other side of Cat's Eye from Ayesha. Doing so kept it hidden from the refueling station's sensors. The frigate had now left the A3 orbital anchorage and was underway for Haven. The shuttle had been ordered to make an orbital rendezvous with the frigate in two T-days. When they reached the shuttle, ground personnel had been packing up the expedition's equipment. The two Imperials had made it back in the nick of time. Just before their departure, Dmitry learned of a strange discovery.

"Franny, one of our collection teams came down with a strange illness. They had taken genome samples from some pigs. A few days later they came down with a bad case of the flu. Our antiviral medicines didn't help their recovery. We sequenced the virus and discovered a combination of both Earth and Haven life. A type of chimera. It's extraordinarily unusual for native life from two different planets to combine. Another strange thing, once the team members were over the flu, they seem to have developed the ability to pull more oxygen from your thin air. On further investigation we found their genome had been changed. Genes had been added. Have you heard of anything like this before?"

"This sounds familiar. Years ago, when I was a little girl, there was a plague ravaging Haven. It was called the Red Plague. It was a combination of Earth virus and Haven genetic material. Something thought highly unlikely. Scientists at the University found a cure.

"Upon further research our scientists found that the Red Plague was a mutation of a disease that swept Haven five hundred T-years ago. Back then it helped the people of this world acclimate to the thin air here. We don't know where it came from but the Harmonies thought it a gift from God. A boon given to them to help harmonize with Haven, this Promised Land of theirs. We thought the original virus extinct once it ran its course. It sounds like there are hidden reservoirs of it still in some of the animal populations."

"So, people didn't die from it?"

"No more than from a normal flu virus. But the Red Plague was different. It did have a very high mortality rate. If your people haven't died from it, they don't have the Red Plague."

"Thanks, Franny, that's very helpful. I'll pass what you've told me along to the medic."

SIX

2640 A.D., INSS *Cassiopeia's Daughter*, Beyond the orbit of Hel, Byers' System

Academician Ivanov floated onto the bridge escorted by a security officer. *Strange, the Cassie D isn't under acceleration and the ring isn't rotating.* Then he looked at the bridge screens. *And, where is that piece of ice we were topping off from? What's going on? Did we cut it that close?* The Admiral was strapped into his command chair. He nodded to the security officer and said, "Carry on." The officer turned by grabbing hold of a workstation, pushed himself off and floated back to the entrance hatch.

"Welcome back, Academician. It looks like you and your expedition were successful. Congratulations. While you were hiking across northern Cracovia, your colleagues found a variety of cocoa bean that grows in the extreme conditions found on Haven. We had nothing like it in the gene banks. And I understand the turkey and potato varieties you found are both of keen interest to your colleagues. Fortunately, you returned with them just in time."

"Admiral Blaine, I returned under protest."

"I read the Sitrep from the frigate's captain."

"Then you know I left some unfinished business behind."

The Admiral responded disapprovingly. "You mean that girl you got pregnant?"

The biologist blushed. "Yes, damn it. My child is on Haven. We're leaving the galaxy because of the Saurons. I can't leave my child to those monsters."

"Don't worry. Remember the Emperor ordered all traces of Haven removed from the Imperial astrogation databases. And, even if they have it in their database, it'll be a long time before they get there."

"Admiral, please. I need to go back."

At that moment the Captain interrupted the conversation. "Excuse me, Admiral; look at the patterns in the Alderson force readings. Betelgeuse is getting ready to explode. The time is nigh."

"Captain, put me on the ship-wide 1MC. I want to address the crew."

"Aye aye, Admiral. You are on."

"Shipmates, this is the Admiral. We are about to engage on a mission of vital importance to the Empire of Man. The Emperor himself, in his wisdom, has commanded that we Jump to the Andromeda galaxy and plant new colonies to ensure nothing less than the survival of the human race. We will never know if the Saurons were successful in defeating the Empire but we will know that they never defeated the human race. Hail Lysander! Hail the Empire!"

Throughout the ship the crew's response reverberated.

"HAIL LYSANDER. HAIL THE EMPIRE!"

The Admiral looked over at the highest-ranking member of the Church on the expedition, Cardinal Peterson. The Admiral thought he looked a little out-of-place with his regal vestments draped over his spacesuit. But the Cardinal had insisted. Just as he had insisted on being awakened from frozen sleep for this moment. Something about looking into the face of God as they Jumped.

"Now I'd like Cardinal Peterson to lead us in prayer."

The Cardinal cleared his throat, bowed his head and spoke into his mic. "Almighty God, we your humble servants, are about to Jump into the unknown to a new promised land. We do so to ensure your glory is not lost to the universe and that you did not give us your only Son in vain. We beseech you to bless this expedition in the name of the Father, and of the Son, and of the Holy Spirit. Amen."

"Amen. Thank you, Cardinal Peterson. Captain, make the final preparations to Jump. I want everyone, not just the bridge, in their spacesuits and on suit air. I want Damage Control manned and ready."

"Aye aye, Admiral. Officer of the Deck, sound General Quarters, then sound Jump Stations. Bring the Jump engine capacitors up to one hundred percent of rated storage. Activate the Field."

The biologist pleaded, "Please, Admiral. I promised her I'd come back."

"I'm not going to discuss this, Academician. Get off the bridge and get to your GQ station or I'll have the master-at-arms remove you."

The biologist's head slumped. He knew the Admiral was right. And he knew there was nothing he could do about it. Distraught, he launched himself toward the hatch leading to his station.

A few minutes later the OOD said, "All stations report at General Quarters, Captain. Jump Stations are manned and ready. Jump engine capacitors fully charged. The Field is activated and stable. We have a green board."

"Very well. Captain, I want you to set Condition Zebra throughout the ship. Manual Lockdown."

"Aye, Admiral. We'll lock her down tight all around. OOD, set Condition Zebra Manual Lockdown."

Over the 1MC came, "Set Condition Zebra Manual Lockdown. I say again, set Condition Zebra Manual Lockdown."

All over the great ship hatches were manually closed and dogged.

"Captain, all stations report Condition Zebra Manual Lockdown set."

"Very well. Power down all computers."

"All computers are shut down. We are ready to engage the mechanical initiators."

"On my command, Captain."

"Aye aye Admiral."

A minute later the Alderson force detectors pegged. The OOD said redundantly, "There she goes!"

Admiral Blaine paused. *A massive star is dying in an explosion so immense it will outshine all the stars in the galaxy for months. Yet interstellar distances are so vast it will take hundreds of years for the light from that explosion to reach here and much of the rest of the Empire. The Alderson force from that death is a different beast, though. It is here now. The pulse of Alderson force released is a herald announcing to the universe that Betelgeuse has died. And that death knell will hurl us to another galaxy. Will we survive the Jump?*

Admiral Blaine took a deep breath. *God's Will be done.*

"JUMP."

Amalgam

ONE

2640 A.D., Haven

Even with gale force winds, ice built up on the exterior of the dome. Outside was the middle of truenight. The dome was located far to the west of the usual inhabited areas of the Shangri-La Valley on Haven, south of the mountain range called the Iron Limpers.

Inside the dome it was morning, based on St. Ekaterina mean time. The dome not only protected the dig from the extremes in weather, it also increased the air pressure for the inhabitants. The fusion reactor ticked up a bit, lighting and warming the interior. The heat began to seep through the outer covering and melt the ice on the outside of the dome. As they had been doing for the past seventeen T-years, the two astropaleontologists, Vasily Petrov and Sergei Sobol, followed their usual routine. They rose, showered, had breakfast from the food synthesizer and returned to work on the fossil bed.

The two academicians from the Imperial University on St. Ekaterina almost had the imaging system wrestled into place above their latest fossil find. They had laid down rails on either side of the fossilized bones for the heavy system to run along, scanning through the rock below. The men were excited because this was the largest fossil they had yet found. About the size of a man. From the part they had uncovered, it looked like it was almost intact. From zircon dating, the find was from a period in Haven's past just before a mass extinction fifty-seven million years ago. One thought to be caused by a large comet hitting the moon.

Sobol paused from his physical exertion. "Why are we doing this, Vasily? They are never going to come for us. We will never be able to publish."

"Sergei, my friend. We have spoken of this before. What else can we do? It wasn't our fault we missed the last Imperial evacuation ship. Our flyer remains broken. The outer world is too harsh for us to try going somewhere else on foot. And, where would that somewhere else be? No, the Empire promised they would return. They will. We have left the Imperial IFF system on the flyer engaged to automatically signal us when that happens. In the meantime, we have our work. We will earn accolades for these discoveries. No one else has found the fossil record on this world that we have."

"Yes, sedimentary rock is rare on this world. Fossil beds even more so. Volcanic activity changes the surface rocks so quickly. Very well, Vasily. I will try and continue to focus on my work." Pushing hard one more time he continued, "There. That sets the imager on the tracks."

A short while later, Sobol asked, "What in hades is that?"

The two men were sitting in front of the Tri-V, looking at the holographic image from the scan. Hanging in the air in front of them was the reddish outline of the slab of rock in which the fossil was imbedded. Inside was the ghostly image of the fossil. Sobol enlarged the head.

Petrov was working his tablet. Next to the image, another popped into existence. "The head looks a little like this velociraptor fossil from old Earth."

"Convergent evolution."

"Of course, but what is this?" he asked, pointing to a solid, dark area on one of the fossil's dagger-like teeth.

"An artifact of the system? It would be unfortunate if the imager was beginning to fail."

"The status lights are all green."

"Then we should focus our work there," Sobol said.

"I agree, my friend."

* * *

After several T-months of painstakingly slow work, the two men finished excavating the head from the rock entombing it.

Petrov was carefully holding the anomalous tooth in his gloved hands. He was amazed at their find. It was clear that the tooth had been drilled out and a filling inserted into the space. The amalgam was similar to what ancient dentists would have used on old Earth back in the twentieth century. He was holding something in his hands that proved the existence of an alien intelligence far in the past. This was more than he had ever hoped for.

"We must get news of this discovery out," Sobol said.

"And, how do we do that, my friend? We haven't made radio contact with anyone else on Haven for years. The mountains around us shield our signals and the comsats have been offline for a long time."

"Have we really tried? We have been passively waiting for rescue. Can we broadcast our discovery widely? Or try routing the signal through the refueling station on Ayesha. The fusion reactor puts out plenty of power."

"I doubt we can reach Ayesha. It's not a matter of power. Our radio equipment is designed only to reach comsats in orbit and the radio storms from Cat's Eye makes even that difficult. But, yes. This is a world-changing discovery. Some type of broadcast might work. We must try."

"Very well. Let's work on the transmission. What do we want to say?"

* * *

The Talon class heavy cruiser *Fomoria* was the lone surviving Sauron warship from the Battle of Sauron. It had escaped by chance. Just as it was getting ready to make a Jump, Betelgeuse exploded in a supernova. The

Alderson force released by that explosion caused the warship to make a Random Jump. A Jump that took it to a little visited, out-of-the-way place called Byers' System. Now the ship was engaged in a contra-orbital attack run on the system's only habitable world, a moon of the gas giant Cat's Eye. Softening it up for invasion.

"First Rank, we are receiving a broadcast from the surface. Its point of origin coincides with an Imperial IFF signal."

"My orders were to nuke the point of origin of any Imperial transmission from the surface."

"Yes, First Rank. This one makes a claim of an alien artifact."

"Not important, Second Rank. Nuke it."

"Acknowledged, First Rank."

Between Haven and Hel

Hel, what can you say about it? A gas giant named after a legendary being in Norse mythology who rules over a kingdom of the same name. In other cultures, a realm known as Hades, Hell or Inferno. That says it all.

* * *

These sagas began many Cat's Eye orbits ago and further away than a man can sail in countless lifetimes. Like most tales of adventure, there are great challenges, hard sacrifices and heroic deeds. These stories have much truth in them. But remember, history is written by the survivors.

* * *

That ancient mariner Bligh had it easy.

— The Soltyk Sagas - Book I, *2695 A.D.*

ONE

2636 A.D., Imperial Navy Shipyard, Eden System

Fleet Admiral George Sergei Carlton Blaine had a problem. The *INSS Cassiopeia's Daughter's* construction was falling behind schedule. He had to find places where he could pull it up. *If I can't get the schedule back on track, our trajectory across the Byers' System is going to take us through the outermost planet's leading Trojan point. I need a scouting mission to search out asteroids and comet heads in that region. And of course, to look out for any human activity. The system hasn't been visited in thirteen years. Anything could have been going on there.*

A day later, the Admiral was behind his desk in his underway cabin. His flagship was in orbit around the Imperial Navy Shipyard in Eden System, a rock rich in metals, like 16 Psyche in Sol System. The ring of his flagship was rotating to provide one standard gee. Less than he was used to on Sparta but still better than weightlessness. Someone entering the Admiral's cabin would see a man who looked like he was sitting in a fighter cockpit; one surrounded by screens and instrument panels. He wasn't in a cockpit, but all the electronics served a necessary purpose. They allowed the Admiral to track the progress of the redoubt program. From video feeds of the construction, to computer database access, to Tri-V calls, he could lead the entire project from this one place.

The Admiral didn't personally manage the details or give detailed orders to the myriad of program personnel. He had an entire department to do that. No, for want of a better term, he was the overwatch. Still, the Admiral felt that talking to his subordinates in person when he could, was the best way to communicate. He was just ending a Tri-V call when his orderly knocked on his entry hatch.

The Admiral responded, "Come."

A young officer came through the hatch, made his way to the front of his desk, stood at attention and said, "Lieutenant Commander Ramsey, reporting as ordered. Sir."

The Admiral looked up at the officer. While the Admiral was appraising the officer in front of him, that officer was discreetly looking around the compartment. Not at the electronics but at the personnel mementoes the Admiral had collected during his distinguished career. Like most senior officers, the Admiral furnished his in-space cabin with possessions acquired during a dozen planetary assignments.

"At ease, Lieutenant Commander."

The Lieutenant Commander relaxed but remained standing.

The Admiral continued looking over the young officer. A member of the Ramseys, an aristocratic family like his that had their roots in the early days of the Empire. He was of medium height, blond hair and alert eyes taking in his surroundings. Like many Spartans, Ramsey was muscular and stocky. Not for the first time, a thought unbidden came to him. *So many of our high-ranking officers come from the Peerage. Political influence instead of competence. I can understand why some of the Commoners are unenthusiastic about this war. One of the fault lines in the Empire the Saurons and their allies have been able to exploit successfully. But it's not my job to reengineer the Empire. That's his Majesty's responsibility. Back to the matter at hand.*

"Lieutenant Commander, you come highly recommended. I have a mission for you. It is Imperial High Secret. Your mission is to take your scoutship and recon in the Byers' System. Our last contact with it was in 2623 when the Empire withdrew its forces." Then the Admiral touched a control in front of him. The Tri-V tank lit up and displayed the solar system he wanted intel on.

"Byers' System, as far as we know, has two inhabited bodies. Both are moons of the gas giant Cat's Eye. Haven is a terrestrial world while Ayesha is a small, airless body, composed of rock and ice. There is a hydrogen cracking station on Ayesha's surface connected by a tether to fuel bladders in orbit.

"You are to remain outside of detection range of both of those moons unless an emergency requires you to do otherwise. Specifically, you are to scout Hel's leading Trojan point," he said referring to the outermost gas giant in Byers' System. "Take only a skeleton crew, Lieutenant Commander. This is a 'need-to-know' mission. Do you have any questions?"

Ramsey didn't understand why the mission, which appeared so simple, was so highly classified but that was quite literally above his pay grade. So, he just replied, "No, sir."

"Very well, Lieutenant Commander Ramsey. Godspeed. Dismissed."

TWO

2637 A.D., INSS Vasily Zaytsev, Hel's Leading Trojan point, Byers' System

Lieutenant Commander Ramsey was looking forward to returning home to his family. *It has been a long, uneventful mission. Nothing here for the Admiral to worry about. One last check of this Trojan point and then we head for the Alderson point and home. Time to focus on the launch.*

The scoutship's weapons loadout for this mission consisted of two Damocles IXm torpedoes carried internally in the ship's weapons bay. One had already been deployed to look at Hel's leading Trojan point from above. They were about to launch the second torpedo, this time from below the point. The radar reflections from both detonations would then be combined by the computers with the pulsar positioning system data to calculate the orbital parameters of any object in the region.

Damocles IXm Torpedo – Missile with a variable effect nuclear warhead. Yield can be dialed in between 500 kilotons and 50 megatons. Directionality can be chosen between 1 degree (pencil beam) and 360 degrees (omnidirectional). All parameters can be chosen by the weapons operator. Primary energy output: microwaves.

Nuclear weapons of this type are not as efficient as weapons that are designed for a single, specific effect; however, they provide the warfighter with more choices. The missiles can be carried by all Navy warships.

The weapon is a variation of the ancient CoDominium missile now known as the Damocles Ig which was armed with a nuclear pumped graser warhead. The Imperial Corp of Engineers has been known to use microwave warheads to rapidly map asteroid orbits within large regions of space.

- From *Jane's All the Galaxy's Warships*, 18th Edition (Montagu Ltd Press, 2632)

"Ops, did our SIGNIT suite pick up any radio traffic or other signals out here?"

"No, Skipper. Not a peep from anywhere in the Trojan point. Or, anywhere else for that matter."

"You sure it's working correctly?"

"Yes, sir. I run diagnostics daily."

"Astrogator, did our IR survey pick up any rocks out here while we were crossing the leading Trojan?"

"No, Captain. Everything out here is colder than a witc—"

The Captain interrupted him. "Belay that kind of talk, Mister. I'll have no such vulgarity on my bridge." He looked at the Astrogator and then nodded slightly toward the Midshipman. *Don't you know better than to speak that way in front of the Middie here? It's our job to teach him how to be an officer and a gentleman.*

"Aye aye, sir. Sorry, sir. No rocks or ice, Captain." Then the Astrogator expanded on his response to cover his misstep. "That's not too surprising, sir. At its closest approach, Cat's Eye is just under six Astronomical Units away. And being thirty percent more massive than Jupiter back in Sol System, Cat's Eye disrupts the gravitational stability of Hel's Trojan points. We expect asteroids and cometary nuclei to spend only a brief period of time in the points before being ejected."

"Thank you, Gator," the Captain said, using his nickname for the Astrogator. Then he turned to the Operations Officer. "Ops."

"Aye, Captain"

"Prepare to launch the Damocles."

"Aye, Skipper."

"Set the yield at fifty megatons."

"Fifty megatons. Aye, Captain."

"Set the energy dispersal to ninety degrees."

"Ninety degrees, aye. All parameters dialed in, sir."

"Ops, is the radar antenna array deployed through the Field?"

"Affirmative, Captain."

"Are the radar receivers online?"

"Yes, sir."

"And the system test results?"

"Green board, Skipper."

"Gator, status of the PPS?"

"Everything checks out, Captain."

"Engineering."

"CHENG here, Captain."

"What's the status of the Field and Field generator, Chief Engineer?"

"Captain, the Field is at maximum. The Field generator is working within specs."

"Very well. Ops, you have weapons release."

"Weapons release. Aye, Captain." The Operations Officer flipped up the red protective cap covering the launch button and said formally, "Three, two, one. Launch." Then he toggled the weapons release switch.

Almost immediately, the ship lurched backward. The forward view screen went blank as the bow cameras burned out. The stern cameras showed a Field turned violet-white. Close to failing. The normal bridge lighting died. Emergency lights came on. Smoke rose from the astrogation controls. It was a surreal scene. Burn throughs arced through the red, hazy bridge. One of the energy bolts jumped from the instrument panel in front of Lieutenant Commander Ramsey, killing him instantly. Then the Astrogator died as he was struck by another bolt.

The Operations Officer activated the 1MC communication circuit. "This is Lieutenant Johansen; the Captain is dead. As the highest-ranking line officer on board, I am assuming command. General quarters. Set condition Zebra throughout the ship. Close up your suites. Prepare for hard vacuum." Hatches could be heard banging shut and being dogged.

"Engineering, this is the Captain."

Chief Gunner's Mate Kowalski replied, "Captain. The comm lines to the engine rooms are down."

"Use the emergency lines, Chief. Get me comm."

"Aye, sir.' After a few moments the Chief said, "Okay, Captain. Try it now."

"Engineering, Bridge. What happened to the Field?"

"Captain, immediately after launch, we got hit by a huge spike of energy. I think just after the warhead passed through the Field it misfired and detonated. It wasn't even supposed to arm itself until it was a safe distance away from us. We received all the energy in the microwave backlobe close up. Thank God we had the Field up but even then, it's near collapse. We have burn-throughs in multiple locations. We're trying to dump the energy as fast as we can but the Field generator is failing."

"Keep on it, CHENG. Give me a damage control report when you can."

"Aye, Captain."

Long minutes later the CHENG hailed the Captain. "I'm in the Langston Field generator compartment, Captain. Here's my damage control report. Most of the ship's electrical systems are fried. We have system failures throughout the ship. The most important are the life support systems. The radar array channeled a huge surge of electrical energy into the ship overwhelming the trip switches. Backup systems are spotty. We have fires in the commissary and the port engine room. We are venting fuel to space. Several compartments have lost their structural integrity and atmosphere. Two of my people are securing the starboard engine room. We are having trouble sealing the hatch from here to the port engine room.

"Some good news. The Alderson Drive is unaffected. And, Sickbay, with its own self-contained power supply and extra armor, is all green."

"Here in the generator compartment, we're still trying to dump the energy from the Field generator. I think we've been able to radiate enough energy from the Field so that, if we lose the generator, we won't lose the ship." The CHENG paused for a moment. The Captain could hear him say to someone in the background, "Smitty. The power couplings! They're arc—" Suddenly, CHENG's voice cut off.

An explosion rocked the ship. The aft view screen went blank.

"Get me external cameras. Now," the Captain said to Midshipman Stewart, the Junior Officer of the Watch.

The aft view screen came on. It didn't show the Field, it showed only stars. The hull was glowing red-hot in places but it had survived the Field's death, and its remaining energy release.

The Langston Field generator had failed, melting into slag and explosively releasing the energy remaining in its capacitors. Fortunately, the generator room was armored and the ensuing destruction was, for the most part, confined to it. CHENG and the engineering gang's heroic sacrifice had saved the ship. At least for now.

THREE

Scoutships were designed to be deployed on detached duty for long periods. Built for independent operations, they were designed to withstand attacks or breakdowns and then to repair themselves.

The fires were out, the fuel tank leaks plugged and the air leaks sealed. The *Vasily Zaytsev* was stable for the moment, but it was in bad shape. The six survivors huddled around one of the red emergency lights on the bridge, like it was a campfire in the wilderness. And, in a way, that's where they were. In the wilderness of space. But there was no warmth to be had from the emergency light. All the survivors were wearing spacesuits with their helmets doffed even though the ship was losing heat. The cold condensed the moisture in their breath as they spoke. They were taking stock of their situation and deciding on their next steps. Ones that would decide if they lived or died.

Lieutenant Johansen, now the Vee Zee's Captain looked around the cramped bridge. Fifteen dead. Fifteen. *Thank God we had a skeleton crew. Only half our normal compliment was on board. What a disaster. Back on Earth, when I was going through the Academy, I never imagined I'd find myself in a situation like this. Who did? But, it's my job now. My job is to do everything I can to get us through this. To get everyone to safety.*

"Captain, we're in a world of hurt."

Chief Kowalski's words brought him out of his brooding.

"That's pretty obvious, Chief. Do you have any useful thoughts?"

"Yes, sir. I think it would be good if we didn't die."

The Captain just looked at Chief Kowalski. He wasn't sure if the man was in shock or just exhausted like the rest of them. "My thoughts exactly, Chief. We need a plan. First, what's the status of the major systems?"

After everyone ran through their status reports, the Captain summarized: "We need to work on the life support systems first, energy, heat, air, water, food. In that order. After that, we'll work on the other systems. Therefore, the first priority is to get the fusion reactor in the starboard engine room back online. We're running on emergency battery power and that won't last long. Chief Engineering Petty Officer Wagner, you and Propulsion Mate First Class Williams get that fusion reactor running again. Chief Kowalski, you work the electrical lines to the life support machinery. Coordinate with Chief Wagner. I don't want anyone electrocuted. Midshipman Stewart, you help Chief Kowalski. Boatswain's Mate Second Class Martinez, you're with me." Then to the group. "Let me know if there is anything you need. Questions?"

Midshipman Stewart, spoke up. "Sir?"

"Yes, Midshipman?"

"Sir, I was wondering ..." The Midshipman's voice trailed off.

"Speak up, son."

"Well, I was wondering about the bodies, sir. The bodies of our shipmates, sir."

"We will have services for our brothers and commit their remains to the depths of space once we get the life support systems working again."

"Yes, sir. Thank you, sir."

Several days later, everyone was exhausted. Everyone had been working round the clock with just a few hours' sleep. Finally, the fusion reactor and the electrical distribution wiring were repaired. At least enough to run the critical systems, heat, air and water.

The water system had to be extensively reworked. Chief Wagner and Propulsion Mate Williams had to cannibalize parts from the unofficial alcohol still to make it work. Then, they began to work on the food synthesizer.

Two days later, Chief Wagner reported to the Captain on their progress of repairing the food synthesizer. "Captain, I don't think we're going to be able to fix the food synthesizer."

"Why is that?"

"We don't have the parts."

"Can't we make them with the micro-fabricators?"

"They aren't working either. I programed them for the parts I needed, what I got was a mess."

"Can you fix the micro-fabricators?"

"No, sir. I've tried. It's the electronics. We don't have any way to make new large-scale semiconductors and there is nothing else like them we can use instead."

"What alternatives do we have?

"We have the emergency rations. But they won't last long."

"What about using an emergency converter from one of the lifeboats?

"We can do that, Skipper. I thought you didn't want to cannibalize the lifeboats."

"I don't but we've got three of them. If I have to use one for spare parts so we don't starve, so be it."

"You know all they'll produce is a thick gruel that will keep us alive. It'll be like eating soggy flavored cardboard."

"Yeah, I know, Chief. Would you rather be dead or bored with what you eat?"

The Captain knew the Chief was a chowhound so he wasn't surprised at his answer.

The Chief smiled and said, "Give me a minute, sir."

Good, the Chief's smartass reply means his morale is picking up. And that means he doesn't see our problems as insurmountable. "Carry on, Chief."

"Before I leave, sir. I would like your permission to use the rest of the lifeboat for spare parts. Starting with the computer. I'll network it with our tablets. It'll beef up their processing power."

"Permission granted, Chief. Use whatever you need. But use only that one lifeboat for spare parts, not the others."

"Aye aye, sir."

Once the life support systems were repaired the Captain had the engineers go to work on the propulsion system. That took a week of grueling work.

"Captain, I've got the starboard fusion drive back on line. The port drive was destroyed when the Langston Field generator went. A more serious problem, we don't have much hydrogen." The Chief showed the Captain the screen of his tablet. One of the few tablets on the *VeeZee* that weren't plugged in for recharging at the time of accident. One of the few that weren't fried by it.

"That's all the fuel we have left?"

"Yes, sir. We lost a lot of it when the tanks ruptured."

Another all-hands meeting. The Captain smiled to himself. *At least we are alive and still working the problems.* He looked around, everyone looked bone tired. *I have to keep them going.*

"We are making progress. We have come farther than many of you expected we could. Today's problem is another hard one."

"They're all hard ones." Then thinking better of it, Chief Kowalski added, "Sir."

"Our astrogation computer and the PPS were both destroyed. We need to find a way to figure out where we are and where we can get to. Any ideas?"

Midshipmen Stewart spoke up. "Sir, I have my textbook astrogation programs on my tablet. Would they help?"

The Captain just looked at him in amazement. "And this is the first you thought to mention that?"

"Well, Captain. Like everyone else I've been pretty busy. Sorry, sir."

"Don't worry Mr. Stewart. I didn't tell you it was important." *Though, as an officer, I expect you to know what's important. No reason to say that in front of the others. I'll tell him that when the others aren't around.* "Is the telescope working, Chief Kowalski?"

"I had to realign some of the lenses but it seems to be functional."

"What can we get out of its control system?"

"If we aim it at something, we can get the pointing coordinates. And we can take photos but I don't see how that's going to help us right now."

"Mr. Stewart, we need backups. Copy your astrogation programs to all the other tablets."

The Midshipman picked up his tablet and, with a pen, started writing on it. "Yes, sir." A moment later he said, "Done."

"Chief, now send me the data on our fuel status and the performance data on the starboard fusion engine."

A few minutes later, the Chief said, "Done, sir. By the way, I have already factored in the loss of the Langston Field, and the resulting inefficiency to the engine's performance."

"Thank you, Chief."

The Captain sat with his tablet for a few minutes, then put it down. "I've got to look at this in more detail. It doesn't look like we have enough fuel for a direct trajectory to Ayesha and the refueling station."

"Captain," the Midshipman, said remembering his astrogation lessons. "Perhaps we can trade time for fuel. What about a Hohmann orbit?"

"Good thinking." *Maybe he is learning.* The Captain went back to work. A few minutes later, he looked up. "That helps but it takes just under five years to get from here to Cat's Eye. And even then, we're in the wrong place in Hel's orbit. We won't be in the correct orbital position for such an orbit for at least another six years. We can't last that long."

"Why six years, sir?"

"The orbital mechanics only allow us to travel along a minimum energy orbit between Hel and Cat's Eye at certain times. These times are called the synodic period. It means both bodies have to be in the right position relative to each other for the trajectory to work. For Hel and Cat's Eye, that's every ten years. Given our position in the leading Trojan, we have six years, a little more than half a synodic period, before the next window opens that will allow us to get to Cat's Eye."

"Captain," Martinez said. "What about the frozen sleep tanks in sickbay? There are six of them and six of us."

"Let me look into that. In the meantime, our next project is to get the Wheel turning. We need some artificial gravity. Anything would be helpful. Chief Wagner, can you get it moving again?"

"Williams and I will take a look, Captain."

"Okay, we'll meet again tomorrow. Same time. Dismissed."

The next day, the Captain had some good news. "I've run the numbers; we can do it. We have just enough fuel to make it to Ayesha.

"There is bad news too. We won't be able to make the Hohmann orbital burn for sixteen years, not the six we talked about yesterday. After the burn, it will still take five years to reach Cat's Eye. Once there, we pass close behind the gas giant and, at closest approach, make another burn slowing us down. That injects us into an orbit that will take us to Ayesha and the refueling station. Once there, we make a third burn to slow ourselves down to the station's orbital speed. We actually get there will a little fuel to spare. That means that if we can't get fuel from Ayesha, we still have enough fuel to get to Haven."

"Why the additional ten years, Captain?" Williams, asked.

"We have to wait through more than one complete Hel-Cat's Eye synodic period for Ayesha to be in the correct orbital position around Cat's Eye so we can match orbits with it." Then he paused and looked at the Midshipmen. "Mister Stewart, I would like you to check my calculations."

"Aye aye, Captain."

Then the Captain addressed the crew, "Yesterday, Martinez asked about the frozen sleep tanks in sickbay. I looked at them. They are fully functional. While they were designed to keep seriously wounded personnel alive until we could reach Fleet hospital facilities, they will work for our needs. This means we will all be in frozen sleep for the majority of the trip."

"Captain, aren't those tanks designed to be used only for a few years, at most? We're talking about twenty-one years here."

"You are right, Chief Wagner. They weren't designed for how we're going to use them. But medical frozen sleep tanks have the largest safety margins designed into them of any frozen sleep tanks. Take a look at them and satisfy yourself. Let me know if you have any concerns after you've done a deep dive into the specs."

"Aye aye, Skipper."

"Captain, who's gonna wake us?" Martinez asked.

"We're going to have to rely on our tablets to initiate the thawing."

Chief Kowalski spoke up. "Captain, is there any other way?"

"Chief, our radio transmitters are dead. Even if we had the power to spare and could pierce the static around Cat's Eye from here to contact Ayesha or Haven, they don't have the ships to reach us. We don't have the consumables to survive the trip. And, even if we did, I'm not sure any of us could stay sane for twenty-one years waiting. No, this is the only way. We can network the tablets together to make sure they initiate the waking process. However, for two of us, there will be two waking events."

Chief Wagner suspecting what the Captain had in mind said, "What do you mean? Or, more precisely, who do you mean, Skipper?"

"Chief, in sixteen years the computers will wake you and me so we can ensure the burn is made that puts us on the proper trajectory to Cat's Eye. Then we'll go back into frozen sleep. You and I will be awakened a month before the gravity assist around the giant planet. We'll need to make sure we're lined up properly. If we need to wake any of the others, we will. Just before we reach Ayesha, everyone will be awakened."

"Thanks for the explanation, Captain. I don't like it but you are right. I need to be awake for the burns." The Chief thought for a moment. "If we can get rid of excess mass, that will increase our fuel reserves." He thought for a moment and said, "Or, more correctly, it will increase our available delta vee."

Chief Kowalski asked, "What about the radar array? It's a fused mess. We can cut it loose from the hardpoints with a laser pistol."

"Good thinking, Chief. Anyone else?"

"Captain, these scoutships were built by linking prefabricated modules together. Can we remove one or more of them?"

"I don't think so, Martinez. The modules are integral to the structural integrity of the ship. Removing one might weaken the ship enough so we break apart during a propulsion burn. And, to remove one properly would require a shipyard. Still, that's what I want, out of the box ideas."

"Captain, another question."

"Go ahead, Martinez."

"With our Langston Field gone, what about the radiation fields around Cat's Eye?"

"Our hull platting is designed to shield us against radiation. Sickbay is shielded more than the rest of the ship. That's where we'll ride out the passage. If anyone has other ideas, I'm open to listening. Bring them up now or come to me individually. Let's meet again tomorrow."

Lieutenant Johansen hadn't moved into his old CO's quarters. He still felt uncomfortable doing that, although he couldn't exactly say why. It might have been superstition or it might have been respect. Maybe it was a little of both. As he was thinking about it, Chief Wagner knocked on his hatch.

"Come."

The Chief entered. The Captain's stateroom was small and very crowded for a meeting; even a meeting of only two people.

"What did you want to see me about, Chief?"

"Two things. First, the frozen sleep tanks. I agree with you. I've had a chance to look them over. I think mechanically they'll hold up for the duration. However, I am concerned about their self-contained power supply lasting long enough."

"Is there anything you can do, Chief?"

"I can run an electrical line from the ship's emergency batteries directly to sickbay. It's a jury-rigged solution but it should work. In addition, I'll add sickbay's power status to the computer monitoring programs. The computers will initiate a thaw for you and me, if the sickbay battery levels drop below fifteen percent. If the batteries drop below that level, we will have to restart the fusion reactor to recharge the batteries."

"So, we'll be awakened if the makeshift plan doesn't work?"

"Yes, Captain. This minimizes our risk."

"Very well. And your second item?"

"I had an idea for getting rid of some more mass."

"I'm listening."

"Captain, the port engine room was destroyed in the accident and that engine is useless to us. I was thinking we could cut the port engine nozzle off with our laser pistols. It's massive enough to help."

"Is there any way it could be repaired at Ayesha?"

"It's possible, Captain. It depends what kind of spare parts they can make for us."

"In that case, let's not go down that road as long as we have enough delta vee. But, thank you."

"Captain, before I go, can I ask you a personal question?"

"Sure, Chief. What would you like to know?"

Chief Wagner pointed to a model of a boat above the Captain's desk. "That model, what is it? I've never seen anything like it."

"Chief, I built that when I was a boy. Before I went to the Academy. I come from Dalarna. A planet settled by Scandinavians back in the CoDominium days. So, my ancestors are Vikings. Or, at least they were sixteen hundred years ago. I was interested in their history. With my fader's help, I built this model of a Viking longship. It's an exact replica, best I know. My fader was killed in the Sauron surprise attack on Dalarna a few years ago. I keep the model to remember him." Then with steel in his voice, he added. "And to remember what this war is all about." Changing the subject, he asked. "How about you, Chief. Where are you from?"

"Churchill, sir. My ancestors were German. They also colonized Churchill during the CoDominium period. Before we arrived, Churchill was colonized by our cousins, the English. We didn't get along well at first. After the Troubles, we learned how to live and work together. Like many in my homeland, I had a knack for making things. There weren't many engineering jobs on Churchill, so I joined the Navy. Never regretted it."

"Thanks, Chief. Now, I've got to get back to these astrogation calculations. Dismissed."

FOUR

2658 A.D., INSS Vasily Zaytsev, Between the Orbit of Hel and Cat's Eye

Lieutenant Johansen had just finished injecting Chief Wagner with adrenaline. Straight into his heart. He then continued CPR. "Come on, Chief. Breathe! Breathe! You can't die on me!" The Chief was lying on the medtable in sickbay. The computer had awakened the Captain early, when its algorithms determined the Chief's frozen sleep tank was failing.

The Chief finally gasped for air. The heart monitor showed an irregular beat. Then slowly, it began to stabilize and return to a normal cadence. The Chief opened his eyes. Shivering, he tried to talk. The Captain put his ear close to the Chief's mouth.

"Co…co…cold."

The Captain wrapped him in a warm blanket. Then he made him a cup of what seemed to be broth. Warm, but not too hot. Something that would help raise the Chief's internal temperature slowly. It tasted like beef bouillon but it contained nutrients and medicines a body needed to recover from the ordeal it had just gone through. Standard fare when waking from frozen sleep.

"Wh…where are we?"

"Take it easy, Chief. You're going to be all right."

"Are we there?"

"No, Chief. We were awakened early."

"Wh … why, sir?"

"It's not an immediate problem. I'll fill you in once you've recovered."

Two days later the Chief was chomping at the bit. "Captain, what's happened? Why are we awake?"

"Chief, your frozen sleep tank was failing. The computer woke me in time to get you out of it and wake you. Once you are up to it, I need you to repair it. While you're awake, I want you to start up the fusion reactor. Might as well give all the batteries a full charge. And run routine checks on all our other equipment too."

A few days later the Chief came to see the Captain. "Sir, I have bad news. I can't fix the frozen sleep tank. I don't have the parts."

"No spare parts in inventory?"

"No, sir."

"The micro-fabricators?"

"Still the same, Captain. They're broken. And there's nothing I can cannibalize to fix them."

"Then Chief, the only answer I can see is that you use my tank and go back into frozen sleep. I'll stand watch here. Do we have enough battery power to run the life-support systems?"

"For a year, sir? No."

"Can you set the fusion reactor to run at its lowest power setting?"

"I can set it up that way, Captain. But it'll still use some of our hydrogen fuel."

"How much?"

"I'll give you an estimate. At the very least, it will reduce our reserve. Can you handle being alone for that long?"

"I can do it, Chief."

"Captain, wouldn't it be better for me to stay awake. After all, I can fix things if they break."

"No, Chief. I'm not going to ask you to do that."

"But, Captain ..."

"Do I have to make it an order, Chief?"

The Chief just looked at the Captain. He shook his head sideways. "No, sir. You don't."

"Don't worry, Chief. I can handle a year by myself. And, if I run into any engineering issues, I'll wake you."

"Yes, sir."

FIVE

2659 A.D., INSS Vasily Zaytsev,
Approaching Cat's Eye

They were close enough to see the giant planet on the forward view screen. A small banded crescent of orange, and cream and yellow on a background of black. It looked small but it was big enough to swallow Sparta, Dalarma or old Earth a thousand times over.

"That's it Chief. That's our destination."

"Twenty-one years," Chief Wagner said, shaking his head. "I didn't believe we'd make it, sir. We…Captain, we wouldn't have made it this far if you hadn't kept us moving forward. And…well, I wouldn't have made it if you hadn't saved my life. You never gave up on me. Thank you, sir."

The Captain turned slightly red at the Chief's praise and thanks. "You're welcome, Chief." Then the Captain changed the subject.

"Now, we still have a way to go. By my calculations, we need to adjust our orbit. We're not quite lined up correctly for the gravity assist maneuver."

"Captain, let me check the fusion engine. It's been idle for five years and may need a tune up."

"Make it quick, Chief. The longer we wait to make the burn, the more fuel we'll have to use to correct our course. And that eats into our reserve. My last year awake has already done that some."

"Yes, sir. But before I do, Captain. Can I ask what the last year was like for you? Awake here. Alone."

The Captain smiled. Almost a sigh of relief. "Chief, let's just say I'm really glad for the company."

The Chief gave him a questioning look. Silently asking for more than just a simple answer.

The Captain expanded on his reply. "I developed and followed a very precise routine. The same one every day. And I made myself a short-timer's calendar. Not much more than scratches on my stateroom wall. But it kept me focused."

"I see. Thank you, Skipper."

"One more thing, I hate the gruel your Rube Goldberg food synthesizer makes. I really hate it." Then the Captain got back down to business. "Okay, enough reminiscing. Chief, I also want you to check the telescope after you check the fusion engine. I'm making a small adjustment to our course that will take us near Haven. I want to do a recon of it."

"Why, Captain?"

"We don't know what's been going on there for what? Over thirty-five years? Just caution."

2659 *A.D.*, INSS *Vasily Zaytsev*, Ayesha

The entire crew was awake and crowded onto the bridge. They were excited. All were looking forward to the end of their remarkable voyage.

"Captain, I'm not receiving the refueling station's IFF beacon. I also don't have visuals on either the tether or the fuel bladder's flashing safety lights, and at this range I should. Lastly, I'm still not receiving any radio traffic from the station."

"How far to the fuel bladders, Boats?"

Martinez looked at his tablet. "We should be coming up on them in nine kilometers, Skipper."

"I wish we had radar. Does the telescope show anything at the fuel bladder coordinates?"

"Wait a moment, sir…" Chief Kowalski replied. Then he added, "No, Captain. That's strange. I double checked them. They're input correctly."

The Captain had a bad feeling. "Chief, aim the telescope straight down at the moon's surface where the station is located."

The image that was displayed on the forward view screen showed a mass of wreckage; the collapsed tether piled on top of the ground station.

Someone cried out, "God, no!"

Another voice, "Damn!"

Chief Kowalski simply said, "ATTENTION." The chatter ended.

The Captain addressed the group. "Now we know why there is no beacon, no radio traffic. Remember, we talked about this. Our backup plan is Haven. I'm disappointed too but we are still alive and we have work to do. First off, Chief Kowalski, do we have any sensors that can tell us about the weapon that destroyed the station?"

"Yes, sir. Those sensors amazingly were not burned out in the accident. I'll see what they can tell us."

An hour later, Chief Kowalski had an answer. "Captain, the weapon that severed the tether was a small nuclear charge. It looks like it has a Sauron signature."

"You're sure, Chief?"

"Not one hundred percent but it's the closest match to my readings."

"Can you determine how long ago it happened?"

"Only a range. Eighteen to twenty years ago, sir."

"Mr. Stewart, let's see those photos we took of Haven as we past it."

On the forward view screen, a composite photo of the Shangri-La Valley came up. It was Chief Kowalski who spoke first. "Captain, it looks like the major cities have been nuked. And, if I read the maps correctly, the military installations as well. It's the type of attack the Saurons would execute. But why do it here? Haven is the ass end of nowhere. Nothing strategic here."

"I want everyone to look over the photos."

Chief Wagner scratched his beard. "What are we looking for, Skipper?"

"I don't know, Chief. Anything that looks unusual. We need more information. Mr. Stewart, do we have image analysis software on any of the tablets?"

"Yes, sir."

"Good, then run the photos through whatever we have."

Several hours later, the crew met again.

"Anyone find anything we didn't see before?"

Midshipman Stewart, spoke up. "Captain, my image recognition program found something at the far west end of the Shangri-La Valley. See these squares and rectangles? And what looks like an arrow pointing from them to the east? That's unusual."

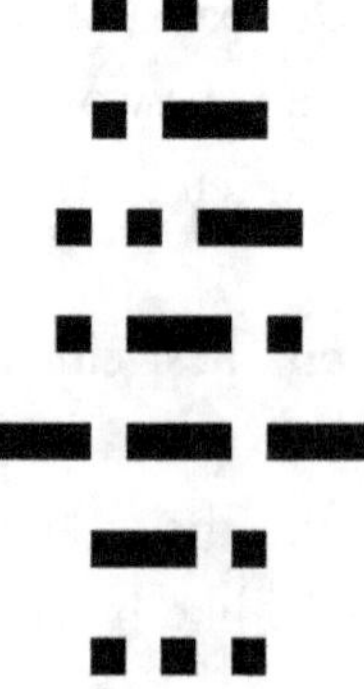

"Anyone else?"

Williams responded. "Captain, look here at the southeast end of the valley. Another set of them squares. But the arrow is pointing differently. Looks to be north."

"Anybody have any idea what these are?" the Captain asked.

Williams said, "I'm from Tabletop, Captain. Born and raised on a farm. We grew New Washington cornplant. After our harvest, we used to burn our fields to get them ready for the next planting. I saw them from the sky once, after we did that. My brothers had built a homemade glider and they took me up. It looked like this. I think somebody burned some fields to make those."

Martinez said, "They remind me of photos I saw when I was a kid. A photo of something called the Nazca lines back on old Earth. In a region called Peru. Images of insects and animals and whatnot. Things that were said could only be seen by the space gods or some such horse exhaust."

Chief Kowalski said, "I've heard that if you squint your eyes, it can sometimes make a broken image take more solid form."

The Middie tried it. Then said, "All I see are a bunch of circles and dashes."

Chief Kowalski was talking to himself now. "Circles and dashes. Dots and dashes." Then he tried it. He turned to the rest of the crew and said, "Captain. When I was a kid, I learned an ancient coding system called Morse code. It was made up of dots and dashes with spaces between them. My friends and I used it to exchange messages our parents couldn't read."

"And you think those squares and rectangles are this Morse code?"

"They may be, sir."

"If they are, can you tell us what it says, Chief?"

"It's been a long time, sir. I'll try."

The Chief looked at the photos, then his face changed to horror and he mumbled, "Oh, Mother of God."

"Chief?"

"Saurons, Captain. It says, Saurons."

The Captain had a hunch. "Midshipmen, the two arrows. Where do they cross?"

The Midshipman went to work on his tablet. A minute later he said, "Karakul Pass. A place called Fort Stony Point, sir." Then he showed everyone the map of the area on his tablet. "Here."

"Bring up the best photo we have of that area on the forward view screen, Mr. Stewart."

After seeing the photo of the pass, Lieutenant Johansen gave the crew his analysis. "They didn't nuke the fort. I'll bet my pension, they took it for their own." The Captain then paused for a minute before he added, "That explains what the Saurons are doing here. They were running away, looking for a place to hide. A place to takeover and rebuild. The good news is, that means the Empire is winning the war against them. The bad news, this limits where we can land. Where else can we make landfall on Haven?"

"Captain, I was born on Haven. Got off of it as soon as I was old enough to join the Navy. I never wanted to go back."

"And now?"

"And now, sir. It sure beats the alternative," Chief Kowalski said smiling. Then turning more serious, "Haven is a cold world. Its air is very thin and its day night cycle is long and complex. Trueday, dimday, truenight. One orbital cycle around Cat's Eye is a hundred and thirty standard hours long. But, because Haven's rotation is eighty-seven hours, it takes two orbital cycles to bring someone on the surface back to see the exact same sky. In other words, Haven rotates three times on its axis for each two orbits of Cat's Eye. On the other hand, when Cat's Eye is up, it's one of most beautiful sights I've ever seen. And it's slightly warmer since Cat's Eye is still radiating heat from its formation.

"The eastern continent is called Tierra de la Muerte, the Land of Death. It's overrun with stobor. Wild packs of your worst nightmare. It has never been colonized. The Western continent contains the Shangri-La Valley and the steppes of the north plus maybe a few other barely habitable areas. The southern ocean contains a small continent, also a few large islands but we're better off if we stay near the equator. It's warmer there."

The Chief pointed to a big island in the middle of the Occidental Ocean between the western and eastern continents. "This is Cracovia. It's where I was raised before I joined the Navy." The Captain gave him a questioning look. *Keep going, Chief.* "Cracovia was mostly barren when Haven was first discovered but it was extensively terraformed with Earth-stock plants and animals. The air pressure is low there. At least lower than the Shangri-La Valley. As I said, being on the equator is good and, as a result, Cracovia is one of the more temperate places on Haven. The volcanos don't have carbon dioxide glaciers on them like most of the high mountains on the planet."

"The western continent is out. The Shangri-La Valley and the northern steppes are really the only habitable areas there. The Saurons obviously control the passage between the two, which means they control both areas. Those messages are a couple of thousand kilometers from Fort Stony Point. That implies the Saurons have taken over a large swath of the Shangri-La Valley. It also implies some long range coordinated resistance. Anyone who keeps those patches up knows they'd be on the south end of a Sauron expeditionary force if the Saurons ever discovered them. That suggests to me the Saurons don't have satellites or aircraft anymore. Not something we should bet on though."

"A lot of guesses, Captain."

The Captain smiled. "Best I can do, Chief." Then the Captain paused for a moment before continuing. "I don't want to set down on the same continent as the Saurons. Eventually we would run into them. It sounds to me like Cracovia is the best choice. Anyone have a better idea than Cracovia?" The Captain looked around. "No? Then Cracovia it is. Do we have enough fuel to get there? Mr. Stewart, what do your astrogation programs say about a Hohmann orbit to Haven and landing us in Cracovia?"

"Captain, the ship doesn't have enough fuel to do it. We don't have enough fuel to slow down or land. Even the burn to get us there is on the bubble."

"Chief Wagner had an idea to deep six some more mass. Chief, would you explain?"

"I talked to the Captain about cutting off the port fusion nozzle. Like we did with the radar array. The magnetic containment coils surrounding the nozzle are massive. Just take our laser pistols and lop it off. It'll change our center of mass but we should be able to compensate for that."

"I think it's time we did that, Chief. We're not getting the port engine repaired here any time soon and we need every bit of delta vee we can get. Mr. Stewart, get the mass of the nozzle from the Chief and recalculate. Tell me what that does for us."

The Chief transferred the data to the Midshipman's tablet. The Midshipman worked his tablet. "Still not enough to land, Captain. Or to go into orbit about Haven. But there's no question about making the Hohmann orbit. This will give us enough delta vee with the fuel we've got."

"How long to make the transit, Mr. Stewart?"

"A day and a half, Skipper. But the Hohmann window is only open once every eleven days. I assume you're thinking of taking one of the lifeboats down. They can get us to the surface but we'll lose the *VeeZee.* If it survives reentry, it will crash into the Occidental Ocean. The next window that will allow us to get to Cracovia is in twenty-seven days. Just like at Hel's leading Trojan, we have to wait a couple of synodic periods before we can make our insertion burn. We're five days into the current synodic period between Ayesha and Haven now. And then we have to wait for Haven's rotation to line us up with Cracovia. That will take two more synodic periods. We are all going to be pretty sick of gruel by the time we make planetfall."

"Anybody have a better idea?"

Chief Kowalski asked, "What about taking both good lifeboats, Skipper?"

Chief Wagner responded instead. "Someone has to be physically in the lifeboat for it to function. That's the way they were designed. So, it means we would have to split up. And if we do that, there's no guarantee we'll make planetfall anywhere near each other. I don't know about the rest of you but we've stuck together this long; I'd like to finish this together."

The Captain looked around. "Anyone else?" No one said anything. "That's it then. We stay together. Chief Wagner, can we disable the IFF and emergency beacon on the lifeboat?"

"I'm not sure, Skipper. They're not designed to be turned off, for the obvious reason. I'll see what I can do."

"Thanks, Chief. It's important." Then addressing everyone, he asked, "What do we take down with us in the lifeboat?"

2659 A.D., Haven

Chief Wagner had gotten the Wheel working, somewhat. The crew had taken turns exercising in it since they had been awakened from frozen sleep. The Wheel had been designed to simulate up to 1.2 gees; one Spartan gravity. But after the accident and the following repairs, the most it could produce was half a gee. Even though Haven's gravity was point nine one gee, more than the Wheel could generate, it was better preparation than nothing.

Before the crew abandoned the *VeeZee*, they opened all the exterior hatches and weapons bay doors. They needed the ship to sink to the bottom of the ocean after it crashed. The last thing they wanted was all or part of the *VeeZee* to wash up on some distant shore and be found by the Saurons.

The squat cone-shaped lifeboat capsule had a design history that went back to the old United States Apollo moon program. Except this capsule was over twice as big and constructed with twenty-seventh century materials. Inside, the crew couches were arranged in a six-point star with the crew member's feet pointed toward the center.

The atmospheric entry was hard on the crew. As the capsule entered the atmosphere, it was engulfed in a glowing shroud of plasma. Deceleration pressed the crew deep into the padding of their couches. Finally, after the capsule's speed had been bled off, the gees subsided. The next thing they felt was a small jolt as the pilot chute opened. That was followed by a much stronger jolt as the three big parachutes opened. After what seemed like an eternity, the retrorockets fired, cushioning their touchdown.

Lieutenant Johansen had kept his promise to himself. All of the surviving crewmembers of the *INSS Vasily* Zaytsev had made it safely to Haven.

Persistence of Memory

ONE

2640 A.D., INSS *Cassiopeia's Daughter,* Location Unknown

Dimity woke in a daze. Where was he? Then he realized he was weightless. Wearing a spacesuit. Red emergency lights reflected off the bulkhead in the compartment where he floated. His mind was a jumble of thoughts and emotions. Slowly, he began to regain control. He remembered. They had Jumped. He must have Jump shock. That was it. He was relieved.

I have survived.

The ship has survived.

The Race has survived.

Dmitry wondered where that last thought came from. Then he remembered his unborn child and forgot all else. The child he had to leave behind on the world called Haven, now in another galaxy. A child he would never meet. He let his grief and anger wash over him until he blacked out again.

* * *

Admiral Blaine was a child, sitting with his mother in the main garden of his family's manor. It felt like dusk but the sky was the color of marmalade. Instead of the sun or stars, there were diamonds in the sky. Sitting under a tangerine tree, his mother was trying to tell him something but he couldn't understand. He looked up and saw an ancient mechanical pocket watch. It looked half-melted, draped over one of the tree limbs. The hands on its face frozen, unmoving. It reminded him of something he had seen in the Imperial Art Museum on a class field trip.

He tried again. "Mother, what are you saying?"

"Georgie, your father and I love you very much but you will need to make your own way in this world. Your older brothers will inherit the titles and lands before you do."

"Why, Mother?"

"It's the law." Then she lowered her voice and added reverently, "Lysander I, established the precedent long ago. It has served the Empire well."

"What will I do?"

"Your father and I think you should go into the Navy."

"How do I do that?"

"You will need to go to the Naval Academy."

"Is that here on Sparta?"

"No, Georgie. It's on Earth."

"Mother, I am not …"

Another voice interrupted, like thunder booming out of the marmalade sky. "Admiral. Admiral Blaine, sir. You need to wake up."

His world began to shake. The garden receded from his mind. His mother shattered into a thousand pieces like a mirror dropped on the floor. He was confused. Then he felt his stomach churning.

"Admiral, sir. You have Jump shock. Admiral, can you hear me?"

Returning to consciousness, Admiral Blaine answered. "Yes, thank you, Ensign. Sitrep."

* * *

The *INSS Cassiopeia's Daughter*, the largest, most advanced spaceship humans ever built, had survived the Random Jump, but just barely. Most of the crew had also survived the Jump shock that came with using the Alderson Drive. Everyone's reaction to an Alderson Jump was different. The distance of the Jump didn't seem to affect the severity of the malady. No one knew what did or what caused Jump shock in the first place.

In over six hundred years, no one had ever been able to measure the time it took to make a Jump. But, in that timeless instant some people swore they knew everything there was to know about the universe. But it was only the memory of having known they remembered, not the knowledge itself. Others remembered experiencing synesthesia; they could hear colors, smell noises or taste shapes. Some remembered dreams. In rare cases, minds never came back at all. Their bodies became mere husks. Confusion and nausea were common symptoms. Both were usually temporary. Sophisticated computers reacted much the same as people. After several disasters, computers had been shut down for every Jump since the beginning of interstellar flight.

The crew had taken twenty minutes to recover from their ordeal. Now, damage control teams swarmed through the ship. Several DC teams were out on the hull, manually pushing sensor arrays through the protective black bubble of the Langston Field.

Fleet Admiral George Sergei Carlton Blaine was on the flag bridge waiting for the first image from the sensors. The first arrays through pointed aft, away from the bow of the ship. As the image appeared on the screen in front of him, a dense star field could be seen. Five more such sensor arrays needed to be deployed before the Admiral could get a complete picture of where the ship had materialized.

Looking at the images from the final sensor array to be deployed, one bright star stood out. "Put the telescope on that one," Admiral Blaine ordered.

"Now, magnify it."

As the enlarged image came up on the screen, his most junior staff officer Ensign Vasiliev said in a shocked voice, "My God. What is that? It looks like something out of a Jump dream."

The Admiral looked disapprovingly at the young Ensign who had spoken. He didn't like blasphemy and he didn't want his watch officers to speak unnecessarily. The Admiral just said one word.

"Ensign."

"My apologies, Admiral."

On the screen was a small black globe, blacker than black. It was embedded in the middle of a folded disk of bright sun fire. There might be stars further out from that disk but the human eye couldn't make them out. The contrast was too much like that of daylight.

Because of the Ensign's apology, the Admiral was inclined to answer his question. "I believe, Ensign, that is something no man has ever seen this close before. That is a black hole with an active accretion disk." He looked down at the instrument readouts. "As it is, based on the sensor readings, we can't drop the Field. Too much radiation out there. Thankfully, we materialized far from it."

The Admiral keyed a comm circuit. "Captain Fainchurch, Admiral Blaine here. What does Astrogation say about where we are and what we are looking at?"

"We're working on it, Admiral."

"There is a Command Staff meeting in a half an hour. Come with answers, Captain."

"Aye aye, Admiral."

* * *

Admiral Blaine looked around the table at his Command Staff. He was saddened to see two of the chairs empty. They were left empty as a sign of respect for the two Command Staff officers killed in the Jump and its aftermath, the ship's First officer and the Admiral's Chief of Staff. *None of us will ever see the Imperial stars again. Well, time to get on with it.* The Admiral cleared his throat to speak and the room went silent.

"We survived the Jump. Although we have had casualties. Cardinal

Peterson, would you lead us in prayer for our fallen shipmates?"

The Cardinal, the highest member of the Church on the expedition, still felt weak from Jump shock but he pulled himself together. "Of course, Admiral." Then he turned to the assembled personnel, bowed his head and prayed.

"All powerful and merciful God, we commend our fallen shipmates to you. In your mercy and love, forgive them the sins they have committed through human weakness. Let them live forever with you. Through Christ our Lord. Amen."

Cardinal Peterson paused for a moment before continuing. "Let us pray."

The assembled personnel joined him. "Our Father in heaven, hallowed be your name. Your kingdom come, your will be done, on earth as it is in heaven. Give us this day our daily bread, and forgive us our debts, as we have also forgiven our debtors. And lead us not into temptation, but deliver us from evil. Amen."

"Thank you, Cardinal Peterson. Captain Fainchurch, what has your Astrogation department determined? Where precisely are we?"

Captain Fainchurch came from one of the aristocratic families on Churchill, with a line that went back to the CoDominium period. Depending on your perspective, part of the famous, or infamous Niles line. He was tall at six-two, had light colored eyes and light brown hair with a touch of gray in it. He had a reputation as an exceptional naval officer. Like the Admiral, he was a younger son who joined the Navy to make his own way in the world. After pausing for a moment to look around the table, he called up an image of the black hole and displayed it on the big war room screen. The image had a much higher definition than the one they first saw on the bridge. The captain used a pointer to highlight the black globe in the center.

"Admiral, you are looking at the black hole at the center of the Andromeda galaxy. This is a close-up of the hole. All two hundred million solar masses of it." The image then pulled back. "This bright, multicolored region across the middle of the black hole is the accretion disk. The bright areas above and below the hole are a mirage caused by gravitational lensing.

It's like an interstellar Fata Morgana. In this case, we are seeing light from the far side of the disk bent around the hole by its intense gravity. It will take us some time to analyze it in detail.

"We materialized about fourteen thousand astronomical units from it, almost edge on. The size of that thing is enormous. The black hole alone is seven AU across. The Capitol; Agamemnon, Sparta and all the gas giants, could fit neatly inside. Fortunately, we materialized a fifth of a light-year out from it." Captain Fainchurch then used his pointer to designate the ghostly vortexes above the north and south poles of the hole. "Here and here are relativistic jets."

The Admiral looked at the image. *Up close, that disk looks like a folded, swirling rainbow. Each color blending with the one next to it, surrounding a small, impossibly black balloon. What terrible beauty. Interesting. That fiery maelstrom is colored with the same hues a Langston Field sequences through before it overloads; red, orange, yellow, and then white. That means the disk is producing black-body radiation, the same as the Field. Though obviously, from a different process.*

The Captain changed the display to a split screen. On the left was an image of the center of the Andromeda galaxy taken from the Milky Way before they Jumped. It was two and a half million years out of date. On the right was a picture of the region as it looked now. The two were very different.

"Now, our Astrogator, Commander Anderson will give you some background on the large-scale structure of the central region and what has happened here over the last two and a half million years. Commander."

The Captain handed the pointer to the Astrogator and he began his portion of the briefing. "Admiral, as you can see, there have been a lot of changes. The central black hole has become much more active over that time.

"This bright area on the left seems to have decreased in intensity. We think these were a group of stars orbiting five light-years away from the center that, because of their orbital parameters, temporarily clumped together. They no longer show such a grouping."

Next, the Commander highlighted a region closer to the accretion disk containing hundreds of very hot, blue giant stars. "Over the last two and a half million years, these stars seem to have orbited closer and closer to the accretion disk until they were absorbed into it. We haven't had time to model the stellar dynamics yet but it makes sense given what we know. In any case, the disk is much larger and more massive than it was two and a half million years ago. As a result, it is also much more active today than it was. We suspected something like this might have happened based on the information collected by astronomers at the Imperial Alderson force observatories."

The Commander shifted his pointer again. "Now for the accretion disk. There are sites of embedded turbulence in the disk which the astrophysicists think are caused by neutron stars or stellar black holes. However, in general, the disk is distinguished by regions of different temperatures and therefore, of different colors. The innermost region is the hottest and produces white light. This is where vast amounts of X-rays are produced; just before the infalling matter passes through the hole's event horizon and is lost to this universe."

The Astrogator moved the pointer away from the white region. "Outward from here the disk is wider and cooler and produces yellow light. Moving out from there is a broader and cooler region still, producing orange light. And further out is an even cooler, larger region producing red light. The outer region beyond that is the widest, producing infrared radiation. Most of the light is produced by friction as the gas streams inward toward the hole.

"The inner region of the disk is hot enough for fusion which produces huge amounts of Alderson force. That and the gravitational field of the hole is why we materialized here."

The Admiral thought about that for a moment. Then he said, "A star can be thought of as a point source for the Alderson force. This source is ring shaped. Do we know what that does to the location of the Jump points?"

"No, Admiral. Some of the models developed by the Imperial Alderson force observatories suggest that the Jump regions are further out than what we would normally expect. But we haven't begun looking into that yet.

One of the unknowns is: does the gravitational warping, that causes the accretion disk to look like it does, affect the Alderson force distribution around the hole?"

Captain Fainchurch added, "I have given that a lower priority for now, Admiral. Damage control is more important."

"Agreed, Captain. Now, Astrogator. What about gravity waves?"

"Admiral, I don't understand your question."

"Back in the early days of interstellar flight, several CoDominium spaceships were trapped around a black hole. They experienced destructive episodes of intense gravity waves. Are we at risk of the same?"

"Admiral, the short answer is that we do not know yet but we think it unlikely. Let me explain. Gravity waves are normally extremely weak however we know black holes can produce intense gravity waves. The ships you are referring to materialized one AU from a black hole of about ten solar masses. That black hole's accretion disk was only occasionally feeding matter into its hole and therefore only occasionally producing gravity waves.

"The accretion disk of this black hole is continuously feeding matter past the hole's event horizon and, therefore, is continuously producing gravity waves. We materialized over fourteen thousand AUs from the event horizon of the central black hole here. Gravity waves follow the inverse square law, so gravity waves produced at the event horizon are much weaker out here. Since we haven't experienced any destructive effects from gravity waves, we do not think they will become a problem for us.

"However, if there are density fluctuations in the accretion disk, that could change. We haven't been able to untangle the gravitational lensing effect yet. So, we cannot be sure. If there are knots of higher density close to the inner edge of the disk that we haven't seen, then it is possible we will experience a ringdown of more intense gravity waves in the future. I'm sorry, Admiral. That is the best answer I can give you at the moment."

"Thank you, Commander. So, if we move a lot closer to the hole or if there are higher concentrations of matter approaching the event horizon, we could experience more destructive effects?"

"Yes, Admiral. From our cursory examination of the disk, there aren't any matter concentrations near the event horizon that are a danger to us.

But we need more time to examine it in detail."

The Admiral thought about the presentation. *Gravity and the Alderson force. We have been exposed to these two forces at intensities rarely seen by man. I hope we don't need to worry about gravity waves. The Langston Field won't protect us from those. But we need to study the disk more before we can be confident we won't be hit with them.*

As far as the Alderson force is concerned, there are few astronomical objects that could produce as much of it as we have experienced. When we Jumped from the Byers' System, we were six hundred light-years from the Betelgeuse supernova. That explosion, even at such a distance, produced Alderson force intensities that could only be rivaled by a supermassive black hole's accretion disk, or another supernova. The resulting tramline was stable, but short-lived. Its life measured in minutes. That monster in front of us has the largest gravitational cross-section of anything in the Andromeda galaxy. Making it more likely to drop a ship out of hyperspace than anything else. Yes, in retrospect, this was the most likely place for a Random Jump to the Andromeda galaxy to terminate.

"Very well. Can your people tell yet if we are moving with respect to that thing?"

"We're working on it, Admiral. My people are trying to get a Doppler shift but it's difficult because of the hole's gravitational redshift."

"Try the stars on the other side of the ship. Away from the hole."

Commander Anderson looked surprised. *I should have thought of that.* But he only said, "Aye aye, Admiral."

"Our instruments indicate the radiation levels are very high outside the Field. Is that coming from the inner disk's X-rays?"

"Yes, Admiral. If we were closer to the plane of the accretion disk, I would recommend we move into it to maximize the shielding effect the outer regions of the accretion disk provide. But the plane is over three thousand AUs away. Too far. I think our best hope is to move outward and find a rogue planet to get behind. Given all the mass floating around the center here we might be able to find one."

"Let's come back to that." The Admiral addressed Captain Fainchurch. "Have we heard anything from the other two Imperial ships?"

"No, Admiral. We have our receivers tuned to the Fleet frequencies they would use. Given we were all making a Random Jump from different locations in the Empire, we didn't expect to end up anywhere near each other if our Jumps were successful. Even if they materialized here at the center, this is a huge region. None of us can send or receive omnidirectional signals very far."

"Thank you, Captain. Now, what is the ship's status?"

The Captain turned to his Damage Control Officer, Commander Durant. "DCO, make your report." Commander Anderson handed the pointer to Commander Durant and sat down, strapping himself into the chair so he wouldn't float away.

Commander Durant didn't stand. Instead he touched the workstation controls in front of him. The Commander said in his Tabletop accent, "Admiral, Captain, if you don't mind, I need to stay seated to use the workstation controls for my presentation."

The Admiral responded. "Continue, Commander."

The image of the black hole disappeared from the main screen. Then the Tri-V tank lit up and displayed a large, three-dimensional wireframe model of the spherical ship. The model was color coded to designate damaged equipment and systems. Floating in the tank next to the model was the DCO's prioritized list of damage to repair. It was long. Highlighting an entry allowed the DCO to bring up more detail.

"This report is for the *Cassie D only,* the auxiliary ships we carry aren't included. We haven't had time to compile reports for each of them yet. Alderson Drive #1 is burned out. We lost the engine room for it too. Ten good men died. It would have been much worse if the compartment containing the Drive hadn't been armored. Alderson Drive #2 and #3 are offline and in need of extensive realignment. No Estimated Time to Repair. Main fusion engine #3 is offline and in need of repairs. No ETR, yet. Engines #2 and #3 are serviceable. We lost hydrogen fuel bunker #7. It was holed somehow and vented into space. We lost one twelfth of our fuel."

Commander Smirnov, the Comm Officer from St. Ekaterina, spoke up. "It would have vented inside the Field, da? Shouldn't we be able to recover some of it?"

"No, Commander. The fuel was hydrogen slush. Almost as cold as you can get. The Field allows slow moving objects through rather easily. The temperature of the fuel allowed it to pass unimpeded through the Field and it all escaped."

The Admiral didn't like the interruption. "Questions at the end. Now, continue your report, DCO."

"Yes, sir. Langston Field generators #1, #2 and #3 are all functional. Although #2's capacitors seem to be experiencing some minor fluctuations. The ring has seized up. The tracks are warped. We cannot spin it to provide artificial gravity. We cannot repair it under acceleration. It will require zero gee to repair.

"Weapon systems are eighty-seven percent operational. Seven missile launch tubes are down due to loading system warpage. Two more tubes are down due to misaligned magnetic accelerators. Three high powered lasers have cracks in their optical cavities. We are still checking the particle beam systems. We are still checking the missiles themselves for damage.

"All life support systems are working within their design parameters. Although we lost one hundred and forty-three of the colonist's frozen sleep tanks. The rest are functional. Some minor power problems throughout the ship but we're working them. A long list of other minor problems. In general, Admiral, we saw chaotic damage. Some delicate instruments were left untouched while hardened systems next to them were badly damaged. And in other places, just the opposite occurred."

"And the Alderson force sensors we need to plot a Jump?"

"Some of the Alderson force sensors survived, Admiral. We have enough to plot a Jump once the Drives are repaired."

"So, there is nothing damaged that is currently critical to our short-term survival. Medium term, there are several items. And we can't attempt a Jump. Is that what you're saying, DCO?"

"Yes, Admiral. That is a concise summary. My detailed report is posted in the main computer nodes and available to all Command Staff."

"Very well. Questions? No? Captain, let me know when your Astrogation people have determined our velocity vector relative to that hole. Start searching for nearby rogue planets. Also, take samples from the deceased for the gene banks before processing their bodies through the recycling tanks. Continue your repairs. That is all for now. Carry on."

* * *

"Why are the repairs scheduled to take so long, Chief Engineer?"

"Captain, as the Astrogator has told you and Admiral Blaine, he thinks our voyage to a region of the galaxy where we can find either habitable planets or terraformable ones is going to take at least a hundred years. Doctor Volkov tells me that we must have the ring repaired so it can provide the artificial gravity we need to remain healthy for the long voyage ahead of us.

"To repair the ring, we have to construct zero-gee scaffolding around the *Cassie D* amidships. We can't do that until we have ceased accelerating and have a planetary mass between us and the black hole at the center. Once we are shielded from the radiation coming from the center, we can drop the Field and get to work. At the same time, we need to find sufficient titanium, mine it, process it, transport it to the ship and then form it into the things we need. That is an industrial-scale undertaking.

"Then we need to remove the hull plating around the ring. Next, we need to remove portions of the outer keel structure that supports the ring in order to access and replace the warped rails and magnetic induction motors. While the designers thought that using titanium would make the ship sturdier, it also makes it more difficult to repair.

"At the same time we are finding the metals we need, we must build large scale fabricators to process the titanium and other materials into replacement parts. Things like hull plates, ring tracks and keel implants. The tolerances we need to achieve are quite tight, Captain. Especially on the keel and ring structures. Once the repairs on the ring are completed, we need to test everything and then replace the hull plates. Detailed plans are available to the Command Staff for your review and feedback.

"We also have other critical repairs to make. We need to bring the third fusion drive back online. As well as repairing our auxiliary spaceships that were damaged. A lot of work to do."

"Can we use the damaged parts from the ship as feedstock? That would reduce the amount of material we have to mine and shorten the repair time."

"That's an interesting idea, Captain. The keel and hull plating are made of one of the hardest and strongest materials known. I suspect the conversion will be difficult but I'll investigate it."

"What other steps can we take to pull up the schedule, Commander Sheffield?"

"We can delay the repairs to our auxiliary spaceships and focus those men and material on the *Cassie D's* repairs. The risk there is, if we need the auxiliary ships before they are repaired, they will not be available. We also need to rely more on the immersive interfaces to run the robotic constructors. I know the Admiral doesn't like to use them because they make us more like Sauron cyborgs but we need to make our people more productive, and using them is the quickest way to do that. Lastly, we need to wake a few more sleepers. The ones with spaceship construction experience. Here's a list of the people I think would be most useful."

The Chief Engineer touched a control and the list opened in a window on the main damage control center screen.

The Captain took a moment to scan through it. Then he said, "Very well, Commander. I'll talk to the Admiral."

TWO

Academician Dmitry Ivanov floated just above a bench surrounded by Earth-stock greenery. He had forgotten to velcro himself down so that, in the ship's current zero gee environment, he wouldn't float off the bench. The compartment he was in was a huge spherical shell in the center of the *Cassie D* nicknamed the Garden by the ship's crew. It was a humid space with many different natural smells mixing and drifting through the air. The overhead was hidden by a Tri-V image of Sparta's sky and primary sun, Agamemnon.

By far, most of the plants in the Garden were originally from Earth. A few, very few, had evolved on other planets. The Empire didn't allow many non-native plants to be transported from planet to planet. Inserting Earth-stock plants into an alien ecology was fraught with unknown consequences. Allowing native life from hundreds of planets to mix together haphazardly was a recipe for economic and ecological disaster. The New Washington cornplant was one of the few exceptions. It had been allowed to grow on many planets since the CoDominium period.

The ship's designers knew that the *Cassie D's* voyage might be a long one. And, if it was, some greenery was important for the psychological health of the crew. Not to mention the fresh fruits and vegetables that it would provide as well. Food synthesizers alone were fine for a few years of space travel but not for decades.

The Garden contained both hydroponic reservoirs as well as traditional soil beds. In a zero-gee environment, the trees and plants grew in a riot of directions. But when the ship was under acceleration, they grew upward. The resulting growth patterns created one of the most bizarre forests Ivanov had ever seen. Many crew members spent what little time they had off here. It was a calming and peaceful place, away from the stress of their long, daily work assignments.

A small plot had been walled off from the rest of the Garden so that the plants Ivanov brought back from Haven could be grown in an environment similar to that in which they were found. They were samples of Earth-stock life not found in the Imperial gene banks. Life that had adapted itself over six hundred years to one of the most extreme environments man had ever colonized. Ivanov was floating next to the newly planted section. Green shoots were just breaking through the zero-gee soil restrainers.

Above the plot was a Tri-V image of Cat's Eye, the banded gas giant Haven orbited as a moon. More distant in the sky was an image of Byers' Star, the sun Cat's Eye orbited. Ivanov was lost deep in thought, as he remembered his trek across the northern reaches of the island of Cracovia on that moon. A trek he had taken with Franciszka Soltyk, the woman he had fallen in love with along the way. He could see her face in his mind. Ash blonde hair, blue eyes, a brilliant smile. Then, in the back of his mind he became aware of a voice. Then he heard it again. This time it pulled him out of his daydreaming.

"Are you all right, my son?"

Ivanov looked up to see Cardinal Peterson watching him. In a voice that held deep sorrow, Ivanov replied, "Yes. Thank you, Your Eminence. I'm...well, I was just thinking about...someone lost to me."

"Are you sure you're all right? You look pale and you don't sound very well. It can be helpful to talk about these things. I see you are holding a small gold cross. I don't recall seeing you at Sunday services. Are you a member of my flock?"

Ivanov looked at him and shook his head from side to side.

The Cardinal offered again, "You're not? Well, no matter, my son. I've been told I'm a good listener."

He started to respond. "Your Eminence…Please, I…" Then Ivanov, overwhelmed by his loss, broke down and cried.

The Cardinal pulled himself down to the bench next to Ivanov, velcroed himself to it and then put his arm around Ivanov. The Cardinal waited until Ivanov had finished. "My son, what is hurting you so?"

Ivanov blurted out the story of how he had been forced to leave behind the woman he loved and their unborn child in the Milky Way galaxy.

"Your Eminence, what can I do? I promised her I would return. With all my heart I want to return but I know that is impossible." He finished by saying, "She must hate me."

"My son. We can never physically return to the Milky Way galaxy but we can be reunited with our loved ones in Heaven."

Ivanov looked at the Cardinal. The academician in him couldn't see how that would be possible but, in his heart, he felt a flicker of hope. He knew Franciszka believed in God and Heaven with all her heart. How could he not? Finally, after a few moments, he knew he had to fan that spark. He said, "Please, Your Eminence, tell me more."

After a half an hour, Ivanov heard his tablet chime and said, "Thank you, Cardinal. I have to go. My break time is over and I have to get back to my damage control team."

The Cardinal took a small, well-worn book out of his pocket and handed it to Ivanov. "Here, take this. I think you will find some comfort reading it. Especially, the New Testament. Come talk with me whenever you feel the need."

"Thank you again, Your Eminence."

Although Ivanov was one of the expedition's leading biologists, he had been assigned to a DC team. Something not the least in his area of expertise. But what the ship needed right now were strong backs. Men who could wrestle machinery and equipment around, since most of the automated repair units remained out of commission. Ivanov got the job for two reasons. He was strong and he was not in frozen sleep. He was awake because he had just returned from Haven shortly before the *Cassie D* made its Random Jump.

The problem with Ivanov's job wasn't the manual labor. The problem was that it gave him too much time to think. If he had spent that time thinking about academic matters, that might have been different. That might have been productive. But no, he kept thinking about Franciszka. But now at least he was a bit more hopeful after talking with Cardinal Peterson. Then, for some unknown reason, his mind jumped to another thought.

The universe exists in chaos.

What does that mean? Was my mind affected by the Jump? Is this what too many Jumps does to someone?

Joe Conrad, an Imperial Marine pilot and friend, saw Ivanov staring off in the distance, looking confused and holding the small gold cross Franciszka had given him. Conrad knew Ivanov was thinking about her. Conrad also knew Ivanov needed to get his mind off her.

"Hey, Ivanov." Conrad called across the compartment. "Get over here and help me move this thing," he said, referring to a damaged micro-fabrication unit one of the engineering officers wanted moved to a repair station. "Stop your daydreaming."

Ivanov's hand dropped from the cross. "Damn it, Joe. It's not your job to babysit me."

"Who else is going to keep your sorry ass out of trouble?"

Ivanov grinned at that, his reverie broken. For now.

* * *

"Admiral Blaine, Captain Fainchurch here. Astrogation has determined that we are heading toward the black hole at four hundred and eight-two thousand kilometers per hour. Roughly, the distance from old Earth to Luna each hour. That's the same speed that the Milky Way and Andromeda galaxies are approaching each other."

"Thank you, Captain. Cancel that vector and return us to the same distance from the black hole where we materialized."

"Aye aye, Admiral."

"I know Astrogation has been scanning the space around us. Have they found anything?"

"Possibly, Admiral. They may have found a rogue gas giant. It will be ahead of us on our new heading. It may be somewhere we can refuel. If it has moons or captured some comets and asteroids, we may be able to mine those for the minerals we need. We should also be able to get behind the planet and drop our Field to make repairs. It is at the extreme range of our sensors and still might be just a glitch. We need more time to confirm it."

"Very well, Captain. Keep me informed."

"Admiral, one other thing. Astrogation has also picked up some weak gravity waves along the same vector. They aren't sure if the two sightings are related but they are investigating."

"What could produce such gravity waves, Captain?"

"Given their frequency, two very dense objects in a binary orbit, sir."

"Are they a danger to us?"

"No, sir. The waves are very low frequency."

THREE

2641 A.D., INSS Ira Hayes,
Andromeda Center

The *INSS Ira Hayes* was the eighth ship to carry that name since Lysander I had set Sparta on the path of empire. It raced ahead of the *Cassie D* at two point four gees. All the frigate's personnel were in acceleration tanks due to the prolonged acceleration. They needed to reach and recon the rogue system before the *Cassie D* reached the turnover point for it. It could save valuable fuel for the big ship.

Ivanov was chosen to be on the exploration team because of his expertise in biology. They needed someone with his background if they came across any life, unlikely as that was. Conrad was chosen to be part of the team because of a combination of his military training and his experience with Ivanov on Haven. Other members of the exploratory team included an astrogeologist and an astronomer.

Be careful what you wish for, Ivanov thought. *I didn't like being on that damage control team. Now I'm here. What was Joe's metaphor for it? From the frying pan into the fire.* Feeling crushed by the acceleration even in the tanks, all he could do was smile at his latest predicament. Then another thought came unbidden to him.

Man is the measure of the universe.

What? Another non-sequitur. These seem to be coming more often.

"Hey, Dmitry," Conrad, said in a strained voice. "Tell me why this is better than being on a DC team?"

Parroting how Joe responded to such a question before, Dmitry responded. "We're seeing the galaxy, my friend. And the Admiral is paying for it."

"Yeah, but the galaxy's mostly empty space."

It was a strain but Ivanov smiled at that. For a Marine pilot, Conrad had an interesting sense of humor.

2641 A.D., INSS Cassiopeia's Daughter, Andromeda Center

It was the middle of the night and the ship was accelerating at a constant point six gee. A moment later the acceleration had dropped in half. The sudden change came as a shock to the ship's personnel who were awake. Anything or anyone who wasn't secured hit the deck, a bulkhead or the overhead. The next thing all hands heard was the General Quarters klaxon.

Ensign Noland, the Officer of the Deck, had ordered the ship's computer to make an emergency shutdown of one of the two fusion engines powering the ship's drive. Both the Admiral and the Captain were angry. But the OOD repeated their primary standing order to them, "Do whatever is necessary to ensure the safety of the ship."

"In my judgment, the engine was quickly falling out of its safety limits and I had to act. There was no time to call anyone else. I had already ordered Lieutenant Stuart, the Engineering Watch Officer, to shut it down. When he didn't respond quickly enough, I shut it down from here." Nervously, he added. "I stand by my decision, Admiral, Captain."

"Yes, you will, Ensign Noland. Captain, I want a formal inquiry. Make it quick."

"Yes, sir."

The Admiral turned to Commander Durant. "DCO, what damage have we sustained because of the unexpected change to our acceleration?"

"We lost two ratings who were crushed when the micro-fabricator they were moving shifted unexpectedly. The unit itself was damaged too. The crewmen were in the process of moving the repaired unit to a new compartment. A small mystery, no one seems to know who ordered them to do that. We will follow up on that later. Other than that, several crew members were injured. Sprains, contusions, one broken arm. Nothing life threatening. We were lucky that's all we lost," the Damage Control Officer said, looking pointedly at Ensign Noland. "Of course, Captain it would have been worse if the standing orders to secure all equipment when under acceleration weren't in place."

"And the auxiliary spaceships in the hanger decks, DCO?"

"Per standing orders, they were all tied down, Admiral. No damage to any of them."

"Thank you, DCO. Chief Engineer, I want your and the Engineering Watch Officer's reports in one hour."

Both men responded with, "Yes, sir."

"Dismissed."

Then Captain Fainchurch turned to Ensign Noland. "Ensign, turn your watch over to the Astrogator. Go write up your report. Have it to me within the hour."

"Aye aye, Captain."

Several days later, Ensign Nolan was called to meet with Admiral Blaine and Captain Fainchurch. He was nervous as he entered the war room. The Ensign knew his career was on the line. The Captain got right to the point.

"You are exonerated, Ensign," the Captain said. "You took exactly the correct actions. You saved this ship and possibly the human race.

Congratulations, Lieutenant."

Lieutenant Noland smiled that the inquest was over and he had been acquitted. Then he broke into a wider grin as he realized he had just received a spot promotion.

"Dismissed, Lieutenant."

"Thank you, Captain. Admiral."

Lieutenant Noland turned and left the compartment. After he had gone, the Captain dogged the hatch.

"We were lucky, Admiral. That young officer saved the ship. That report suggests sabotage."

"I see that, Captain. But how could a traitor get on this ship? This program had the strongest security I have ever seen."

"I don't know, Admiral but we have got to assume the worst."

"I want you to review all of the security footage and logs from the engine room. I know the Chief Engineer has done that but he wasn't looking for sabotage. And, look into the background of Lieutenant Stuart. He didn't respond quickly enough. Yes, watches are boring but he is only standing one in six. That shouldn't be overly tiring. Until we know more, this stays between you and me. Understood, Captain?"

"Aye aye, sir."

2641 A.D., INSS Ira Hayes, Andromeda Center

The *Hayes* backed into orbit around the gas giant on a pillar of light. Like the *Cassie D*, the frigate's thrust came from a two-step process. Fusion engines exhausted into the ship's Langston Field. The Field, in turn, transformed all of that energy into a cone of pure light producing acceleration.

The frigate's primary mission was to find water ice that could be cracked to produce hydrogen fuel. Secondarily, it was to search for metal ores needed for the repairs. Asteroid or cometary resources were preferred for the ease of extraction. Secondarily, the frigate was tasked with evaluating the gas giant for scoopship mining, if necessary. A risky activity, that, diving into a gas giant's atmosphere to collect hydrogen.

As they came in over the north pole of the gas giant, the survey team discovered four moons. The system, however, was devoid of any smaller bodies. The expedition began their survey with the outermost moon. They left probes in orbit outfitted with hyperspectral sensors, magnetometers, neutrino detectors, gravity field sensors and a half dozen other remote sensing instruments. Software shifted through the resulting data sets to find signs of what they sought.

The outermost moon was a disappointment. The small, rocky world was in a highly eccentric orbit that took it far from the gas giant. It had metal deposits under its impact craters but there was no water ice.

The third moon out was the smallest of the four. Its mass and surface gravity were slightly less than half of Sparta's moon Cythera. It had a moderately eccentric orbit. It had stopped its share of asteroids during its lifetime and had masses of metals buried under the surface in the middle of the larger craters. And, most importantly, it had water ice on its surface.

The second moon was the largest of the four. It looked different from the first two moons they had reconned. The second moon had an atmosphere. The color of the moon was a hazy yellow until they were in orbit around it. Then, they could see more detail. If the atmosphere had been composed of oxygen and nitrogen, it would have been habitable. But it wasn't. Instead, the turbulent atmosphere was composed of nitrogen, methane and water vapor. It had its own magnetic field and a surface gravity of point nine three gees. The moon seemed to have significant volcanic activity. The central black hole's accretion disk produced daylight equivalent to just under Earth standard at this distance. The moon's rotation was long at thirty hours, which when combined with its orbit around the gas giant made for a complex day-night cycle.

The innermost moon orbited so close to the gas giant that tidal heating kept much of it molten. The gas giant's magnetic field also induced currents in the body, causing additional internal heating. As a result, through endless volcanic activity, the innermost moon had a constantly changing surface. Like the moon Io in orbit around Jupiter in Sol System, the constant volcanic eruptions created a plasma torus around the gas giant. The moon orbited within this tube, causing its surface to be bathed in high energy radiation. The astronomer on the expedition noted that the body orbited close to its Roche limit. Within a hundred thousand years, a relatively short time astronomically speaking, it would be pulled apart and form rings around the gas giant.

The recon team named the gas giant Refuge. They concluded that it must have lost its outer moons in close encounters with other astronomical objects here at the center. Refuge reminded Ivanov of Cat's Eye. Unlike the second moon of Cat's Eye, the gas giant's second moon didn't have any life on it. But the second moon's atmospheric composition was similar to New Scotland's before it was terraformed. Unfortunately, Refuge system's illumination depended on the mass flowing into the black hole's accretion disk. And that could change over relatively short geological periods of time.

Ivanov had studied the terraforming of New Scotland during his post-doctoral research. In particular, he had identified the mistakes made during the terraforming process and proposed how to correct them. That is, if the Empire ever tried such a project again. Now he began to think about whether such a project could be successful here. To that end, Ivanov offered up the name of New Haven for the second moon and no one on the recon mission objected.

After completing its reconnaissance, the *Hayes* masered its findings back to the *Cassie D.*

FLASH MESSAGE BEGINS

CONFIDENTIAL

TO: FLEET ADMIRAL GEORGE BLAINE, COMMANDING OFFICER, IMPERIAL ANDROMEDA EXPEDITION ONE

FROM: COMMANDER ANATOLY PORTNOV, COMMANDING OFFICER, INSS IRA HAYES

SUBJECT: RECON SITREP

SYSTEM SUMMARY:

CONFIRM GAS GIANT IN HIGHLY ECCENTRIC ORBIT AROUND DOUBLE NEUTRON STAR BINARY. FIVE AU AVERAGE DISTANCE FROM PRIMARIES.

GAS GIANT HAS FOUR MOONS, ZERO ASTEROIDS, ZERO RINGS.

THIRD MOON HAS WATER ICE ON SURFACE. CONFIRMED BY SAMPLE RETURN.

THIRD MOON HAS METAL ORES BURIED UNDER SURFACE PER REMOTE SENSORS.

THIRD MOON GRAVITY POINT ONE FIVE STANDARD.

MOONS ONE, TWO AND FOUR LESS VIABLE RESOURCE EXTRACTION.

DO NOT RECOMMEND SCOOPSHIP MINING OF GAS GIANT DUE TO EXTREME TURBULENCE IN ATMOSPHERE.

INTERROGATIVE: ADVISE HAYES TASKING.

LOGS AND REPORTS TO FOLLOW.

FLASH MESSAGE ENDS

The reply was a shock to the crew of the *Hayes*. The *Cassie D* had suffered a near catastrophic failure of one of its main fusion drives. The ship was now operating on a single fusion drive. In turn, that had caused the ship to decrease its acceleration to a conservative two point five gees, causing a delay in its expected arrival in the Refuge System. The frigate was ordered to go into orbit around moon number three and continue its remote sensing of that body while conserving resources.

Ivanov hated asking military authority for permission to do things he, as an academician, felt were important. But he knew he had no other choice. Deployment of resources for further investigation of the moons around Refuge were controlled by the captain.

Like every commanding officer of a spaceship, no matter what their actual rank, Commander Portnov was called captain or skipper.

"Captain, we have several landers in our hold. Our micro-fabricator can produce more if needed. I only want to use one to land on New Haven and release a fusion powered drone to explore."

"Academician Ivanov, you have seen orders. We are to conserve resources. Sending probe to land on New Haven does not meet criteria."

"Captain, the *Cassie D* is damaged and making its way slowly toward us. What if these moons are all we've got? We need to understand them better. New Haven reminds me of New Scotland before it was terraformed. We brought that technology with us. What if we need to terraform that moon? Yes, it would take decades but we need to be prepared to move forward as quickly as we can, if that becomes necessary."

"Academician, why are we still discussing? My orders not clear?"

"Captain, we have been tasked with exploring this system. Isn't it within our previous orders to continue that mission? After all, we know there are metals under the surface of this moon but we aren't sure what they are. I'm only asking for one probe. There may be minerals we need down on the surface of New Haven. The atmosphere is unusually turbulent. To mine any minerals, we will need to understand the atmospheric profile. The *Hayes* will stay in orbit here. We can use the probes currently in orbit around New Haven as a telecom relay."

Then, for no reason he could understand, a new thought formed in Ivanov's mind. *The ultimate chaos of man's existence is the human endeavor called War.*

Another one? Damn, where are these one-liners coming from? Focus on the meeting.

"If we are so low on supplies that we can't use one lander, then it means we may really be stuck here and we will need to terraform New Haven. This will reduce the risk for our mission, Captain."

That argument seemed to give the Captain pause. "Academician, if I approve, you will cease complaining and focus on planetary profile, da?"

"Of course, Captain."

2641 A.D., INSS Cassiopeia's Daughter, Andromeda Center

"Why a micro-fabricator?" Admiral Blaine asked. "An alcohol still I can understand. There has been a long, unofficial tradition of stills on warships. But a micro-fabricator?"

Admiral Blaine was meeting in the war room with Captain Fainchurch, and the DCO. They were reviewing the open issues related to the recent emergency engine shutdown.

"What was the compartment they were moving it into?"

"Captain Fainchurch, it was empty but designated for food-synthesizer expansion once we wake the sleepers," the Commander responded, using the slang for crew and colonists they were carrying who were in frozen sleep.

"Do we know if the micro-fabricator had been programmed to produce anything?"

"That is another strange thing, Admiral. It had been programmed to produce oxy-nanites."

Surprised, the Admiral asked, "Oxy-nanites?"

"Yes, sir."

"What can you tell me about them?"

Commander Durant accessed the ship's Imperial Library from the workstation in front of him. After a few moments, he summarized what he had read. "The oxy-nanites were discovered by Imperial Marines on Novi Kossovo at the end of the campaign to free the planet from the Saurons. They were found in an abandoned Resistance laboratory. The Academicians at the Imperial University on Sparta found they increased the oxygen supply to those injected with them. Documents found in the lab indicated the Resistance scientists were trying to create something to even the odds when fighting Sauron Soldiers. The nanites are flushed out of a person's system about three months after having an injection of them."

Then on a hunch the Admiral asked, "Has anyone used them?"

Commander Durant scrolled through more information. "Interesting, the landing party on Haven used them."

"Who was on that landing party?"

As the list appeared there was surprise all around the table. The list included Lieutenant Stuart whose slow response to shutting down the fusion engine had almost caused a disaster. Also listed were the two ratings killed by the change in acceleration as well as First Lieutenant Conrad, Academician Ivanov and several others.

"That's an interesting list. What does it mean?"

"I don't know, Admiral," Captain Fainchurch replied. "But it doesn't strike me as a coincidence."

"Have autopsies of the two ratings been completed?"

"Yes, sir."

"Have their bodies been recycled yet?"

"No, Admiral. Until our investigation is complete, the bodies will remain in cold storage and will not be released for recycling."

"Good, Captain. Now, what did the autopsies find?"

"The cause of death was as expected. The two ratings were crushed under the machinery."

"Was there any sign of nanites in their bodies?"

"No, Admiral. But the Chief Medical Officer wasn't looking for them."

"Have the Chief Medical Officer conduct another autopsy on both of the deceased ratings. Look specifically for the nanites."

"Yes, sir."

"Captain, where are the other six members of that landing team right now?"

The Captain touched his consoles' controls and a list appeared on the war room's main display.

"As a precaution, take the four men on the *Cassie D* into custody. Very quietly. I'll contact the commanding officer of the *Hayes*."

"Aye aye, Admiral."

"Use the utmost care, Captain. These men may be innocent or they may be very dangerous. Let me know when it's done. As a further precaution, I will put a temporary security lock on the Library's oxy-nanite information and related entries. I'll arrange the lock to propagate to all branch libraries too."

A few hours later the Captain opened a private comm circuit to the Admiral. "Sir, we have detained the *Cassie D* personnel who were exposed to the nanites."

"Thank you, Captain."

"All were stunned simultaneously. They are all now confined to individual cells in the brig. We are beginning interrogations."

"Very well, Captain."

"Admiral, what about Conrad and Ivanov?"

"I have sent a Flash message to the commanding officer of the *Hayes*. Eyes Only. I ordered him to confine both men until we rendezvous."

FOUR

2641 A.D., INSS *Ira Hayes,* Refuge System

Conrad and Ivanov were meeting in Conrad's stateroom on the *Hayes*. They were having what had become a familiar discussion.

"Don't you see, Dmitry? Sauron is the way ahead. It's the future of the human race. We're in a hostile galaxy. We may need to fight aliens for our place here."

"In six hundred years, aliens have never been found, Joe. Theory states they would destroy themselves without both the Drive and the Field. While the Drive can be discovered by studying stars, the Field was such an unlikely discovery that it's possible no one would ever discover it again. The academicians at the Imperial University on Sigismund decided long ago that solved the question of why we haven't made first contact with any alien civilizations."

"From what I've heard, we need to travel at least twenty-thousand light-years to reach a region of the galaxy that's habitable for us. That's going to take a hundred years. In traveling through all that space, you don't think it's possible we could run into aliens?"

"Okay, Joe. I'll grant you that it's possible we could run into aliens before they have destroyed themselves. But, it's so unlikely."

Conrad's eyes glowed with a messianic intensity. "Do you want to take that chance? After all, we may be the only humans in the galaxy. The other two expeditions may not have made it. I tell you Dmitry, the future of the human race in Andromeda is Homo Sauron. You've got to see that."

"Joe, they don't believe in God. How can they be our future?"

"I don't have an answer to that. But I know what I believe is right."

"What do you want to do? Even if we agree that eugenics is the way forward, they will never let us practice those beliefs."

"Exactly, Dmitry. So, we need to convert them and I know how to do that."

"What? Are you crazy?" Out of reflex, Ivanov looked around to see if anyone could hear them. Meeting in Conrad's stateroom, no one could. Still, Ivanov lowered his voice and said, "You're talking mutiny. That's punishable by death. And even if we are successful, what would we do with just a frigate in the middle of nowhere?"

"I have a plan. It's not mutiny. You just need to trust me."

At that moment, Conrad's phone chimed. He picked it up and answered it. "Hello? Yes, Captain. I can be there in a few minutes. Do I know where Ivanov is? Yes, sir. He's here with me. Yes, sir. I'll bring him along."

"What was that about?" Ivanov asked.

"I don't know. He said something about taking a flyer down to New Haven."

Ivanov was excited by this news. "Maybe he sees the value in my research now."

"Let's go find out."

As Conrad and Ivanov entered the Captain's cabin, they saw two security guards. Each guard was stationed on opposite sides of the cabin. Both guards were armed with stunners. Each had their weapon pointed down at the deck but in Conrad's and Ivanov's general direction.

The Captain rose from his desk and addressed the two men. "Gospodin, I'm sorry to do this but I have—"

Before the Captain could finish, Conrad kicked out at the security guard nearest him catching him in his solar plexus, doubling him over. Even before the guard hit the deck, Conrad was on the second guard. Conrad was a tall and muscular pilot. But like all Marines, he was trained to fight hand-to-hand. He wrestled the stunner away from the guard and shot him at point blank range. Then Conrad turned and shot the other security guard. Finally, he stunned the Captain. He set the stunner down, made sure the hatch was dogged shut and searched the guards for plastic handcuffs. Ivanov simply stood there, dumbfounded.

"Joe, what are you doing? Joe, are you crazy? You just shot the Captain."

"They were going to arrest us, Dmitry. I could see it. I had to act. There was no time for an academic discussion."

While he was talking, Conrad put the plastic handcuffs on the Captain and the two security guards. Then he walked over to the Captain's desk and found a flimsy printout from the Captain's encryption unit. As he read it, he nodded.

"Dmitry, this is an order from Admiral Blaine to take us into custody."

"Why, Joe? Why would the Admiral want to arrest us?"

"I don't know. I need to go check on something. I need you to stay here and guard these three. I'll be back soon."

"But, Joe. What if they wake up?"

"Stun them again."

Ivanov began to protest but Conrad stopped him. "Just do as I say, my friend. This is important."

When Conrad returned, he found Ivanov holding the cross Franciszka had given him and staring off into space. Tears were running down his face. Ivanov wasn't paying attention to the guards who were beginning to stir.

"Dmitry, I told you to guard these people." Then, seemingly in anger, Conrad grabbed the cross from Ivanov's hand, ripped it off his neck and threw it on the deck.

That was too much for Ivanov. "Joe, do you know what you've done? You have included me in your sin. I'll never see Franny again. I'll never be reunited with my child. Damn you." Then louder, "Damn you!" He looked at Conrad with a feral grin, raised his stunner and fired. Conrad fell to the deck unconscious.

2641 A.D., INSS Cassiopeia's Daughter, Andromeda Center

Admiral Blaine, Captain Fainchurch and three of the Captain's senior staff were meeting in the war room to review the most recent findings in the nanite investigation. Admiral Blaine started the meeting.

"I want to remind you all, everything said or discussed here has the highest security classification. Now, what have the interrogations found, Captain?"

Captain Fainchurch got right to the point. "Admiral, all four of the remaining Haven expedition members on the *Cassie D* seem to be Sauron sympathizers."

The Admiral was shocked. Captain Fainchurch continued. "My Security Chief will give the detailed update. Master Chief Moore."

"Thank you, Captain. Admiral, the four detainees claim they have had no known contact with Sauron or its agents. We interrogated them with, and without, the standard truth drugs. The results were the same in both cases. Medical sensor results were also the same in both cases. All the subjects reported hearing almost constant voices or whispers. They all reported seeing images, or what two called ghosts. All reported hearing Sauron martial music, remembering Sauron ideology, seeing images of Sauron's greatness; that sort of thing. To varying degrees, all believe in the Sauron eugenics program as the future of the human race and not the Empire."

"Any idea on how they got through our security screening with those beliefs?"

"Admiral, they all claim to have begun having these thoughts in the last few months."

"Do we know why, Master Chief?"

Dr. Volkov, the expedition's Chief Medical Officer, answered. "Admiral, I may have an answer to that. However, I would like to wait until Master Chief Moore finishes."

"Very well, Doctor."

"As I was saying, Admiral, we interrogated all four of the detainees. Lieutenant Stuart gave us insight into what happened to the two deceased ratings. He told us that he had repaired the micro-fabricator in his time off and then ordered the two of them to move it to the compartment next to the ship's food synthesizer. He couldn't say how he knew the two ratings had been compromised, only that he knew they shared his beliefs. One of the open questions we have is how he could have known that.

"With regard to the emergency shutdown, Lieutenant Stuart said he knew that the two men were moving the heavy micro-fabricator. He was trying to avoid unexpectedly changing the acceleration by delaying the shutdown."

"Did he say why he wanted the micro-fabricator installed in that particular compartment?"

"Yes, Admiral. We are getting ahead of ourselves but he was going to link it into the food synthesizer. He was trying to infect everyone on the ship with oxy-nanites."

"What! Why?"

"Admiral, I think the Doctor can answer that question."

"Very well. Doctor Volkov, you're up."

"Admiral, you asked that I conduct a second autopsy on the two ratings who were killed by that sudden change in acceleration. In particular, you wanted me to look for signs of nanites in their bodies. In both men I found inflammation on their auditory, optical and spinal nerve bundles. Upon further investigation I found small lesions on those bundles. Inside the lesions, I found several thousand nanites clustered around the nerves. They were in roughly the same location on both of the ratings."

Captain Fainchurch asked, "Any idea of what they do there?"

"Take a look at this electron microscope view." The screen displayed a roughly spherical nanite extruding what looked like a harpoon. The tip of the harpoon appeared to be imbedded in the wall of a nerve cell. The Chief Medical Officer then added a second image next to it. "This is from the Imperial Library. It is an image of what the nanite is supposed to look like. Do you see the difference?"

"The nanite in our crewmen has grown a harpoon-like structure and embedded it into that nerve cell."

"Yes, Captain. All the nanites I found look this way now."

"Do you know what the purpose of that structure is, Doctor?"

"Admiral, I believe it is twofold. First, it is a way for the nanites to attach themselves to a specific type of nerve cell receptor as they pass it. Second, once attached, it is used to feed information into the nerve cell. To control it, if you will."

"The attachments to auditory and optical nerves would explain the voices and ghostly images. But, what about the connections to the spinal cord?"

"Admiral, we did a complete work-up of the biochemical markers in both crewmen. We found that they all had high levels of biomarkers for sexual arousal."

The Admiral looked uncomfortable. "Doctor, what does this have to do with anything we are discussing?"

"Admiral, I'm getting there. We then compared the results to the same biomarkers found in the four crew members in confinement. They exhibited the same increased levels. It appears that the spinal nerves compromised by the nanites are tied into the pleasure center of the brain."

"I don't quite understand what you are suggesting, Doctor."

"It's called positive feedback. I believe the nanites are subliminally feeding information into an infected person's nervous system while at the same time rewarding them with a low-level stimulation of their pleasure centers."

"So, these little beasts brainwash people by making them sexually aroused? What truly nasty buggers."

"Yes, Captain. I agree. But we still don't have all the answers."

"What do you mean, Doctor?"

"Admiral, we have just begun to study them. I think the nanites must coordinate their activity among themselves to produce the effects we see. But, if so, how? Is it some form of ultra-short-range mesh network? Do the nanites work together to form a high-level computer or do they simply act like a memory cube player? Are the nanites active twenty-four seven? Are they programmed to do more than just brainwash people? How long does it take to brainwash someone? Most importantly, how can we safely remove the nanites?"

For the first time in the meeting, Commander Sheffield, the Chief Engineer spoke up. "Doctor. Since the nanite-nerve cell union combines both cyber and organic elements, I should work with you to answer those questions."

The Admiral turned toward the Doctor. "Do these nanites reproduce on their own?"

"No, Admiral. There is no evidence of that. I think the micro-fabricator was intended to be used for that purpose."

"How are the nanites powered, Doctor?"

"Captain, they use the same blood sugar that our cells use. However, the nanites do use more energy than normal cells. As a result, an infected person eats more food than normal."

"How do we detect if a person is infected with them, Doctor?"

"We don't have an answer to that, Admiral. If Lieutenant Stuart could sense who was infected, it implies that there is some physical manifestation that we can detect. Maybe radio comm or some type of chemical signaling.

"We know the kidneys filter the nanites out of the body if they haven't attached to nerve cells. That may give us a place to start." The Doctor's eyes went glassy as he fell deep in thought for a moment. Then he mumbled, "The Chief Engineer and I will work on it."

"Doctor." When the Doctor didn't respond, the Admiral addressed him again, louder this time. "Doctor."

The Doctor's focus returned to the meeting. "Yes, Admiral. Sorry, sir. What was your question?"

"Not so much a question as an admonition, Doctor. Remember Occam's razor."

"What do you mean, Admiral?"

"Don't overlook the simple explanations, Doctor. Maybe they just used hand signs to recognize each other."

The Doctor felt sheepish. He had immediately jumped to a sophisticated technological solution when a simple explanation might just as well be the answer. "Of course, Admiral."

The Admiral nodded to himself. Then he said, "It's clear to me now how these men got through our security screening. They didn't. They weren't infected until they traveled to Haven and used the oxy-nanites. Oxy-nanites created from the Imperial Library. A trusted source. The Saurons must have realized toward the end of the Novi Kossovo campaign that they were going to lose the planet. They probably decided that they could gain some strategic advantage from their loss. To that end, I would wager they left the nanites for the Imperial forces to find. An extremely useful technology. Of course, we would take the nanites and use them. Insidious.

"I think your choice of words earlier are terrifyingly accurate, Chief Engineer. The nanites create a blend of the machine and the organic. The same general idea behind the Sauron cyborgs." The Admiral paused for a moment. "Maybe these things were originally developed for their cyborgs. I suppose it doesn't matter. What is important is that they are a Trojan Horse with the goal of creating a fifth column. Intending to take us over from the inside. I suspect they were not aimed specifically at this expedition but at the Empire and mankind, in general. I wish we could warn the Empire of Man but there's no way we can do that. Just like us, they are on their own."

Then the Admiral looked at the men assembled in the war room. "Have we contained the nanite infection?"

The four men all indicated they did not know.

"So, we have lost the eight men from the Haven expedition. Two of those are currently on a frigate not under our direct control. We need to stop this Sauron infection dead in its tracks. First, we need a way to detect a nanite infected person, Doctor. That is your highest priority.

"I am permanently restricting information about the oxy-nanites in the Imperial Library to the four of us. All, and I mean all, existing oxy-nanites are to be disposed of by vaporizing them with a fusion flame. Any place exposed to them is to be cleaned with plasma torches. And, that includes the recyclers. This has a higher priority than any of our repairs.

"Furthermore, no new physical nanites will be created. Only virtual recreations are allowed. And those need the highest level of sandboxing. No files outside the Library are to be made or kept. Complete your analysis soonest."

The four men all responded. "Aye aye, Admiral."

After the meeting ended, the Admiral made his way back to his cabin. He carefully closed the hatch and dogged it.

I wasn't completely honest with those men. There may be one way to alert the Empire of Man to the danger of the nanites. I was hoping I wouldn't need to use it again. Just attempting to use it might destroy it. But this is too important. There's nothing to be done about it.

The Admiral made his way to his desk. Behind it, on the floor, was a hidden hatch. He placed the palm of his hand on the deck in a special location and spoke a code phrase.

FIVE

"Admiral, the Astrogator and I would like to meet with you. He has some additional information about our situation."

"Captain, why don't we review it at my next staff meeting?"

"We can, Admiral. But I think you need to hear this before we bring more personnel in on it."

"Very well, Captain. Meet me in the war room in an hour."

The Astrogator began the meeting. "Admiral, Captain, I need to cover two topics today. First, something that will be a danger to the ship in about three years. And, second, the location of the Jump region."

The Astrogator called up an image of the central black hole. He slowly enlarged it until the pointer was on one region that looked like a small whirlpool. "Admiral, in your initial Command Staff meeting after the Jump, I talked about some areas of turbulence in the accretion disk. We have probed them more closely. There is bad news on that front. One of the areas near the central hole contains a stellar black hole of thirty solar masses. Our estimate is that it will merge with the supermassive black hole in three years plus or minus three months."

"How will that affect us, Commander?"

"I expect there will be a massive release of gravity waves when that happens. If the merger takes place on this side of the hole the release could damage or destroy the *Cassie D.* If the merger is on the other side of the hole it would be less intense but, just as light from the far side of the accretion disk is bent around the hole, the gravity waves would be too. It could still damage us."

"How confident are you about this, Commander?"

"Very confident, Admiral. We also have evidence suggesting these types of mergers create very intense gravity wave bursts. In their first Sitrep, the *Hayes* reported that the atmosphere of Refuge was far too turbulent for a scoopship to mine. We have modeled what a burst of gravity waves from a stellar black hole merger with the central supermassive black hole would do to Refuge's atmosphere. Past mergers would explain the turbulence they observed."

"Will the merger produce any Alderson force?"

"No, Admiral. That occurred in the past when the stellar black hole first formed."

"Again, how long until the merger?"

"Three years plus or minus three months, Admiral."

Captain Fainchurch spoke up. "There is more, Admiral."

"Admiral, we have also been able to model the Jump region around the central hole. Please note that, because the Alderson force is being produced by an accretion disk and not a star, it is a region and not a point. There is both good news and bad news here. The bad news is that, because of the intensity of the Alderson force produced by the central hole, the Jump region is two thousand AU further outward from our current position. It will take considerable time and fuel to get there. Once there, it will be difficult to pick a specific tramline to Jump along. Here is a computer model of what the Jump region looks like."

In the Tri-V tank, an image that looked like a spoked bicycle wheel formed. "As you can see, the Jump region is complex. If you look closely, you can see the end points of the tramlines shift constantly, jumping from one star to another as the intensity of the Alderson force from the accretion disk fluctuates. The good news is that, because of that intensity, our first Jump will be a long one. I estimate between sixteen hundred and seventeen hundred light-years. After that, we can expect Jumps to be of more normal length."

"You are saying that we need to complete our repairs, refuel, travel to the Jump region and Jump, within just over two and a half years. Is that correct?"

"Yes, Admiral."

"I see why you wanted to present this to me privately. Thank you. Captain, I'm sure you have given this some thought. Can we do it?"

"We may be able to, Admiral. We have some critical repairs we must make like the ones to the ring that spins to give us our artificial gravity. What worries me is that everything in the schedule must go almost perfectly. We both know that never happens. Even if everything goes right, the timing will be close and we get to the Jump region with dry tanks."

* * *

The *Cassie D* limped into the Refuge System on one fusion drive. The *Hayes* rendezvoused with the damaged ship and returned to its berth in hanger bay #2. In an unusual procedure after docking, the hanger bay was kept in vacuum. Under heavy guard, Conrad and Ivanov were transferred to the *Cassie D's* brig.

Admiral Blaine was in his spacesuit waiting for the frigate's return. As the *Hayes'* crew disembarked, he addressed the ship's commanding officer. "Welcome home, Commander Portnov." Then the Admiral added, "Bravo Zulu," an old naval signal code meaning "Well done."

"Thank you, Admiral."

"From your Sitrep, it sounds like you were lucky that Conrad and Ivanov didn't take control of your ship."

"Da, Admiral. After I received Flash message, I attempt to take Conrad and Ivanov into custody but Conrad broke free. He captured me and my two security guards. Only reason we here today is Ivanov turned on Conrad. He stunned him and released the rest of us. I immediately confined both to brig. I still do not understand what they hoped to accomplish. They would be lone ship against *Cassie D*. Even if they did not attack the *Cassie D*, where would they have gone? They would have been alone in Andromeda galaxy."

"Commander, did either First Lieutenant Conrad or Ivanov ever use the micro-fabricator?"

Commander Portnov seemed to struggle with his response. "That is unusual question, Admiral. I do not think so. But I cannot say for certain."

The Admiral signaled to the nearby security personnel. They all raised their weapons. Not directly at the *Hayes'* crew but not far away from that position either.

"Commander, I need to ask you and your people to stand down for an enhanced security check. I have no doubt you will pass but the threat Conrad and Ivanov represent is so great I can't take any chances. Master Chief Moore and his people will escort you to the security area."

Commander Portnov was shocked. Still, all he said was, "If you say so, sir."

In the meantime, Chief Engineer Sheffield entered the *Hayes* to check the micro-fabricator. He reviewed its recent programming and took samples from its print chamber. Next, he reviewed access records for the frigate's branch of the Imperial Library.

The Chief Engineer discovered that, contrary to the Commander's belief, the *Hayes'* micro-fabricator had been used by Conrad. And, he had used it to make oxy-nanites. He also found that a jury-rigged connection between the micro-fabricator and the food synthesizer next to it had been hastily made and then, before the sealing compound dried, removed. It appeared Conrad and Ivanov had tried to spread the nanite infection to the ship's personnel. Doctor Volkov's recently developed antibody test confirmed the *Hayes'* crew were all infected with the nanites. The entire crew of the *Hayes*, all seventy personnel, were locked up in the brig. Admiral Blaine thanked God that his extreme caution had been vindicated.

2642 A.D., INSS Cassiopeia's Daughter, Refuge

"Captain Fainchurch, what is the status of our repairs?"

"Admiral, we have made significant progress on most repairs but we've fallen behind on others. I'll let Commander Sheffield talk about specifics." He turned to the Chief Engineer and said, "Commander."

Commander Sheffield looked around the big war room table. He turned back to the Admiral and began. "Admiral, the good news is that we have repaired fuel bunker #7 that was holed during our Random Jump. Our auxiliary ships have begun transporting fuel from the hydrogen cracking plant we built on the moon below. We should have full bunkers within sixty days. Both fusion engines have been repaired and are fully operational.

"Weapons systems are ninety seven percent functional. We have repaired all missile launching systems. We are still working on repairing the laser weapon's optical cavities. But we are on schedule for those repairs. Alderson Drive's #2 and #3 have been realigned.

"The repairs to the ring are behind schedule. Even though the *Hayes* deployed a drone to search the surface of the second moon, they didn't find any titanium minerals. Therefore, we are reprocessing the damaged single crystal titanium alloys we are removing from the ship. The technology we have to do that does not allow us to do it very quickly. At least, not with the equipment we currently have."

"What can we do to get back on track, Commander?"

"Admiral, there isn't much. We have already pulled out all the stops. My people are working twenty-four seven. We will continue to look for opportunities to increase the titanium alloy reprocessing capacity, but I fear they are limited within the time frame we have available."

"Thank you, Commander."

"Admiral."

"Yes, Captain."

I am working on a different approach but I need another week. I will be ready to brief you on it after we complete the courts martial."

"Very well, Captain."

* * *

"This court finds you guilty of sedation and mutiny. Since you were brainwashed without your knowledge or consent, this court will not impose the death penalty. Instead, the nanites will be removed. Once your nerves have been regrown by the regeneration stimulators you will be placed in frozen sleep for the remainder of the voyage. Once reawakened, you will undergo a year of re-education. At the end of that time, an assessment will be made as to the effectiveness of the reeducation process. If the process is deemed ineffective, you will serve at the Navy's pleasure for the rest of your natural life. This court martial is concluded. God save the Empire."

Conrad raised his voice. "You mean I will be your slave. Is that the empire you want to create? One with slaves? You think an empire run on slavery is better than one run on eugenics? At least my philosophy gives everyone a chance to succeed and rise to the top."

The Admiral only said, "Master Chief. Remove the prisoner."

After Conrad had been escorted out of the compartment and they were alone, Captain Fainchurch turned to Admiral Blaine. "That's the last one, Admiral." Then he paused and added, "If I may, sir. I think he's right. What kind of empire do we want to create? Do we want slaves? I believe that would be a mistake. It is well established that slavery corrupts everyone who would touch that vile practice. Remember the Naval Academy motto: Duty, Honor, Empire. Slavery is not honorable."

The Admiral winced. "You are right, Captain. But I wasn't thinking about slavery. We may be strangers in a strange land but we don't need to reinvent the wheel. The Empire, and the CoDominium before it, has always had prison planets. Alexander IV turned old Earth into one a few years back. No, I was thinking of something smaller. Maybe a penal colony on an island. But dropping discontents who believe the Sauron philosophy onto an island to develop doesn't strike me as a good idea either. I need to think on this more. I'll talk with Cardinal Peterson before making a final decision."

"Thank you, Admiral."

* * *

"The Dioscuri System is unusual, Admiral. Both neutron stars, Pollux and Castor, appear very old. Well past their pulsar stage. They have spun down and lost most of their magnetic fields. But the orbital eccentricity of the system is about as large as it can be. Something usually seen only in young systems."

Admiral Blaine was looking like he'd rather be somewhere else. He looked to Captain Fainchurch and raised his eyebrows, silently asking, "What am I doing here?"

Captain Fainchurch spoke up. "Commander Anderson has a theory about Dioscuri System, Admiral. I think it important you hear it. This is what I was referring to at the end of our last repair status meeting."

"Very well, Captain. I'm listening."

The Astrogator continued. "Admiral, I think this is an old system but it recently underwent a close encounter with a stellar black hole or a neutron star. That encounter almost tore the system apart. Instead, Castor came out of it with a highly eccentric orbit."

"That sounds unlikely, Commander."

"Yes, Admiral. Normally, I would agree with you. But, here in the center, we have found a number of extremely dense stellar objects in close proximity. So, it's not as unlikely as you might expect."

"Why is this important, Commander?"

"Admiral, if these were young neutron stars and we passed close to them, their magnetic fields would easily overload our Field. If they are old neutron stars, they should be orbiting each other in a very tight, circular orbit producing gravity waves that would damage or destroy our ship. Again, if we came near to them."

The Admiral said, "But, as you said, these aren't acting entirely like young or old neutron stars."

"No, Admiral. They aren't. Which makes them ideal for us to use."

The Admiral hadn't expected the Astrogator's last comment. Now he leaned forward, his interest piqued. "Use them how, Commander Anderson?"

"We can use them to pick up speed and travel to the Alderson region much faster than otherwise. At closest approach to Pollux, Castor is moving at six percent the speed of light. We can use a gravitational slingshot maneuver to acquire that speed."

2643 A.D., INSS Cassiopeia's Daughter, Dioscuri System

The black globe that was *Cassiopeia's Daughter* fell toward the neutron star. Precautions for the passage were taken as best they could. The fusion reactors were taken off line and the ship run on stored energy. The ring spun down and locked into place. Air evacuated from the hanger bays and all personnel withdrawn from the outer compartments.

The ship was aimed at a small keyhole in space. A special region where Castor's gravity would alter the spaceship's course and speed. Both changes without exposing the *Cassie D* to dangerous tides. More importantly, instead of dry tanks when the *Cassie D* reached the distant Alderson region and slowed to Jump, her fuel bunkers would be half full.

It was a dangerous maneuver. Small masses in orbit around the neutron stars or impacting on them as they passed could be deadly, potentially overwhelming the ship's Langston Field. But this was the fastest way to reach the region from where they could make a Jump. And, because of the impending merger of a stellar black hole with the Andromeda super-massive black hole, they needed to get there quickly.

Captain Fainchurch opened a comm circuit from his station on the main bridge. "Admiral, we are at General Quarters. Condition Zebra is set throughout the ship."

From the flag bridge, Admiral Blaine answered. "Very well, Captain." *The ship is repaired and locked down as tight as it can be, all the crew are in spacesuits, our fate is now in His hands.*

The Tri-V tanks on both bridges were synced. They were displaying a real-time view of the neutron stars along with the *Cassie D's* projected and actual trajectories. So far, there was no deviation between the two paths. They hadn't expected any. Over the past year they had launched recon probes along the same trajectory. Both the Admiral and the Captain had thought it wise to test the feasibility of what the Astrogator called their Nantucket Sleighride.

The Admiral glanced at the countdown timer. Less than ten seconds remained. They were nearing perihelion, the ship's closest approach to Castor, itself approaching its closest point in its orbit around Pollux. The Admiral knew they would feel a slight pull toward the star as they whipped around it. But the tide would not be a danger to the ship or crew; not if they followed their trajectory correctly.

The Admiral unconsciously gripped the arms of his command chair and braced himself. *We are, as always, in His Hands.*

The House of Soltyk

ONE

There is an old proverb, 'For want of a nail the kingdom fell.' That's just a variation of the Butterfly Effect. If a nail can cause the loss of a kingdom, what can a mere speck of dust do? Turns out, one very small speck of dust in the wrong place, at the wrong time can do even more. In this case, the speck must have been on one of the reticles used by the Imperial Navy to produce an integrated circuit. One speck that caused a weakness in the wall of a circuit. A circuit that failed after the test systems passed it. A circuit in a chip that ended up in a nuclear warhead's detonation circuity. Bad luck. One of the *VeeZee's* nukes. A speck that would set off a series of events far wider than a warhead's detonation would normally produce. A speck of dust that would change a people and a world.

— The Soltyk Sagas, Book II, *2695 A.D.*

2640 A.D., Haven

Simultaneity across intergalactic space has little meaning. However, personal human events continued to move forward in both the Andromeda and Milky Way galaxies. On Haven, in the Milky Way, the Kingdom of Gletscherheim tried to contact the Sauron heavy cruiser *Fomoria* which was masquerading as the *Dol Guldur*. The Kingdom was nuked for its trouble.

On the island of Cracovia, the Sauron orbital bombardment included the city of Nowy Kraków, the single spaceport, the main seaport and several ground-based radar installations and radio sources. The three most important targets were nuked. The lesser ones received beam weapon fire or a hypervelocity rod bundle, known technically as a HVRB. In Imperial Navy slang, it was called a Rod From God. Because the island had little industry and therefore limited targets, the damage was light compared to the Shangri-La Valley. Still, three quarters of the population died over the next three years.

Three groups of people on Earth had naturally evolved adaptations for breathing high altitude air; the kind of air that was found at sea level on Haven. The Inca, the Amhara and the Tibetans. Each group had evolved a different genetic response. Over the six hundred years since those peoples came to Haven, their genes spread rapidly through the others who had colonized this world. While their other genetic characteristics had been diluted over time, the ability to use the thin air had been combined and reinforced throughout the general population. As had their ability to withstand cold and higher than Earth standard ultraviolet light.

In spite of the adaptation to the thin air of Haven, birthing areas were still used to increase the success of childbirth. The Shangri-La Valley located on the western continent, with its higher air pressure, was the largest of these. On the windward side of Cracovia, the western flank of a volcano had collapsed and slid into the sea creating a box canyon. As the westerly winds came ashore, they blew up the canyon. This increased the air pressure at the eastern end, which is where the Cracovians built their birthing centers. Three months after the Saurons invaded Haven and settled on the main continent, Franciszka Soltyk saw the inside of a Cracovian birthing center and bore a daughter. She named her Demetria.

Demetria's first three standard T-years were more difficult than normal because of the unusual cold brought on by the Sauron planetary bombardment. But, to paraphrase the nineteenth century philosopher Friedrich Nietzsche, what does not kill you makes you stronger. An adage that defined Haven and its people.

2659 A.D., Haven

The lifeboat floated gently to earth under three large bright orange parachutes. Just before touchdown, several small rockets flared, slowing the capsule further, ensuring a soft landing. The capsule landed on the lower slopes of the Góra Rog volcano on uneven ground that gave the lifeboat a distinct tilt. After a few minutes, the hatch opened. The air inside rushed out and was replaced by the thin, cold air of Haven. Each man quickly put on a breathing mask, a device that concentrated oxygen so the men could breathe the thin air. It made them look like some type of monster but it kept them alive and allowed them to exert themselves without passing out.

They were lucky they didn't land in deep snow higher on the sides of the volcano. If they had, the heat of the reentry shield would have melted through the snow, trapping them at the bottom of a deep, icy hole. Or, they might have landed on an ice-covered lake. Melting through the ice and, if their flotation devices had become fouled, being trapped underwater. Even worse, if they had landed in the Occidental Ocean and their flotation device had deployed, they would have been set adrift, far from land and rescue. Adrift in rough seas to slowly starve. But the lifeboats were designed to seek out the most favorable landing location within range of their limited maneuverability. The capsule did its job well.

Lieutenant Johansen was a tall, burly man from the planet Dalarna. A planet settled by Scandinavians back during the CoDominium days of man's interstellar expansion. When he was at the Academy, his friends nicknamed him Thor because of his planet of origin and his physique. He was the first one out of the capsule. He began to look around the area. After a few minutes, he turned back to his crew. "Everyone out. The air is fine. But it's a bit cold, even with survival gear."

Chief Wagner responded from inside the capsule, "Captain—"

Lieutenant Johansen cut him off, "Chief, I am no longer Captain of the *VeeZee*. Now that we're here, I don't rate the title."

The Chief said, "With due respect, sir. That's just horse exhaust. You're the one who got us here. Alive. We wouldn't be here without you. You are still our Captain." The Chief looked at the others in the lifeboat. "Agreed?"

Ayes were heard all around.

"Thank you for your vote of confidence. I'll do my best to live up to it."

Then the five other castaways climbed out of the capsule to view their new home. Chief Kowalski looked up in the sky. "Captain, Cat's Eye isn't visible right now but Byers' Star is. That means this is a trueday. Based on where the sun is in the sky, it will only last a few more hours before truenight falls. We need to have our camp set up before then. Truenights are long and cold. We should be on our way as soon as possible."

"Okay, everyone. You heard the Chief. We need to pack up what we've brought and get down to a lower altitude so we can make camp. Chief Kowalski, you're our local guide. Which way should we go?"

The Chief unfolded a map of Cracovia he had printed before leaving the *VeeZee*. "Let me look at the map and I'll let you know, Skipper."

"Okay, the rest of you. Once you've packed up, I want you to get the parachutes and the canopy lines. Roll them up, we're taking them with us."

"Good idea, Captain. We don't want to leave them here where their bright orange color can be seen from afar."

The Captain regarded the Midshipman for a moment. *Still halfway between a midshipman and an officer. Not thinking far enough into the future.* Then he said, "Yes, Mr. Stewart. That's one reason. But we're taking them with us for another reason too. Trade goods."

"Trade goods, sir?"

"The chute materials are made of super-strong artificial fibers. More advanced than anything the natives are bound to have. We can cut it with our laser pistols and trade it."

"I see, sir. Thank …"

At that moment a bullet ricocheted off a rock near Lieutenant Johansen. Then several more. Chief Kowalski yelled, "Incoming. Take cover. Prepare to return fire."

Diving behind a large boulder, Lieutenant Johansen countermanded the last part of the Chief's order. "Belay the Chief's last. No return fire. I repeat no return fire. Retreat. Chief Kowalski, lead us out of here. We don't know how many of them there are. Or who they are. I don't want to get into a firefight."

"Aye aye, Captain. This way. Follow me. Keep your heads down." Then to the Captain he added. "Given they're terrible shots, they're probably just bandits, sir."

While running with his head down, Midshipman Stewart spoke up, "Captain, what about the parachutes?"

"Leave 'em."

* * *

"Fourth Rank Dagor, why did you call me here?"

"First Citizen, our last operational reconnaissance satellite picked up several frames of a spaceship crashing into the eastern ocean. The images were blurry but I believe it was an Imperial scoutship."

"What is the confidence level of your ship classification, Fourth Rank?"

"Eighty-five percent, First Citizen."

"And your confidence that the ship was destroyed?"

"Ninety-eight percent, First Citizen. It didn't slow much. Only what you would expect of an unpowered atmospheric reentry. It broke apart on impact and sank."

"Task the satellite to look for lifeboat capsules, Fourth Rank."

"Immediately, First Citizen."

It took another two orbits of the satellite for the TAC to find the infrared signature of the capsule. It had landed on the side of a Cracovian volcano. Its heat shield still cooling from reentry.

The image on the tactical view screen showed five glowing hot spots moving around the capsule. The First Citizen responded immediately, "How many HVRBs do we have left in orbit, Fourth Rank?"

"Three, First Citizen."

"Destroy that capsule. Assign the nearest bundle to it."

"Immediately, First Citizen."

* * *

Two hours after retreating from their lifeboat, dusk was setting in. The crew stopped at the mouth of a cave for a rest and drink of water from a small spring. After an hour's rest, they began to pack up, getting ready to resume their trek. Suddenly, there was a bright flash of light in the sky. Chief Kowalski yelled, "Cover!"

They all dove further into the cave. Then, a large sonic boom rang out. That was followed by a huge explosion on the side of the mountain far above them. Up near where they had landed. The ground shook. Dust and small rocks fell on them. Then there was an eerie quiet.

Lieutenant Johansen looked up and asked, "What was that?"

Chief Kowalski, replied. "That Captain, was a Rod From God. The Saurons must have had a few in orbit plus at least one reconnaissance satellite. Those poor bandits. They got more than they bargained for."

"We should get farther away from here."

"Captain, respectfully, I disagree. If they knew we were here, we would have been on the south end of one of them rods already. I believe we need to lay low until the next trueday. At truenight, our infrared signatures will be easy for them to pick up. The trueday warmth will mask our signatures better."

"Very well, Chief. We'll make camp in here until the next trueday."

It was morning of the next trueday. Chief Kowalski shook Lieutenant Johansen's shoulder. "Captain? Captain?"

The Lieutenant woke up and opened his eyes. "What, Chief?"

"Captain, it's trueday out."

"How long have we been here, Chief?"

"About forty standard hours, sir. By the way, the locals call them

T-hours."

"Yeah, forty T-hours. That should be long enough. Wake the men. We need to saddle up."

"Will do, Skipper."

Several hours later they took another break, "Chief, let's talk about where we're heading."

The Chief pulled out his map and unfolded it. "Here's where I think we landed, Skipper. On Góra Rog, a volcano in the northern Wielki Lato. We're moving down this valley, heading toward Nowy Kraków, the capital city here."

"Wielki Lato, Chief?"

"It's Polski, sir. It's what they speak here. It means big summer. It's the largest temperate area on the island."

"Chief, you need to start teaching us the local language."

"Yes, sir. I'll do that. Now, back to the map."

Looking at the map, Lieutenant Johansen said, "Don't you think the Saurons would have nuked Nowy Kraków, just as they did to all of the major cities in the Shangri-La Valley?"

Nodding his head, the Chief responded, "I guess they would have at that, Captain."

"What's this river?"

"That's where I was heading. It's called the Rzeka and it flows through Nowy Kraków to the sea. I figured if there are people around, that's where we'd find them."

"Okay, let's continue along this tributary toward it and see where it leads."

"Aye, Captain. Everyone. We're going to be hiking along this stream. There is a native species that lives in both the fresh water and salt water of Haven. It's very dangerous. It's called a river jack. They can grow up to a meter in length and they sometimes school like Earth-stock fish. They are bony, have spear-shaped heads and tentacles. River jacks can be caught and eaten but they will attack people and animals in turn. Be careful when drinking from streams, rivers or lakes. Or when crossing them."

Lieutenant Johansen had one more order before they started hiking.

"We will not move in any type of a military formation. Remember, our enemies have eyes in the sky and could be watching."

As they hiked along the stream, Midshipman Stewart posed a question to Lieutenant Johansen. "Captain, if the Saurons have a reconnaissance satellite that picked up our landing on Góra Rog, why didn't it pick up the Nazca type Morse code in the Shangri-La Valley?"

"Mr. Stewart, I can't say for sure, except, maybe the Saurons don't know Morse code."

"Yes, sir. That would make sense."

"Mr. Stewart, where are you from?"

"Covenant, sir."

"Why did you join the Navy?"

"Covenant has been part of the Empire for over five hundred years. Like several worlds settled during the CoDominium period, we needed capital. To get it, we raised and then rented out our military forces as mercenaries. Their motto was, as it is today, 'Stand and Deliver.' So, we have a military tradition that goes a long way back.

"We believe in keeping our promises, Captain. When my ancestors settled the planet, they made a covenant with God to keep the faith. They named the planet for their commitment, but to keep the faith, they realized they needed to be allied with something larger. Something stronger. That was the Empire of Man.

"The Empire allows us self-rule and doesn't impose their religious beliefs on us. We are Presbyterians, by and large. People of great faith. The Saurons are godless. They would destroy our beliefs and our souls. I joined to stand and deliver. It was an easy decision for me to make."

"Don't most Covenanters join the infantry or the marines?"

"Yes, sir. But I have always liked sailing. I thought the Imperial Navy would be the way to serve."

"Tell me more about Covenant, Mr. Stewart, I've never been there."

Slipping further into his Covenant burr, he said, "Aye. It's the most beautiful of planets, Captain. The habitable land is near the equator and is all rolling hills and mountains; nothing over fifteen hundred meters. In school, I learned that the hills are similar to those our forbearers inhabited, in a country called Scotland on old Earth. Even though the habitable land is on the equator, we have seasons. The planet has a high eccentricity. In late summer and early fall, the highlands are covered by heather with their purple hues. They have a fragrance that is indescribable," he said, remembering back to his boyhood days.

"We don't have a lot of interstellar trade. Agriculture and aquaculture are the most important industries on the planet. Few large cities, mostly villages. And each of those is centered on a kirk; a church in Anglic. Winters are cold and snowy. Most Imperial citizens visiting call the gale force winter winds fierce. We call them brisk," the Midshipman said with pride.

"You should feel right at home here, Mr. Stewart."

The Midshipman was not as surprised as he thought he would be when his suspicions were confirmed. "You don't think we will ever get off this rock, do you, Captain?"

"No, Mr. Stewart. I don't. I wish I could tell you differently but I think we are here to stay. I think this is where we will leave our bones."

At that moment, Chief Wagner came running toward them with a grin on his face. "Captain, Captain. Sorry to interrupt. I spotted a group of wild pigs up ahead. No more gruel!"

TWO

The crew of the *VeeZee* had made their camp next to a rock face under sheltering trees. A spring ran out of the rock face nearby. They had plenty of pork left from their early kills and wood for the fire. They had found some potatoes and carrots growing wild nearby. So, they had enough to eat. This was all good since they didn't have the strength to find more of either.

They didn't know it, but they had come down with a sickness acquired from the pigs they ate. A flu that combined an Earth-stock virus with a native Haven virus. Plus, some genetic material from the Tibetans, which they in turn had acquired from one of mankind's long extinct relatives, the Denisovans. A chimera virus that had been created by the Saurons in a secret Shangri-La Valley research laboratory over half a thousand T-years before. The virus was designed to insert genes into a person's DNA that allowed them to pull more oxygen out of Haven's thin air. A virus that, to the benefit of many Haveners, had accidently escaped from the lab.

They were sick with the worst flu they had ever had. For two T-weeks, they lay around their makeshift camp. None of their medical knowledge or pharmaceuticals had any effect on the bug. Like anyone who came down with a flu, they just had to live through it. They just had to let their bodies heal themselves. If they could.

As they recovered, they once again began to do the things they needed to do for their survival. One such activity was to clean their breathing masks, since they required periodic maintenance. Specifically, the semipermeable membrane in the masks had to be cleaned. It was an easy process but the mask had to be removed to do it.

Midshipman Stewart had taken his mask off when a gust of wind blew his cap away. Without thinking, he went running after it. It was only after he recovered the cap that he realized he had sprinted in the thin air without any ill effects. That was the crew's aha moment.

A few T-weeks later, Martinez ran up to Lieutenant Johansen. "Captain, Captain,"

"What is it Martinez?"

Even with the new genes, he was out of breath and took a minute before he said, "Captain, I was checking out the area over the hill there. There's a rundown farm house. Looks deserted. Might be a better place to lay over through the truenight."

The Captain was cold. Even though his ancestors had come from Scandinavia on Earth and he was wearing a survival jacket, he hadn't yet acclimated to the truenight temperatures on Haven. Lieutenant Johansen scratched his curly red beard and thought about moving their camp. But he didn't think about it for long.

"Chief Wagner, Chief Kowalski. Pack up. We're moving. Martinez says he found a better place to lay over during truenight. Sounds to be more comfortable than where we are."

Both Chiefs responded, "Aye aye, Captain."

As they approached the farmhouse, they saw it was occupied.

"Martinez, I thought you said it was abandoned."

"It was, Captain. Those men must have just arrived."

Chief Kowalski put his hand on the Captain's shoulder and made a sign for quiet. Then he pointed to the right of the farmhouse. It looked like the men were tying a woman to a tree. A very unhappy woman who was swearing at them in Polski.

* * *

Demetria Soltyk was angry at herself. How could she had gotten in this situation? Tied to a tree as truenight fell. She could feel the chill beginning to bite through her thick clothing. She guessed she would eventually be brought into the old farmhouse once her captors thought she had become submissive enough.

Yes, she had gotten herself captured on purpose, but her plan had been that she would immediately set upon her captors and retrieve her mother's diamond pendant. The one they had stolen. Something her mother had always said was a connection to her long-lost father and his past. Something she had vowed to recover. Instead, she had been knocked unconscious and restrained. All her training with the hussar sabre had come to naught.

She had wanted to prove herself to her mother. To show her that she was a grown woman of eighteen T-years who could take care of herself. How embarrassing for the daughter of Dama Franciszka Soltyk, leader of a small but successful lenno on the southeastern coast of Cracovia. Dama Soltyk had inherited the stone manor and land around it from her mother. That was after Franciszka's parents had been assassinated by Gletscherheim terrorists; several T-years before Demetria was born.

She thought back to her original plan. It had been a good one. It wasn't her fault that it didn't work. She began to think about how she was going to get out of this mess when she felt a hand cover her mouth and a voice say in very bad Polski, "Quiet, miss. We're here to rescue you."

She had no idea who these people were but at the very least they would provide her an opportunity to get untied. She felt someone cut the ropes restraining her. Then instead of turning to go with her rescuers, she ran toward the farmhouse.

"What the hell are you doing? It's this way."

She turned and said, "Thank you, but I have something to do first."

Demetria, surprised the guard outside the rundown farmhouse with a kick to his solar plexus. She heard the air rush out of his mouth with a loud grunt. He was wearing her captured sabre. She grabbed it and ran him through, killing him. Then she entered the farmhouse and started slashing and stabbing her captors. The result was bedlam.

During the confusion, Demetria found what she had been seeking. She ran out of the farmhouse putting the pendant around her neck while running. Lieutenant Johansen was close enough to see what she was doing. *A funerary diamond. I wonder what the story is behind that. And why it's so important to her.* Before he could say anything, her captors followed her out the doorway. They ran into the crew of the *VeeZee.*

Lieutenant Johansen, told the kidnappers, "Hold, or we will—"

Before he could finish, Demetria's captors attacked the *VeeZee's* crew, men who were armed with laser pistols. The crew of the *VeeZee* made quick work of their attackers.

Now Demetria turned to her rescuers, her sabre covered in blood. She bent down and wiped the blade off on the body of the dead leader. Still breathing hard she stood and said, "Thank you, I can take care of myself from here."

The tallest of the rescuers responded. "I'm sure you can, my lady. You fight like a demon. We have no interest in fighting you. We thought you needed help."

Her curiosity was piqued. *Who were these men who would risk their lives to save her? To save someone they didn't know?* "And just who are you?"

"I am Lieutenant Johansen of the Imperial Navy and these are my men."

"The Imperial Navy? Has the Empire returned to Haven after all these years?"

"No, my lady. Our ship crashed here. We are castaways."

Thinking quickly, she realized her mother would want to talk to these men. "Lieutenant, thank you and your men for rescuing me. My mother will want to reward you and I would like to offer you the hospitality of our home. If you would like to go with me, I will lead you there."

"How far is it?"

"A long T-day hike from here."

"We should hold up here until trueday. Wouldn't you agree, my lady?"

"Yes, but we should bury these bodies. We don't have any large scavengers on Cracovia but between the small ones and the smell the bodies will produce, even in the cold of truenight, we will be better served by properly disposing of them now."

* * *

Pointing to Lieutenant Johansen, the woman sitting on the large wooden throne at the far end of the great hall said, "I am Dama Soltyk. I rule here. My daughter tells me you are a member of the Imperial Navy? Yes?"

Lieutenant Johansen looked at the woman who had spoken to him. She seemed old. Either that or she had had a very hard life. Maybe both. She was a big woman. Her hair was gray. She struck him as tired but even standing this far away from her, he could see her blue eyes glowing with watchfulness. Just as her daughter's eyes did. "Yes, Dama, I am Lieutenant Johansen of the Imperial Navy," he replied in his best Polski.

"Come forward, Lieutenant. Closer. You mangle our language. I speak Anglic. Please speak in your native tongue. Now, what can you tell us about what is going on in the Empire? We have had little news of late." Which was quite the understatement.

"Dama, I do not know. You look surprised but we have been in frozen sleep for the past twenty-one T-years." Lieutenant Johansen then relayed the story of their accident and subsequent journey. Leaving out the fact that the mission was classified as an Imperial High Secret.

"Thank you, Lieutenant. A more personal question. Do you know an Imperial Academician by the name of Dmitry Ivanov? A biologist?"

"No, Dama. I am sorry but I am not familiar with anyone by that name. If I may ask, why?"

Dama Soltyk's face seemed to take on a harder, unhappier look. "You may not." Then changing the subject. "What can you tell us about Haven? Do you know why Cracovia was attacked almost twenty T-years ago?"

"It was the Saurons, Dama. It wasn't just Cracovia. The whole of Haven was attacked."

"Ah, we wondered about that. Especially, after the weather patterns changed. Many people died. We call it *czas zarazy, głodu i zimna*. It means the time of plague, famine and cold. Since then, the weather has returned to normal. For the last fifteen T-years, life has been more normal."

"From space we saw that all the major cities and military installations in the Shangri-La Valley were destroyed. Their bombardment likely caused a little nuclear winter. A worldwide cooling. We saw evidence that the Saurons have made a new home in that valley. They are exceedingly dangerous. And, they are still active. They saw us land and cast down a powerful weapon upon us. Our lifeboat capsule was destroyed but we were no longer in it. Only luck saved us."

"By your own admission, the Saurons are on the other side of the world. How could they attack you here?"

"Do you remember the explosion on Góra Rog, a T-month ago?"

"That little volcanic eruption? Yes, we get them often."

"No, Dama Soltyk. Respectfully, that was not a volcanic eruption. It was a Sauron strike on our lifeboat capsule. They hit it with a weapon called a hypervelocity rod bundle made of poplar sized metal poles. If they have more in orbit, they could bring them down on you and your people. By attacking our capsule, we know they have at least one reconnaissance satellite in orbit. We need to keep out of their sight."

"You have asked for sanctuary. What do you offer us in return?"

"We can fight for you with light."

Dama Soltyk pulled back a portion of the wrap covering her legs. She was holding a laser pistol aimed at the Lieutenant. While he looked on, she shifted the aim to a shield hanging on the far wall of the great hall and fired; melting a hole in it. "I can fight with light, too, Lieutenant. What else?"

Lieutenant Johansen was surprised that she wielded an Imperial Navy laser pistol. The Navy didn't give those to civilians. He wondered how she had come by it. Something he would look into later. He composed himself and answered her question. "Dama, we have tablets, pocket computers if you will. With knowledge in them. If we can find a way to recharge them."

"What kind of knowledge?"

"Recent photos of the Shangri-La Valley from space. Scoutship maintenance manuals, astrogation text books and more."

"Do the maintenance manuals include one for your Langston Field generator?"

"Yes, Dama."

"What else do you bring?"

"We have advanced medical knowledge and some supplies."

"Anything else?"

"We are trained Navy men. We can be of assistance to your military."

"So, you come to us as mercenaries?"

"Yes, Dama Soltyk. If that is the only way you will have us."

"Will you give me your oath of fealty?"

Lieutenant Johansen looked around at his men. They all nodded affirmative. "Yes, Dama. We will."

"Very well. It is enough."

THREE

"Fourth Rank Dagor, this is the second time in a T-month you have called for me. Do you like these visits from me?"

Taken off guard, he responded in a flustered manner. "No, First Citizen. I mean, yes. First Citizen. I—"

The First Citizen looked at Fourth Rank Dagor. *Not one of the brighter ones. Maybe I need to send him out on patrol and let Haven test him.* Instead of that he said, "Never mind, Fourth Rank. Why have you called me here?"

"First Citizen, our last reconnaissance satellite is failing. The TAC projects it will completely cease operations within three T-days. We have two remaining HVRBs in orbit. I recommend we use them before we lose our targeting ability."

"Very good, fourth Rank. What does the TAC recommend?"

"Here is a list of the top ten threats to the Citadel, First Citizen."

The First Citizen looked it over. Then he said, "That island we attacked the last time you called me here, what is it called?"

"Cracovia, First Citizen."

"Yes, Cracovia. Are any targets there on the threat assessment list?"

"Not in the top twenty, First Citizen."

"Is there an overview of the island?"

"Yes, First Citizen."

"Call it up."

"Immediately, First Citizen."

The First Citizen quickly took in the entry.

Cracovia is an island country on the moon called Haven. Haven orbits the gas giant Cat's Eye in the Byers' System. Cracovia is a large volcanic island that covers one million square kilometers of area. It is surrounded by the Occidental Ocean, one of the roughest bodies of water on all of the settled worlds. The island was colonized during the CoDominium era by people of Polish ancestry.

The Cracovian economy is primarily agricultural. They have few fishing boats and their coast guard is not a blue water service. They have no heavy industry and little light industry. The island has little mining. The few metal ores found there come from geothermal deposition. Metals mined include gold, silver, lead, zinc, copper, thallium, antimony and small quantities of iron.

A footnote had been added: Targets on Cracovia were chosen using the same criteria as targets in the Shangri-La Valley. However, the level of orbital bombardment on Cracovia was significantly less than the Shangri-La Valley due to a more limited target set.

The entry contained additional information but the First Citizen stopped reading. "Fourth Rank, what number does the TAC assign to the most important target on that island?"

"Number one hundred eighty-nine, First Citizen. A small castle on the southeastern coast. It is situated on a cliff overlooking the ocean."

"Bring up an image of it for me."

The screen showed a small, badly maintained castle. If it could even be called that.

"That does not look to be much of a threat," the First Citizen said dismissing it. "Now, Fourth Rank, bring back up the top ten TAC threat assessments and order them by the ones that can be destroyed by a HVRB."

"Done, First Citizen. They are all either in the Shangri-La Valley or on the northern steppe."

The First Citizen looked through the list. "Very well. Assign the remaining two HVRBs to priorities one and three. We can take care of the second priority by sending a patrol out."

"At once, First Citizen."

* * *

"Lieutenant Johansen, from what you have told me the Saurons will attack Cracovia if they discover we are rebuilding a technology base. It seems the only way we can shield ourselves from their prying orbital eyes, is by digging tunnels. To that end, I have sent orders to my scouts, I guess that is the best word for them, to send any former miners they capture back here. If they give me their oath of fealty, I let them live."

"Dama, you would kill men who have surrendered or were captured if they don't give you their oath?"

In a hard, sad voice she responded. "It is a harsh world, Lieutenant. As you will find out, if you live very long. My brother Pitor, rest his soul, gave his life for our family and this land." Dama Soltyk changed the tone of her voice again, this time making it softer. "In any case, I did not ask you here to pass judgment on my decisions. I want you to meet one of the Black Monks from the monastery to the south of us. We have had a friendly relationship with them for many years. In fact, they are allies of a sort. I want you to give them one of your tablets.

"Their order is tasked with preserving knowledge. Any books my scouts find are given to them. I recognize that the tablet is more than just a book. But we need permanent access to the information in it to rebuild our civilization as quickly as we can. Therefore, I have asked them to transcribe the information from the tablet onto paper. They will save the knowledge, just as the Black Monks did back on old Earth during the Dark Ages two thousand T-years ago."

"Dama, the batteries in the tablets need to be recharged periodically. I doubt they have the means to do that. Even we don't anymore."

"Lieutenant, much of the electricity on Cracovia was produced by geothermal direct conversion units. Many such generators still exist and produce power but the things that use electricity do not. Their monastery has such a generator. As do we."

"Very well, Dama. At my orders, Ensign Stewart has already consolidated all the information on the tablets and duplicated it across all of them. I am still uncomfortable sharing a tablet with these Black Monks, a group I have never heard of, but I have given my oath of fealty to you and will follow your orders."

"Have you heard of the Benedictines? Sometimes known as the OSB? That is whom I speak. They are an order of the Church headquartered in your New Rome on Sparta. The term Black Monks is one we use to refer to them by the habits they wear. It's easier to say than Benedictines."

"Yes. I have heard of them, Dama. Very well, I suggest we send Chief Wagner and Propulsion Mate First Class Williams along with the tablet. They have a lot of technical knowledge in their heads that is not in the tablet. They can add those things that a practical use requires."

"What do you mean, Lieutenant?" And then with more steel in her voice, "Have you withheld information from me?"

"No, Dama. Theory, schematics, that sort of thing seldom capture everything that's needed to make something work. Or, to repair it. Chief Wagner and Propulsion Mate Williams have much of that practical engineering experience in their heads. That is why they are engineering ratings. They can annotate the ship's maintenance manuals."

"Very well. Two more items, Lieutenant. First, you mentioned Ensign Stewart. Did you promote him?"

"Yes, Dama. It was time. He was ready."

"Lieutenant, I expect you to seek my approval for any promotions of your people."

"Dama, this is an Imperial Navy matter. It does not affect his duties or responsibilities toward you and your fiefdom. Your lenno in Polski. So, with respect, Dama. No, this is outside my oath to you."

Dama Solytk thought about it for a moment. "Agreed."

"And the second item, Dama?"

"I want you and Ensign Stewart to join my army. They are not an army in the traditional sense but a group of farmers. They have rallied around me since my lenno is the strongest one in the eastern Wielki Lato. They have little military training and I have few officers with any experience.

"Surviving forces of the Kingdom of Gletscherheim, landed on the west coast of the Wielki Lato six T-months ago and captured the *kaldera narodzin*. In Anglic that means birthing caldera. Because of its unique geography, it's the one area on Cracovia that has an air pressure comparable to the Shangri-La Valley. It's a box canyon used by the Cracovian people to give birth."

"So, without access, your people will eventually die out?"

"Yes. What is also disturbing is that we have reports that, after they arrived, the Gletscherheimers burned their ships to the ground."

Lieutenant Johansen thought about it for a minute. "They aren't planning on returning to Gletscherheim. They have made an all or nothing bet. Desperate people fighting with their backs against the wall."

"That is my assessment too. The Gletscherheimers are holding the birthing centers in the caldera hostage over our heads to force us to submit to their rule. This is a fight for more than just freedom. It is a fight for our very existence. Birthing centers have been freely accessible to all Cracovians throughout our history. We will ensure they are available again.

"You will report to my army commander as an acting captain." She knew his crew called him Captain and smiled at the happenchance. "Ensign Stewart will be an acting second lieutenant. I believe those are the army ranks that match your navy ones?"

"Yes, Dama."

"Since you have made it clear what the Saurons would do if they detect coherent light from your laser pistols, you will need to leave them here."

"Of course, Dama. It is unfortunate. We could end this invasion with little loss of life to our side. But, I agree, we do not want to attract the attention of the Saurons. Our loss of life would be much greater if they decided we are worthy of their attention. One other thing, Dama. I think Boatswain's Mate Second Class Martinez should go with me. I will leave Chief Kowalski here."

"As I understand, Chief Kowalski is a gunnery chief petty officer. Wouldn't it make more sense to take one of your people who is familiar with weapons?"

"Respectfully, Dama. No. Chief Kowalski is an expert in modern weapons. Lasers, missiles, nuclear warheads, particle beams, HVRBs. Those sorts of weapons."

She thought about it for a minute. Then with a smile on her face she said, "Very well. As I think you would say, make it so."

Where did she come up with that campy reference? One of the men pulling her leg? I guess it doesn't matter. Time to get to work.

* * *

"Eric, I don't want you to go."

"Demetria, you know I have to."

"I can talk to my mother," she said hopefully. But as she said that, she felt him turn cold and draw away from her.

"No, you will not do that. My honor is at stake." Then he softened. "Don't worry, I will return to you. And when this business with the Gletscherheimers is finished, I will ask your mother for your hand in marriage."

Demetria had a quick tongue. "If you value your hand, you will ask me first," she said with fire in her eyes and frost in her voice.

He realized that by being courtly, he had slighted her in her eyes. She was her own woman and wanted to be recognized as such. "I'm sorry, I want to marry you. Will you marry me?"

Demetria's temper wasn't so easily calmed. She quickly replied, "I'll give you my answer when you return." Then she started to leave the room before turning back and adding, "Come back with your shield, not on it."

* * *

It came to be known as the Battle of the Glade. A motley group of Cracovian farmers and ranchers pitted against professionally trained Gletscherheim soldiers. A bloody encounter indeed.

The grand Cracovian strategy was to hit the enemy fast and hard. The Cracovian general planned to open his campaign by attacking across the plain in front of the cliffs on the outside of the caldera. Then after dispatching the defenders, he planned on capturing the tunnel and marching through it, into the caldera. Finally, the Cracovians would attack the birthing center buildings themselves.

The Cracovian intel was very poor. They didn't know if the Gletscherheimers had explosives. If they did and the enemy blew the tunnel, a much longer and bloodier fight would be necessary. The Cracovians would have to fight their way up the side of the collapsed volcano. Then, they would have to fight their way back down into the caldera. Finally, they would have to attack the birthing center buildings and take them. Fighting against an enemy that held the high ground would be costly at best. The baggage train to support the attack on the targets within the caldera would be a nightmare.

Speed was of the essence for the Cracovian strategy to work. Speed and luck. In reality, the strategy was amateurish and didn't take into account the realities on the ground. It didn't consider what the Gletscherheim strategy might be and it didn't plan for more than one contingency. It was a high risk, all or nothing plan.

The Gletscherheim plan was simpler and more professional. Use the attack to decapitate the Cracovian military leadership and then push through the Cracovian army, routing it. Then march on the Soltyk lenno. Once that was taken, the whole southern half of the island would fall to the Gletscherheimers. The northern reaches wouldn't be far behind. If by some unlikely event they lost the first battle, they could retreat to the slopes of the caldera. Then blow the tunnel leading into the dead volcano. They would be in a defensive position but they could outwait the Cracovians. They would still be in the ultimate position of strength.

The Soltyk army was a rag-tag group but they were protecting their homes and families against foreign invaders. History had been made many times before by the likes of them, on Earth, on Sparta and on a dozen other worlds. But those times also required superb leadership and luck.

Once the fighting in the glade began, it was hand-to-hand. The tips of the Cracovian weapons, that is, their crossbow bolts, swords and knives, were all dipped in thallium to make them more deadly. If the Gletscherheimers recognized the poison as such and if they had the antidote, their wounded men would recover. Otherwise, it was a death sentence. And not a quick one.

Captain Johansen's commanding officer and adjutant were both taken out by crossbow fire in the first minutes of the battle. The Captain saw the pattern and realized he was going to be next. So, he kept on moving. Not giving the Gletscherheimers a stationary target. He pursued the original battle plan. A straight-on attack against their line, then retreating. Allowing the Cracovian troops to be pushed back, creating the appearance of a rout. Once the Gletscherheimers followed them, the Cracovians would spring their trap. A pincer movement, encircling the invaders and destroying them.

Long-standing military wisdom held that no battle plan survives contact with the enemy. The Cracovian plan was no exception. It began to go south when the flank that Second Lieutenant Stewart commanded, was itself attacked from the rear by armed Gletscherheimers mounted on muskylopes riding out of the trees. The Second Lieutenant found his command attacked from both the front and rear but he stood his ground. His men were about to break when he raised his sword and yelled, "Stand and Deliver!" Then he yelled it again. This time in Polski. "*Stać i Dostarczyć!*" Again, he yelled it and again; until his troops rallied.

Stewart ordered half of his men to hold and protect their backs. He ordered the other half to follow him. He turned and charged the muskylopes, slashing at the animal's legs with his sword. Causing the animals to fall and spill their riders. Stewart's men immediately pounced on the Gletscherheimers, killing them before they could regain their wounded mounts. The resulting carnage was horrific. Then, he ordered his men to turn and reinforce the men holding off the Gletscherheimers.

The pincher movement was successful. The Gletscherheim survivors retreated to the slopes of the caldera but not before blowing the tunnel. Still, the Soltyk army was victorious at the glade that day. Sadly, late in the engagement, Second Lieutenant Stewart took a crossbow bolt to his chest and was killed.

Dama Soltyk promoted Captain Johansen to Colonel in charge of her troops. While she didn't think he had enough experience to lead her troops fighting on land, she had no one else. No choice. He was the most experienced officer left alive after the battle. She posthumously promoted Second Lieutenant Stewart to the rank of Captain and awarded him the first Saint Pitor's Cross for bravery above and beyond. As a final gesture to Captain Stewart, the Dama added the words Stać i Dostarczyć below the white eagle on her family's coat of arms. Even with all the recognition for the Covenanter, Colonel Johansen felt a deep sense of loss at his death.

FOUR

2660 A.D., Soltyk Manor

"Colonel Johansen, it has been six T-months and we are still in a stalemate with the Gletscherheim invaders. This cannot go on."

"Dama Soltyk, after we beat them at the Battle of the Glade, they fell back and regrouped in front of the caldera tunnel. We tried a frontal assault on their positions but that wasn't successful. They blew the tunnel leading to the birthing centers and retreated up the slope of the caldera. They now hold the high ground. We have tried direct assaults as well as infiltration tactics, none have been successful. I thought we could starve them out but my guess is that they are growing their own food on the floor of the caldera.

"I have not wasted the time, Dama. I have used the time training our men. Building the logistics organization we will need to win."

"We don't have the time to use Sun Tzu's techniques, Colonel."

"You have read Sun Tzu, Dama?" the Colonel responded with a mixture of surprise and admiration.

"Yes, Colonel. I have read Sun Tzu, Falkenberg, Clausewitz and a few others. They are not helpful in our current situation. We need to do something different and soon. Our men are farmers and ranchers. They need to get back to their homes. If it wasn't that they need the birthing centers so badly for their wives and their horses, they would have gone home already. As it is, they are not going to stay with us much longer. Granting them home leave has helped some but you know as well as I do, fewer come back each time."

"I know, Dama. I have been giving another plan some thought. We could send a small force in from the ocean. Make an amphibious landing, hit them hard from behind and disrupt their rear area. Then at the same time, launch another frontal assault. Up the outside of the caldera."

"The seas are treacherous, Colonel."

"I understand that, Dama. I have talked to the Black Monks about building something my ancestors used on old Earth. A longship. I had a model of one I made when I was a child. I gave it to them. Unfortunately, they thought it would take too long to scale it up and build it. Instead, they suggested an outrigger design. It would give us more stability during the rough ocean passage. Also, they are not complex craft. We should be able to build them quickly."

"Do they have designs for these 'outrigger' vessels?"

"They do, Dama."

Dama Soltyk was silent for a few minutes, then said, "I do not think landing a few squads of ten men behind the enemy lines will disrupt their defenses enough. We need to arm a few of the assault team with laser pistols."

"Dama, I have told you what would happen if the Saurons detect such high-tech weapons."

"Yes, you have, Colonel. But maybe we can use that in our favor. I do not think a small force can carry enough weapons to avoid being overwhelmed by the Gletscherheimers inside the caldera. The way I see it is, if your infiltration unit is given overwhelming force, they will be successful. If the Saurons detect the laser pistols' output, the infiltration unit will draw the Sauron's wrath and they will destroy everything in the caldera. Either way, we put an end to this occupation now."

"Dama...."

"We need to roll the dice." Then in a stern voice he had come to recognize as her final words on a subject. "I have decided, Colonel. Who will you send?"

"Since this may be a suicide mission. I will ask for volunteers, Dama. Whoever goes, I should go with them."

"Colonel, you know I cannot allow that. You are my most experienced military officer." Dama Soltyk paused for a moment and then added, "And the father of my future grandchildren. Yes, Colonel. I know how close you and Demetria have become. We need to liberate the caldera for your children's sake too."

* * *

First Citizen Diettinger had called First Cyborg Köln to his Citadel study to discuss the Race's future on Haven. As Köln entered the room, he automatically inspected the First Citizen. *He has aged. Not much longer before he must turn the reins of power over to his son.*

"It has been a T-year since our last reconnaissance satellite died, First Cyborg."

"Your concern, First Citizen?"

"We are losing our ability to maintain our high-tech weapons and equipment. Every year we lose more capabilities and we can't replace what we lose. We still have our genetic superiority over the cattle, so the loss of those capabilities will not put the Race at risk. That is, unless someone, somewhere begins to rebuild a high-tech industry. Or unless we missed something twenty years ago. As it is, we rely on our TAC projections to warn us of threats. We need to recon the planet and compare the latest TAC threat projections to the intel we acquire. I want to ensure the TAC's projections are accurate."

"How do you plan to proceed, First Citizen?"

"I will take one of the flyers and overfly all the major landmasses. I will carry a full recon package. When I say major land masses, I include South Continent and Cracovia. We will compare my flyer's readings with the TAC projections. If they are the same, we can be confident the TAC will project threats against us accurately, even as our ability to gather far flung intel diminishes."

"Why you, First Citizen?"

"Truthfully First Cyborg, I want to fly through the sky one last time. I realize it is an indulgence but I am also fully capable of completing the mission."

The cyborg nodded. A reaction unusual for those of his kind. But he had been working closely with the First Citizen since arriving on Haven and had picked up a few of his mannerisms. He knew that exceptional Soldiers like the First Citizen needed recreation. Something that had been bred out of his kind. "First Citizen, even with a full recon package, your flyer will have two hard points available. I recommend you arm your flyer with two enhanced radiation weapons in case you discover deviations from the TAC projections during your mission."

Diettinger thought about it. "An excellent suggestion, First Cyborg."

* * *

The landing was a disaster. The first outrigger capsized in the heavy surf. Chief Kowalski lost several people. The second outrigger with Boatswain's Mate Martinez fared better. Both Kowalski and Martinez had volunteered for the mission. Laser weapons sound like they are easy to use but the reality is very different. Even minor shaking could throw a beam off target. The two Imperials knew they were best qualified to use the weapons properly. And both men knew the risks. But Cracovia was their home now. They had married and were expecting children soon. It was their duty.

As they struggled up the beach, they came under fire from a roving Gletscherheim patrol. A few well-placed laser shots ended the skirmish. Then they moved into the trees. The team had a few people who were familiar with the canyon floor. They took the lead, heading up the wall of the canyon to set up an observation post to identify where the enemy had established their positions.

They had planned to have a full trueday to recon. The firefight on the beach put that timing at risk. Still, they set up their observation post and began mapping the enemy's positions in the canyon.

* * *

The reconnaissance mission had been uneventful. *Almost boring*, the First Citizen thought. He had covered three quarters of Haven and had not detected any signs of advanced technology. It was truenight out and he was flying over Cracovia. He wanted to see the castle that, one T-year ago, the Threat Analysis Computer had said was the one hundred and eighty-ninth most serious threat to the Citadel. Both his sensors and his enhanced vision detected nothing but wood-burning heat and light from the castle. *So much for the TAC on that target. I wonder why it registered as a threat. I wish we could see into the inner workings of that thing. No matter. I would rather have false positives than false negatives. Time to move on.* The First Citizen changed his course to the northwest heading for the steppe north of the Atlas Mountains on the western continent. North of the Shangri-La Valley.

As he neared the coast, his sensors screamed for attention. He looked at his heads-up display and saw the flyer had intercepted a burst of coherent light. Something that could only come from a laser. His first thought was that he was being targeted, so he put the flyer into a random, twisting maneuver to escape any lock-on. He needn't have bothered. There was no attempt to lock on to his flyer. Only intermittent reflected light from, according to the instruments, several Imperial laser pistols.

He slowed the craft and returned to the area. The synthetic radar painted a picture of an east west canyon with a few buildings at eastern end of it. The infrared detectors identified both the origin and the destination of the laser fire. It appeared two people were using them to attack the buildings. There was no return laser fire. *Someone found a couple of laser pistols and are using them to attack whoever is in those buildings. That isn't good. I need to get rid of those laser pistols now. No guessing where they might end up if I wait to send in Pathfinders to find and kill the owners. Time to use one of my weapons.*

The First Citizen had loaded two neutron bombs onto his flyer at First Cyborg Köln's suggestion. Weapons that had been designed to produce an intense burst of neutrons to sterilize an area without causing much physical damage.

First Citizen Diettinger swung his flyer around and flew back out to sea. He turned again and dropped in altitude until he was flying just above the top of the waves. Now he was approaching the canyon low and fast from the west. As he went feet dry, he pulled back on the stick sending his flyer into a ballistic climb. When he was high enough, he armed the gravity bomb. Then he released the weapon on an unpowered ballistic trajectory, aiming for the far end of the canyon. Diettinger immediately pulled the stick over and down; altering his course ninety degrees to port and picking up speed. For his own protection, he needed to get the canyon's cliffs between him and the detonation. He hadn't felt the thrill of an attack run like this since his early days in the navy. He felt young again, stoked…

…and with a loud popping sound, the bomb detonated in the sky above the canyon floor. Most of the weapon's energy was channeled into an intense pulse of neutrons, killing everyone in the caldera.

Five

The Gletscherheim families and soldiers who were in the caldera, were all killed by the Sauron bomb. Most of the remaining defenders outside the caldera, lost their will to fight. Still, the battle to the top of the ridgeline was not completely unopposed. While it took longer than if an unconditional surrender had occurred, the Soltyk forces were victorious. The caldera with its birthing centers were freed.

The heroic amphibious landing teams were recognized by the Dama. Each of the team members, including Chief Kowalski and Boatswain's Mate Martinez, were posthumously awarded the Saint Pitor's Cross. Their families received land grants and titles.

Trials and executions were held for the few surviving Gletscherheim leaders. The Gletscherheim rank and file troops were disarmed and put to work reopening the tunnel into the caldera. Not a safe job. After the tunnel was cleared and shored up, the prisoners were paroled and released. Reprisals were officially banned by the Dama but some did occur.

After seeing the effect of the fearsome weapon that the Saurons unleashed on the birthing centers, Dama Soltyk issued an edict banning the use of high-tech weapons or devices. At least above ground. The Black Monks were given permission to continue their research and development activities as long as they were underground and couldn't be detected. The Saurons' follow-on recon flights detected no laser or other high-tech emissions from anywhere on Cracovia. They saw only an agrarian landscape. They eventually decided the island was not a threat.

And finally, a cause for celebration. Colonel Johansen married Demetria Soltyk and began what was to become a new dynasty on Cracovia, the House of Soltyk.

Andromeda Nostrum

The Beasts followed us.
How is that possible, Your Holiness?
How many angels can dance on the head of a pin? How many demons?
I do not grasp your meaning, Most Holy Father.
Battles between good and evil can happen at all scales, my son.

* * *

The twins danced.
Danced, Your Holiness? With who?
With each other. The Dioscuris danced until the smaller one that was Castor saw us, reached out for us, grabbed us, threw us out.
Out of Eden?
Out of Purgatory. Out of the Center.
The Dioscuris sound like Gods, Most Holy Father.
No, no, my son. There is only one God. They are but two of His servants.

* * *

…and we wandered through the wilderness for a hundred years before coming upon this Promised Land.
Your Holiness, I don't understand. What wilderness?
The wilderness of stars, my son.

— Excerpts from *Deathbed Conversations with the Supreme Pontiff Peter II*,
Ecumenical Catholic Church of Andromeda,
Second New Rome Press, New Sparta, *2795 A.D.*

November 2, 2798 A.D., New Sparta

George Sergei Carlton, Lord Blaine, DSC, GCMG, Fleet Admiral ISN (Ret.) sat in a wheelchair on the terrace overlooking his country estate. Built into the Marquis' chair was a portable life-support system. These days, he could never detach from it. He was dressed in a tweed coat and cap. Over his lap was draped a wool blanket to keep the morning chill off his legs. Next to him on a side table was a steaming cup of coffee.

Lord Blaine spent much of his time napping these days. When awake, he cast his mind back to the long voyage to this place. This newly terraformed home for humanity in the Andromeda galaxy. His mind wandered back to how it all began …

2624 A.D., Sparta

Admiral Blaine had been driven to the Royal Hunting Lodge in the Phokian Mountains by the Emperor's own guard. Still, he was stopped three times for security checks. Guards with serious weapons stood behind junior officers who checked the car's occupants against their databases. Finally, upon reaching the lodge, Admiral Blaine was escorted into the Emperor's private den. His escort stopped at the door. Then, backing away, his escort closed the double doors leaving the Admiral alone with the only other occupant of the room. Standing there, waiting for him, was His Most Royal and Imperial Highness and Majesty, Lysander V, Emperor of the Empire of Man.

Ruler of a thousand worlds, the Admiral thought. *Fewer each year as this war drags on.*

"Cousin George. Thank you for coming." The Emperor gestured toward a plush chair. "Please sit and make yourself comfortable." On the side table next to the chair was a cup of piping hot Jamaica Blue Mountain coffee. It was imported from Earth and reserved for the Royal Family alone.

The level of intimacy the Emperor was displaying took Admiral Blaine off guard but all he said was, "Thank you, Sire."

"That was quite good work defending New Washington and their Jump point to New Chicago. You prevented the Saurons from cutting one of our most vital supply lines. Yes, quite good work. You remind me of your uncle, Marshal Blaine when he led the Lavaca Campaign and the liberation of Lavaca. Your family has produced some of the Empire's best military minds."

The Emperor clearly wanted something from him, Admiral Blaine just didn't know what. So, he said, "Thank you, Majesty." Then he paused for a moment before continuing. "Sire, I know your time is very valuable. With respect, I suggest we get right to the purpose of this meeting."

"You always were a direct one, George. Very well. What I am about to tell you a classified Imperial High Secret." The Emperor proceeded to tell him of his plan to plant several colonies far from Imperial space. Colonies that would serve as redoubts for the Empire and the human race if the worst came to pass.

"Majesty, have things become so dire?"

"George, they are more serious than is publicly known, however I still think we can win." Then he added more strongly. "Let me restate that. I believe we will win." He paused for a moment and added, "But I also think it prudent to have a backup plan."

"What do you want of me, Majesty?"

"I want you to take command of the redoubt program."

"Sire, I am at a loss for words."

"I know that you joined the Navy to make your own way in the world. That your older brothers will inherit the titles and lands before you do. I'm guessing that has been a sore point with you."

"Majesty …"

The Emperor held up his hand to stop the Admiral from saying any more. “Hear me out, George. This is a chance for you to have the titles and the lands you desire. Your whole family will go with you to start a new line. And something else. You will all receive Imperial longevity treatments. That and frozen sleep will extend your lives by at least a century.”

The Admiral knew the Emperor really needed him. He was offering every inducement.

“Majesty, can I talk this over with my wife?”

“I’m sorry, George, but no. This is too important to the Empire. You have to make the decision for your family by yourself.”

November 2, 2798 A.D., New Sparta

Lord Blaine stirred. His coffee had turned cold. It had been made from Jamaica Blue Mountain coffee beans brought all the way from Earth. Now it was grown here. One of his requests that the Emperor had readily agreed to. He continued to ignore the coffee and settled back into his memories....

2630 A.D., Sigismund

Admiral Blaine joined the Emperor to review the progress on the parts of the redoubt program being pursued at the Imperial University on Sigismund. As a cover story for the Emperor’s visit, a general review was organized. One similar to others that had been conducted in recent years. Department heads received twenty minutes apiece to impress the Emperor and his guest, Admiral Blaine, with their most important scientific investigations and results. Most of the projects struck the Admiral as a rehash of previous research. He wondered why true scientific discovery was rare these days, especially when the war effort required such advances. That concern evaporated at the end of the day when a disheveled looking physicist took the stage and presented a program that caught the Admiral’s attention.

Academician Li Qiang Bhasin's presentation was so esoteric that Admiral Blaine could barely understand it. The Academician threw out terms like quantum scrambling, Hamiltonians, Hawking radiation and qubits. He talked about a deeper meaning to reality that created gravity. None of that made any sense to the Admiral. What the Admiral did understand was that it was about a reinterpretation of the Langston-Ward Grand Unified Field Theory and that it might prove useful to him.

The physicist was investigating how the relativistic and quantum field aspects of the theory interacted. Academician Bhasin theorized that, if two black holes could be entangled, a quantum bit of information fed into one would show up in readable form in the other hole. The information would have instantaneously traveled down the wormhole connecting the two holes, no matter how far apart they were.

The academician knew he would never be able to entangle two black holes to test his theory. Instead, he came up with different approach. He wanted to use Langston Fields to test his theory, since they acted like electromagnetic black holes. He wanted to entangle two Fields and then physically separate them. Then he wanted to send a specially created photon between them; a qubit photon. There was more to it than that. Some form of additional coupling of the Fields would be needed to make it work. But, Academician Bhasin said he had figured out how to do that.

The Academician was careful to point out that entanglement was not bobbling. Bobbling was just two Langston Fields temporarily intersecting, equalizing their stored energy. He wanted to achieve a deeper, more fundamental connection.

If Academician Bhasin could send a qubit from one Field to the other after they were separated, he would prove his interpretation of the theory. Something about quantum entanglement and wormholes being the same; just two sides of the same coin. Admiral Blaine saw something different in his presentation. If the experiment was successful, it might be a way to report back upon the success of the Andromeda missions.

The Admiral immediately classified the academician's research an Imperial High Secret and funded the physicist's experiment. After the first experiment was a success, the Admiral authorized an interstellar version of it. When that was successful, the Admiral authorized the construction of a zero-gee space station in the outer regions of Sigismund System. In addition to the laboratory and maintenance modules, the station included three modules at the end of long support arms. Each of these modules contained one half of a Bhasin comm system. One half for each of the Andromeda expedition's spaceships.

In order to complete the other half of the system, a Langston Field generator with the entangled Field engaged was installed in an armored compartment within each of the three Andromeda spaceships. The armor surrounding the compartments holding the Field generator was a safeguard. If a massive number of qubits were absorbed by an entangled Field, that energy would be transferred to the Field at the other end of the wormhole. That unexpected energy surge would need to be contained to avoid disaster.

All of the Field generators were situated inside vacuum chambers in order to isolate them from the external environment. Each Field generator had triple redundant power supplies. The redundancy was important. If the Field lost power even for an instant, the Field would collapse and the entanglement between it and its distant counterpart would be permanently severed. The communications linkage lost forever.

The Bhasin communication system was highly experimental. It was a low bit-rate system with repetition and error correction built in. Even then, the system required a large amount of computer processing power to recover a simple message.

November 2, 2798 A.D., New Sparta

Lord Blaine was awakened by the laughter of children playing. His great-grandchildren. They were running through the manor's gardens playing Spartans and Saurons. He looked out over the manicured lawns and hedges. *I must remember to ask Lady Amanda to plant roses in the gardens. We need more color here. And of course, you never know when the manor may be in need of defensive shrubbery. So much still to do here to terraform this world. To build an Empire. But it could have been an almost impossible task....*

2640 A.D., INSS Cassiopeia's Daughter, Andromeda Center

"Commander Anderson," Admiral Blaine said. "It's your tank," referring to the Tri-V display.

"Yes, sir."

The Astrogators' department included astronomers, astrophysicists and the ship's sailing masters. The Commander drew the information for his presentation from all of them. He fiddled with the workstation controls in front of him until the Tri-V tank lit up with an image of the Andromeda galaxy. Then he addressed the personnel meeting in the war room.

"Here is an image captured by the Imperial Observatories before our Random Jump to Andromeda. As you know it is two and a half million years out of date. Based on detailed observations, the observatories created a model for us that is able to predict stellar movements since that time. We have confirmed by our own stellar observations that their model is relatively accurate.

"Before we Jumped, the observatories also looked for signs of chlorophyll in the Andromeda light spectrum. They didn't find much. What they did find was a lot of selenium. Back in the Milky Way, selenium-based plant life had been found on several worlds in the Empire closest to the galactic core."

The Commander opened a window and displayed pictures of the jet-black plants. "Imperial xenobiologists have known for some time that selenium-based plant life uses yellow sunlight more efficiently than chlorophyll. So, if it gets established first, chlorophyll plant life doesn't stand a chance. That means, on worlds where selenium-based plant life is present, it would be too difficult to overcome the 'first colonizer' effect and successfully seed Earth-stock plants."

Then Commander Anderson looked at Academician Ivanov, the expedition's only biologist currently awake. Academician Ivanov had a blank look on his face; his mind clearly elsewhere. The Astrogator was expecting some kind of response. Ivanov had enough presence of mind to nod his head in agreement and said, "That is correct, Commander."

The Astrogator continued. "To further illustrate the problem and put it into context, here's what the Andromeda galaxy looks like overlaid with the selenium spectrum information. As you can see, selenium-based plant life appears to be widespread. Academician Ivanov believes that it forms the basis for most food chains in the galaxy. Eating food containing selenium would be poisonous to us. We knew this before we Jumped just as we knew this was a one-way trip. A galaxy is a big place so we assumed we would still be able to find suitable planets to terraform and colonize."

The Astrogator enlarged the selenium overlay. It contained a large void. "I want to draw your attention to this region here," he said pointing to the hole. "This region seems to be devoid of selenium-based plant life."

The Admiral spoke up. "Commander, what could cause that?"

"Admiral, based on the motion of the stars in that region, my department believes that it is the remnants of a small satellite galaxy Andromeda absorbed a hundred million years ago. The planets in that galaxy don't seem to have developed selenium-based plant life. We are fortunate. If this region didn't exist, finding the right planet for us would have been more difficult. Like looking for a needle in a haystack."

"So, this is a region that is more favorable to our biology?"

"Yes, sir. The light spectrum shows signs of chlorophyll there."

"How far away is it?"

"Twenty thousand lightyears, Admiral. And to answer your next question, including the refueling and re-provisioning along the way, my department estimates it will take us about a hundred years to reach it."

"I would think we would be able to reach that region of space in less time than that. Take me through your reasoning, Commander Anderson."

"Admiral, we do not know the route we need to take to get to that region. It's not like traveling through the Empire where Jump points have been well mapped for hundreds of years. Or where the Jump point sequences are available in our navigation database. We need to discover them. We need to explore. And, as you know exploration takes time.

"Since the beginning of the interstellar age and the CoDominium's first Grand Survey, the length of time it takes to discover new pathways across the stars has been remarkably constant at two hundred light-years per annum. Therefore, my department modeled the duration of our voyage based on that metric."

"Drill down for me, Commander."

"Admiral, the astronomers' first need to find the closest stars around each new solar system we arrive at. Then they need to model the Alderson force distribution taking into account interference effects. After we have done that, we need to send our scoutships with their Alderson force sensors ahead of us to pin down the precise location of the points. Granted, our sensors today are better than the ones they had back in the early days of the CoDominium but that has only improved the metric a small amount. That is because the majority of a scoutship's search time is spent in transit. While our drives are more efficient than the ones they had back then, the amount of acceleration a crew can take hasn't changed. So, the efficiency has translated into less fuel used, not faster transit.

"Only after the scoutships Jump through the points and check the conditions on the other side will we follow. That saves us fuel. Even with our best efforts, a system may not have more than one Jump point. That is, we may run into a dead end and have to backtrack. All this will take time.

"Every year or so, we will need to refuel by either finding and mining a small icy body or by sending our scoopships diving into a gas giant to mine its atmosphere for hydrogen. Either approach takes time. And lastly, I assume we will need to stop every twenty years for a more extensive overhaul. In order to do that, we will need to find an asteroid with the right mineral composition to mine. Again, finding the right one takes time.

"Admiral," the Astrogator continued. "I also assumed that you and Captain Fainchurch would be in frozen sleep part of the time. Three years on, three off for each of you overlapping for one month on both ends of your wakefulness."

The Admiral turned to the Captain. "Will our frozen sleep tanks last a hundred years?"

"With proper maintenance, the Chief Medical Officer and the Chief Engineer assure me they will."

"You and your department seem to have thought this through, Astrogator. Well done."

"Thank you, Admiral."

November 2, 2798 A.D., New Sparta

Lord Blaine felt the sun's warmth on his face. He looked up in the sky to see New Agamemnon coming out from behind the clouds. As he enjoyed the morning, his mind wandered back to the first time he used the Bhasin comm system …

2640 A.D., *INSS Cassiopeia's Daughter*, Andromeda Center

Admiral Blaine finished accessing the secret compartment in his cabin. As he entered, the light came on automatically. He looked around and saw a large compartment. In the middle of it was a single device bolted to the deck. The Admiral knew that in the center of that device was a container housing a very small Langston Field. Not just any Field but an entangled one.

The Admiral made his way over to the control panel on the device. All the status lights were green. He mentally breathed a sigh of relief. Next, he plugged his tablet into the panel and reviewed the Bhasin comm system's log. The system had been active since first being entangled with its twin Langston Field in the Sigismund System; although, only an early test message had been logged since then. No surprise there. The system would have notified him if there had been any incoming messages.

While not necessary to use the device, the Admiral felt that zero gee increased the chances of a successful transmission. He knew that this was more superstition than science. But sailors, whether of oceans or stars, had always been superstitious. He had less superstitions than most, but he wasn't without them.

The Admiral opened a comm channel to Captain Fainchurch on his tablet and ordered fifteen minutes of freefall for the *Cassie D*. He then typed his message into the comm system. The Admiral felt the ship's acceleration ebb until he was in freefall. He said a silent prayer and pushed transmit.

FLASH MESSAGE BEGINS

IMPERIAL HIGH SECRET
EYES ONLY

FROM: FLEET ADMIRAL GEORGE BLAINE
TO: EMPEROR LYSANDER V

MATERIALIZED ANDROMEDA CENTER.
HEAVY BUT REPAIRABLE DAMAGE.
NO WORD FROM OTHER SHIPS.

FLASH MESSAGE ENDS

The system acknowledged it had transmitted the message. Unfortunately, there was no way for Admiral Blaine to know if it had been received unless someone at the other end sent back an acknowledgement. He received none. Unknown to the Admiral, the research station had been abandoned a few months prior and left on automatic. The spaceship sent to evacuate the scientists and station personnel had been attacked by Burgess privateers on their return voyage to Sigismund. The ship fought back but was destroyed along with all of its crew and passengers.

Fortunately, automatic meant the communication masers on the station tracked the positions of the Imperial comm buoys located at the Sigismund System's Alderson points. After the buoys received the Flash message, they authenticated it, added the appropriate header and then inserted it into the Imperial interstellar comm network.

The comm network relied on Imperial spaceships to carry messages between the stars. Within a solar system, the network relied on masers to forward them onward. Before a Jump, Imperial comm buoys automatically uploaded message traffic to every passing Imperial spaceship. After a Jump, the messages were automatically downloaded to the Alderson point comm buoys in the new solar system. The buoys then forwarded the message traffic via maser to the other Alderson point comm buoys in the system to await the next passing spaceship. This combination of spaceship Jump and maser transmission continued until messages were eventually delivered to their final destinations, in this case Sparta and the Imperial palace. The process could take days or months, depending on the volume of spaceship traffic passing through the various Jump points.

November 2, 2798 A.D., New Sparta

Lord Blaine was roused from his woolgathering by several nearby quail calls. He cocked his head to figure out where they were coming from. Then, when the bird calls stopped, he found he was looking at the ground. He noticed some crumbs from his breakfast biscuit being carried off by ants. One of the many Earth-stock insects helping to transform the land. That reminded him of another time and place, sending him back to his daydreaming. *Those damn Saurons and their nanites....*

2641 A.D., INSS Cassiopeia's Daughter, Refuge System, Andromeda Center

Dr. Volkov, the expedition's Chief Medical Officer, was stripping off his surgical gloves and gown, preparing to wash up, when Admiral Blaine called. "Doctor Volkov, as soon as you finish up in there, I would like an update."

The Doctor, a native of St. Ekaternia, was angry. He growled at the Admiral and in his Russian accent said, "I can give it to you right now. We lost him."

The Admiral was taken aback. "What happened, Doctor?"

The Doctor remembered who he was talking to and lowered his voice. "I do not know, Admiral. We began removing the oxy-nanites and he went into shock. His blood pressure and heart rate spiked. We tried to lower both but nothing worked. Then he died. We tried to revive him. Nothing worked. I need to conduct an autopsy to know more. Now, please...." The Doctor paused and then started again. "I am sorry, Admiral. I have not lost a patient in long time. I will inform you when I know more."

"Of course, Doctor."

* * *

A few days later, Admiral Blaine was meeting with Captain Fainchurch and Doctor Volkov. Captain Fainchurch started off the meeting. "Doctor, I understand that you have completed the autopsy on Lieutenant Stuart. What did you discover?"

Before answering, the Doctor turned toward Admiral Blaine. "Admiral, I want to apologize for my gruffness the other day. I was upset to lose Stuart. It was very unexpected. I am sorry."

"I understand, Doctor. Thank you, for your apology. Now, please continue with your report."

"Admiral, Captain, I believe the nanites killed Lieutenant Stuart."

Both Admiral Blaine and Captain Fainchurch were shocked. "What do you mean, Doctor?"

"Captain, I had opened him up. I thought the surgery was going to be straightfoward. Just remove the nerves and the nanites attached to them. We started doing that. Then his heart rate sped up. His blood pressure jumped. He started to thrash about on the operating table."

"Didn't you have him secured to the medtable?"

"You mean handcuffed? No, Captain. He was heavily sedated. I did not think it was necessary to do more. And, there was a guard with a stunner in the OR with us. None of that would have mattered, though, because he crashed." The Doctor paused for a moment.

"Doctor?"

"Admiral, he had a massive amount of adrenaline in his system. The only thing I can figure is that, just as nanites sent signals brainwashing him with Sauron propaganda, they sent signals to his brain giving him the manic energy he needed to get away from whatever was attacking them."

"What do we do now, Doctor?"

"We need to figure out a different approach, Admiral. We need to disable all the nanites before we try to remove them. We may be able burn them out with an electromagnetic pulse. I talked with the Chief Engineer about the possibility. He was not sure that would work. The EMP needs a tight focus so all the nanites are fried at same time without cooking the surrounding tissue. His words, Admiral. Not mine."

"Very well, Doctor. Continue looking for a safe way to remove them. I am confident you and the Chief Engineer will solve the problem. Carry on."

"Thank you, Admiral."

A few weeks later Doctor Volkov, Commander Sheffield, Captain Fainchurch and Admiral Blaine met to discuss the progress of removing the nanites from the crewmen's bodies.

Admiral Blaine nodded to Doctor Volkov and Commander Sheffield. "Doctor, Chief Engineer, congratulations. Your EMP procedure seems to have burned out the nanites and allowed you to remove them without any blowback."

"Thank you, Admiral. The EMP fried the little beasts but we aren't out of the woods yet. We need to use the regeneration stimulators to repair the patient's nerves. After that, we need them to go through an extensive reeducation process to reverse the brainwashing."

"We will need to delay their reeducation, Doctor."

"Until when, Admiral? And, why?"

"Until we reach our final destination. I would like to do it before then but we don't have the resources to try and rehabilitate eighty Sauron sympathizers right now."

November 2, 2798 A.D., New Sparta

The sun was getting higher in the sky so Lord Blaine commanded his chair to move him to a position in the shade of a willow tree overlooking the koi ponds. He watched as the occasional ripple spread out across the water. As the little waves bounced off rocks and created interference patterns. *I wonder if my first message using the Bhasin comm system got through. I never did receive an acknowledgement. I never told anyone about the system. The expedition's morale was too important. If I never received a reply, I didn't want anyone thinking the worst happened back home. Has it? I'll guess I'll never know either. I wonder if they got my second message. My warning….*

2641 A.D., INSS Cassiopeia's Daughter, Refuge System, Andromeda Center

The Admiral accessed the hidden compartment in his cabin for only the second time since Jumping to Andromeda. He was loathe to use the Bhasin comm system again. He knew that it was susceptible to something called decoherence. As best the Admiral could tell, that just meant the more it was used, the less likely it was to work. Admiral Blaine had been hoping to use the system again only after they reached a suitable planet to colonize. *Nothing to be done about it. This is too important to the Empire.* He moved quickly to the compartment's center. He noted that the status lights on the comm console were no longer all green. Two were red and one was orange. *The system is still functioning but it could fail at any time. I've got to send the message as soon as possible. No time to reduce our thrust to zero.* The Admiral drafted his warning.

FLASH MESSAGE BEGINS

IMPERIAL HIGH SECRET
EYES ONLY
FROM: FLEET ADMIRAL GEORGE BLAINE
TO: EMPEROR LYSANDER V
WARNING: OXY-NANITES FROM IMPERIAL LIBRARY ARE SAURON TROJAN HORSE AND VERY DANGEROUS. REPEATING: OXY-NANITES FROM IMPERIAL LIBRARY ARE SAURON TROJAN HORSE AND VERY DANGEROUS. WE HAVE CONTAINED THE INFECTION AND ARE PROCEEDING ON OUR MISSION.

FLASH MESSAGE ENDS

The Admiral saw the acknowledgement that the message had been transmitted. He said a silent prayer of thanks. He started to turn back toward the compartment's hatch when he noticed the orange light begin to flicker. As he watched, it turned to red and stayed that color. One of the two remaining green lights then changed to orange. The Admiral knew the comm system was dying.

November 2, 2798 A.D., New Sparta

Lord Blaine watched as his youngest great-grandson played with a sling. He was trying to hit one of the quail running between the hedges. It brought to his mind an early part of their journey to New Sparta. Their departure from the Center. *What was that old saying? E-ticket ride? Didn't that come from one of the early American astronauts? Sally Ride? Yes, that was her name. Well, it certainly described the boost we got from that neutron star ...*

2643 A.D., *INSS Cassiopeia's Daughter*, Dioscuris System, Andromeda Center

It seemed like an eternity before the Admiral felt the gentle tug of the tide and the blurred image of Castor flashed large in the Tri-V tank. At the same instant, he noted the timer had reached zero. Then the image of the neutron star disappeared from the tank. It was over. Only seconds had passed.

The *Cassie D* had survived the passage with no damage. Doppler measurements confirmed they had picked up the speed they needed. In addition to the speed, the ship had acquired some rotation. Captain Fainchurch was already bringing the fusion engines back online to counter the spin. Their risky slingshot maneuver around the neutron star had been successful.

The main bridge crew broke out in a cheer over their comm circuits. The Admiral ignored the break in protocol. If Captain Fainchurch wanted to let his bridge crew cheer, that was his decision. The Admiral was already putting the passage behind him. He was focusing on the challenges that awaited them before their odyssey could be completed and mission accomplished proclaimed. Their next goal was to reach the Alderson region and Jump. Looking at the status board he was now more optimistic than ever they would survive and find a new home.

November 2, 2798 A.D., New Sparta

It was time for Lord Blaine's midday meal. As had been getting more and more common, Lord Blaine didn't have much of an appetite. Still, he picked up a macaron off a plate that had been placed next to his wheelchair but, before he nibbled on the cookie, a cool gust of wind sent his mind back into the past....

2683 A.D., *INSS Cassiopeia's Daughter*, In Transit

Admiral Blaine's first memory on waking from frozen sleep was sitting on the edge of the medtable. He was shivering even though he had a warm blanket wrapped about his shoulders. He looked around the compartment until he found a display showing the date and time. He immediately knew there was a problem. He had been awakened early. He turned to the nurse taking his vital signs. "Wha—" He tried again, slowly forming a different word. "Sitwep."

"Admiral, I have been told the emergency is not immediate. Why don't you recover for an hour? I have called Captain Fainchurch. He is on his way. I'll get you some warm broth in the meantime."

He responded in loud, slurred speech, "Sitwep. Now."

The nurse wasn't used to being yelled at by the Admiral but she composed herself and answered. "Admiral, I don't know any details but I have heard some scuttlebutt. We have detected microwaves coming from the region of space in front of us. Microwaves, that the rumors say, are from aliens. That's all I know, sir. The Captain will tell you more."

The Admiral looked at the nametag on the nurse, paused for a second and then said, "Tha...ou, Nur Symmons."

A few minutes later, Captain Fainchurch arrived in sickbay. "Hello, Admiral. Good to see you are recovering well."

Slowly, the Admiral responded, "Thank...you, Captain. Now what is...going on?"

"Admiral, per your standing orders, you were awakened because there are signals of alien origin on our current heading."

"What… signals, Captain?"

"Microwaves, Admiral. Very powerful microwaves. We looked for modulation and radar waveforms but found none. The astrophysicists believe we are detecting side lobes from solar power satellites beaming power down to a planet's surface."

"How far…away, Captain?"

"Fifteen hundred light-years, Admiral."

"And how long have you been tracking these…emissions?"

"Several Jumps, sir. About a month."

"Why did you wait so…so long to wake…me, Captain?"

"We weren't sure what we were detecting, Admiral. It took some time for the astrophysicists to eliminate all natural explanations and settle on this one."

"Do we have any…xenobiologists awake?"

"No, sir. Our best scientist for the job is Academician Ivanov but since he was infected with the Sauron nanites, he is in frozen sleep for the duration."

"Who…else is available?"

"Both Academicians Witmer and Sonders would be next in line. Do you want me to have one of them awakened?"

"Wake them both, Captain. I think … we need all the expertise … we can get on this one."

"Aye aye, sir."

* * *

It took the expedition another six months to be sure, but the microwaves were coming from more than just one solar system. The implications were enormous. This was evidence of an interstellar civilization. The academicians wanted to study the aliens as much as possible. Admiral Blaine and Captain Fainchurch agreed but for different reasons. This was not an academic exercise to them. The more they knew, the better decisions they could make.

It was six months more before they discovered that the alien microwave sources were coming online faster than the speed of light between the new sources. The meaning was clear. The aliens had discovered the Alderson Drive.

The Admiral called a meeting of the Command Staff. In addition, Academicians Witmer and Sonders were asked to attend.

"I have called this meeting to seek your advice," the Admiral began. "We have an important decision to make. As you all know, we have detected the presence of an alien civilization along our present course. Humans have never made contact with an alien civilization before. This is a momentous discovery.

"Let me summarize what we know. We have not detected any radio or laser broadcasts from them. We have detected the side lobes from their powersats which they use for power generation. The power sat side lobes come from half a dozen solar systems, so they are an interstellar species. The rate of expansion of the power sat sources imply they have the Alderson Drive. This is not surprising since the existence of the Alderson force can be deduced from stellar physics. All their systems have selenium light spectrum signatures, not chlorophyll. Our telescopes are not powerful enough to image their planets and the type of instruments we would need to deploy to do so would take months to capture that information. We can't wait here that long. The question in front of us today is, what do we do?"

Academician Sonders spoke up excitedly. "Admiral, Academician Witmer and I both think this is an incredible opportunity for us. For mankind. As you pointed out, we have never made first contact with an alien species before. Think of what we can learn. How they view the universe. Their technology. They may even be able to help us find a new home. I think we should, no, I think we must, make contact with them."

"Thank you, Academician Sonders. Other views?"

"Admiral."

"Yes, Captain Fainchurch?"

"Admiral, with respect to Academician Sonders, we don't know how they will respond to aliens. To us. We are a single spaceship carrying what could be the last vestiges of the human race. We can ill afford to take chances."

Academician Sonders, responded. "Captain, we are a single, very powerful spaceship. Humans have been in space for over six hundred years and we have the Field. We all know how unlikely a discovery that was. I doubt they have discovered it. I think the risk to us is very low."

"Academician Sonders, they achieved spaceflight fifteen hundred years ago. If they are still alive, and if they have continued their scientific and technological progress, they could be far ahead of us. What levels of technological development could we reach given another thousand years?"

"The answer is speculation, Captain. We don't know."

"Exactly, we don't know. And that, by itself, is extremely dangerous. More to the point, since they have the Alderson Drive, we could run across them at any time. I would not like to run across an alien race where they vastly outnumber us and our only advantage is the Field."

"Captain, with the Alderson Drive they could have reached this part of space hundreds of years ago. But we see no evidence of them. Maybe their desire for outward expansion has waned. After all, the Empire of Man ceased expanding its borders once it reached a distance of about six hundred light-years from Sparta. The Empire found itself limited by the distance effective command and control could be exercised."

Admiral Blaine held up his hand to stop the heated discussion between the Captain and the xenobiologist.

"I think we all understand your positions, Captain Fainchurch, Academician Sonders. Thank you. Anyone else?" The Admiral looked around the table. "No, very well. It doesn't surprise me that we have only two courses of action to choose from. Thank you all for your advice. My decision is that we avoid the aliens. To that end, Captain Fainchurch, you are to set a new course heading to antispinward of the alien expansion. Let's get around them with a fair margin of safety."

"Admiral, I protest."

"Duly noted, Academician Sonders." And then to the entire room, "Dismissed."

November 2, 2798 A.D., New Sparta

Lady Amanda came out of the manor to see how her husband was faring. She had been worried about him for weeks now. He seemed to be getting weaker and weaker. It had taken her and the family some time to forgive him for the decision he made on their behalf. The decision to begin a new life in this place.

Lady Amanda and his family understood that this expedition was part of the Emperor's grand strategy to save the human race and the Empire. They understood that they had been asked to give of themselves for the greater good. They understood that Lysander V hadn't let Admiral Blaine consult with them beforehand. They understood it all with their minds, but it took more time for their hearts to accept it. Eventually, they did. Eventually, they forgave him.

"Georgie." When he didn't immediately respond, she called his name again. This time louder. "Georgie."

That woke the dozing Lord Blaine. "What? Amanda, what is it? I seemed to have dozed off."

"I'm sorry, Georgie. I was worried about you."

"Nothing to worry about Amanda. I'm fine." Then he added more gently, "I'm just enjoying the warmth of the sun and reminiscing."

2684 A.D., INSS Cassiopeia's Daughter, In Transit

"Admiral, the microwave signals from the aliens have ceased."

"All of them, Captain Fainchurch?"

"Yes, sir."

"What do you make of that, Captain?"

"I spoke to the two xenobiologists. They disagree with each other, Admiral. Academician Witmer thinks the aliens destroyed themselves. He used human historical theory to make his case. I'm not sure I buy his argument. Applying our cyclical history theories to aliens strikes me as well, at best, unfounded. But even if I don't agree with his reasoning, I'm not sure he's wrong about their self-destruction."

"You may be right, Captain. Why do you think they destroyed themselves?"

"Do you remember the Astrogator's briefing just after we arrived at the Center? Selenium is more efficient at converting the yellow light of a star into a plant's energy. That suggests to me that these aliens have a more energetic food chain than we do. That may drive them to be more aggressive than we are. And, if so, that suggests to me that they are a more violent species than we are. That leads me to the conclusion that there will be war."

"A long chain of suppositions, Captain. What did the other xenobiologist think? Sonders is her name, isn't it?"

"Yes, sir. She believes the aliens have substituted ground-based fusion power plants for the powersats. Ensign Vasiliev, on your staff, came up with a similar technology-oriented explanation. He thinks the aliens upgraded their powersats to transmit power to the surface using masers. More efficient. No side lobes."

"Good thinking on his part. Any supporting data for either technology scenario?"

"No, sir. We don't have any new information on the aliens."

"As long as we have avoided them, I don't suppose it really matters whether they destroyed themselves or developed new technology." Then, changing the subject, he said, "I'm glad you brought up Ensign Vasiliev's name. He's due for a promotion. I need to do that before I go back into frozen sleep next tomorrow."

November 2, 2798 A.D., New Sparta

Lady Amanda had studied art history at the Imperial University on Sparta before she met and married young Lieutenant Blaine. Now that her family was grown and settled, she wanted to return to those academic roots. She wanted to fill her manor and gardens with classic art. So, she chose art works from the past and Lord Blaine, wanting to please her, commissioned their creation.

They were copies of the originals, some of which had been destroyed over half a thousand years ago during the Great Patriotic War on Earth. Some had been left on Sparta back in the Milky Way. It didn't matter. Here in Andromeda, they were reborn. *David; Spartans, the Helots have killed the King; The Boxer at Rest; The Thinker;* and dozens more. All were recreated by micro-fabricators using locally sourced marble and bronze.

Lord Blaine ordered his chair to take him to *The Boxer at Rest*. As he sat in front of the bronze statue, looking at the boxer's face, he saw a man who had fought many battles. Someone emotionally exhausted, yet still persevering through it all. Lord Blaine understood all too well. The unknown artist had "well those passions read," to quote the ancient poet Shelley. Every time Lord Blaine looked upon the sculpture, he felt a kinship with this man who had lived three thousand years ago.

Time has taken its toll on me. The burden of command. The longer you bear it, the more it wears on you. Lord Blaine's thoughts wandered to the aftermath of a refueling operation gone bad. Just one such burden he carried. The scoopship *John Bea* had been ordered down into the atmosphere of a gas giant to collect hydrogen fuel …

2700 A.D., INSS Cassiopeia's Daughter, In Transit

"Captain Fainchurch, why am I only learning of this now? You lost that scoopship ten months ago. I left standing orders to be awakened if we came across any danger to the ship."

"Admiral, we lost the *John Bea*, but while a tragedy, it did not rise to the level of a danger to the ship or our mission. We had five scoopships remaining. We were refueled. Waking you early would not have altered the resources we had left nor had any bearing on what we could do for those we lost."

The Admiral considered the Captain's response. He realized the Captain was right. Waking him early from frozen sleep would have changed nothing. The Admiral knew that one of the qualities of a good leader was to listen to those around you, keep an open mind, and admit you were wrong when you were. Then learn from it and move on. "Very well, Captain. I agree. Now, tell me more about the accident."

"We Jumped into a new solar system and materialized five Astronomical Units from the primary. About the same distance as Jupiter is from Sol, back in the Milky Way. Nearby, we discovered a gas giant. Nothing unusual about it except for some static-like radio emissions that had the astronomers puzzled. They thought there was some type of pattern to it but they couldn't pin it down. The astronomers also couldn't figure out what was causing the emissions. They finally decided the signals were generated by lightning, since the static seemed to be coming from the areas near towering clouds in the gas giant's atmosphere. In any case, we sent our scoopships down. We have scoop-mined gas giants dozens of times before, Admiral. And the Empire has been scoopship-mining gas giants for over five hundred years. It is a well understood process. Only this time, one of our ships seems to have hit something."

"Hit what, Captain? Ice in the cloud's convection winds? Something like that?"

"No, Admiral. I'll show you what we have." The Captain activated the big war room screen. "We received telemetry and visual transmissions up to the time of the accident."

On the screen was displayed the view through the scoopship's crystalline windscreen. It looked like the ship was going through dense clouds. Suddenly, the sky brightened, then nothing.

"Just that, Captain?"

"No, Admiral. Let me slow it down for you."

The Captain ran it again, toward the end slowing it down to frame-by-frame. Then, he stopped it at the last frame. On the screen was a dark brown mass, almost like a drapery, covering the upper left part of the frame.

"What is that, Captain?"

"I'm getting there, Admiral. Look over here." The Captain highlighted an area to the lower right corner that showed towering clouds floating in the distance. Around one of them, were two small, brown dots. The same color as the mass that covered part of the last frame.

"Do you see these brown dots, Admiral?"

"Yes. They are very small. Can you enlarge them, Captain?"

The Captain did so as much as he could. They each covered only a few pixels. "Admiral, they look small but they are each the size of the *Cassie D.*

"When we checked the filters on the returning scoopships we discovered organic residue in them. After reviewing all the information, I wondered if the scoopship hit one of those brown dots. I thought our two xenobiologists might be helpful in determining what happened, so I ordered both Academicians Witmer and Sonders awakened.

"They found that the organic residue in the scoopship's filters contained cell-like structures. That led the xenobiologists to conclude they were looking at the remains of microscopic life. That in turn, led them to the idea that the microscopic life could be food for the brown dots. And, for that to be true, then the brown dots must be floaters. That is, living dirigibles.

"To summarize, they believe the clouds are thermal upwellings bringing nutrients and microscopic life from below. Dirigibles then feed on that microscopic life. The dirigibles are like the whale sharks of old Earth that grazed on phytoplankton and krill."

"I have never heard of anything like that, Captain."

"Neither had the xenobiologists, Admiral. At least in a gas giant's atmosphere. Life as we do not know it. I looked it up in the Imperial Library and, while there has been speculation about it, no one had found any instances of it. This is still carbon-based life but we don't know how its metabolism works. Since there is no oxygen in the gas giant's atmosphere, it's unlikely they use that in their metabolic cycle."

"You said they have never been discovered in a gas giant's atmosphere. Has anything like them been discovered anywhere?"

"On Haven, in the Byers' System back in the Milky Way, there are balloon-like creatures called float sacs. But they live in an oxygen atmosphere not a hydrogen one. And on Kennicott, there are creatures that make temporary buoyancy sacs to float from one high altitude region of the planet to another. Again, it's in an oxygen atmosphere."

"So, we lost a scoopship but made a scientific discovery? Not a good trade in my opinion."

"No, sir. It's not. But there's more, Admiral."

"Go on, Captain."

"After we Jumped from that solar system, the xenobiologists continued studying the data we had collected. Do you remember those radio emissions I mentioned?"

"Yes, Captain."

"There was a very strong burst at the moment we lost contact with the scoopship. The astronomers determined it came from the same location as the scoopship. The implication is that one of the dirigibles generated it."

"I don't follow, Captain."

"The xenobiologists believe the dirigibles communicate with each other in a rudimentary way using radio emissions, Admiral. Like animals in a herd do when they are grazing. They speculate that the signal we picked up at the time we lost the scoopship was a death cry."

November 2, 2798 A.D., New Sparta

Lord Blaine woke from his nap. He looked around at his country estate and saw the manicured gardens and nicely trimmed lawns. In the distance he saw his orchards and smelled the fragrance of their blossoms. *What a beautiful world we have created. I'm glad we chose this one....*

2739 A.D., New Sparta

The great ship materialized beyond the orbit of the outermost gas giant. After a short while, it began to accelerate inward toward the rocky planets. It almost seemed to be lumbering. Of course, the *Cassie D* had been making its way across the Andromeda galaxy for almost a century now. A long, tiring journey. Jumping from star to star, following the trail blazed across the galaxy by its scoutships. The big ship's crew hoped that this would be their final destination. They were ready for this to be their final destination.

Based on the scoutship's reconnaissance, it seemed this system met all their 'must have' criteria. A Sol type star with half a dozen Alderson points, a habitable planet with a large moon and a chlorophyll biosphere, outer gas giants and an asteroid belt containing mineral resources. This system had all that and more.

Upon finally reaching the habitable planet they hoped would become the capital of a new Empire of Man, Lysander's third son and heir to the Throne on the *Cassiopeia's Daughter* was awakened from frozen sleep. At that moment, the expedition was no longer under military command but under Imperial leadership. Admiral Blaine now reported to the man who had taken the name Lysander VI. This was expected. Something the Admiral had worked toward for over a hundred years.

The Emperor found the planet good and named it New Sparta and its star New Agamemnon. It was similar to the capital of the Empire of Man when it was first discovered: chlorophyll-based sea life producing an oxygen-nitrogen atmosphere with a few native plants just beginning to colonize the land. Ideal for releasing Earth-stock plants and animals. However, the new land ecology would take many years to stabilize. Species' relationships would fluctuate in complex ways until an ecological equilibrium was finally reached. Just as it had on Sparta.

November 2, 2798 A.D., New Sparta

Lord Blaine looked to the south. As the afternoon shadows grew longer, he could barely make out the upper atmospheric glow caused by the launching lasers on the equator. He knew they were sending Earth-stock terraforming packages up to the waiting spaceships.

The industries built to terraform New Sparta were now being redirected to seed Earth-stock life on the eight closest out-system Tier one and Tier two worlds suitable for mankind's future colonization. All were within four Jumps of New Sparta. The new Empire of Man wouldn't need them for hundreds, maybe thousands of years. But when they did, they would be ready for colonization without much additional effort. It was an investment in the future and now was the time to make it, while the industrial capacity and infrastructure was in place and the marginal cost small.

Each world required a different package tailored to it. Lord Blaine recalled the presentation Academician Sonders gave summarizing the different levels of effort needed.

2739 A.D., New Sparta

The war room was packed. Standing room only. Academician Sonders was beginning her presentation.

"Your Majesty, Admiral Blaine, Captain Fainchurch, fellow colonists. I have been asked to give you an overview of our terraforming capabilities. This will be in a lecture format. I have made the material available in the ship's computer nodes along with more detailed follow-up information.

"Over the last five hundred years, the Empire has continually improved its terraforming technologies culminating in the successful transformation of New Scotland and New Ireland in the New Caledonia System. Those worlds are examples of what I show here as Tier three. But I am getting ahead of myself.

"All the worlds that are terraformable have certain parameters in common. Gravity ranges between nine point one gees and one point two gees. They all have magnetic fields that protect the planets from the solar wind. They all have atmospheres that are, or can be converted into, an oxygen-nitrogen composition. With one exception, that being the moon called Haven in the Byers' System, they all reside within the habitable zone of the star they orbit. There are more criteria but these are the main ones they all share. The terraformable worlds are categorized Tier one through Tier five. Each category has many subcategories but I will not be delving into those today. That would be far too much information to cover in an overview.

"I will start with Tier one terraforming." Academician Sonders activated the main viewing screen and displayed a slide summarizing the parameters she just referred to. "Tier one planets have established biospheres with compatible biochemistries to ours. Examples of these worlds include Arrarat, New Washington, Tanith and St. Ekaterina. Not all worlds in this tier are pleasant places to live. The criteria for this tier is that complex life exists in both the oceans and on land. Earth-stock life, when introduced, must fit into an existing ecology, one that has evolved for billions of years. Genemods may be required for the Earth-stock life to thrive but even then, it will not take over and replace the current biosphere. It will only require a small number of Earth-stock seeding packages, which means that the investment is relatively low.

"Next comes Tier two candidates. Tier two planets have an established oxygen-nitrogen atmosphere. Complex life exists in the oceans but not on the land. Again, they have compatible biochemistries. Examples include Sparta, Churchill, and two planets in this system;

the next planet out and New Sparta. The planet we currently orbit. Again, genemod Earth-stock is likely to be required. More Earth-stock terraforming packages are required than are used on Tier one worlds. However, without much native land life, the result is continents that are very Earth-like in the long term.

"Then there are the Tier three candidate worlds. As I mentioned, New Scotland and New Ireland are two examples of our capabilities in this regard. Terraforming planets that have no indigenous life, but have methane, water vapor and nitrogen atmospheres is a very resource-intensive undertaking. The process is begun by injecting large quantities of genemod algae into the planet's atmosphere. Short term, the investment is very high, and even medium-term the investments must continue to ensure the terraforming takes hold. Long term, and by that, I mean hundreds of years, this produces a complete Earth-stock biosphere.

"Next are Tier four planets. These are also known as Venus-lite worlds. They have carbon dioxide atmospheres similar in composition to Venus but far less dense. Examples of Tier four worlds include Taisho and Showa in the Meiji Protectorate and this system's innermost planet. Meiji began two very long-term terraforming projects in systems nearby to them, a half millennium ago. Tier four terraforming is much more expensive than Tier 3 and takes longer. It may require redirecting comets toward the targeted planet to bring in additional water. At the time we departed from the Milky Way, Taisho and Showa still had another five hundred years to go before they radiated enough heat to accept Tier three seeding. Just a side note: The original plan was to have the two planets terraformed by 2600. That means the Meiji project has had a schedule slip rate of one."

"Academician Sonders?"

"Yes, Majesty?"

"What is this schedule slip rate of one you just mentioned?"

"Majesty, a slip rate of one means that the scheduled completion is extended one year for every year that passes. If that continues, the project will never be completed. As it is, Meiji now expects the two worlds to be terraformed by 3100. Or, at least they did before we Jumped to

Andromeda. As a very rough cut, the implication is that the cost of the project has doubled, and the original cost was projected to be very high in the first place. Would you like me to elaborate further, Sire?"

"No. Thank you, Academician Sonders."

"The final category is Tier five worlds. Venus in Sol System is an example of these planets. Terraforming these worlds is currently beyond our capabilities. Their atmospheres are too dense or thick, if you will. The problem isn't breaking down the carbon dioxide in their atmospheres. We believe we can do that. It's just that splitting the oxygen off the carbon dioxide molecule produces an enormous amount of pure carbon. That carbon then has to be removed from, or sequestered within, the planet's surface. In the case of Venus, the amount of carbon produced would create a layer over half a kilometer deep covering the entire planet.

"If that problem could be solved, the amount of oxygen remaining in the atmosphere would still need to be addressed. Adding hydrogen and converting the oxygen into water might be one solution but finding a source of hydrogen would be necessary. It has been proposed that the hydrogen could be obtained from gas giants. However, the number of scoopship dives required to gather enough hydrogen would be enormous. If that problem were solved, the next challenge would be transporting the hydrogen across interplanetary distances. That would require a huge expenditure of energy, even using minimum energy Hohmann orbits.

"In the case of Venus, there would also need to be a significant increase in the atmospheric nitrogen. Saturn's moon Titan has been suggested as a potential source of this nitrogen, but getting it out of Titan's gravity well and into space would be difficult. It has been proposed that space tether technology might be useful to do that, but that still leaves the problem of transporting the nitrogen to Venus.

"Other problems would remain for Venus, such as increasing the day-night cycle to something approaching twenty-four hours and restarting the planet's magnetic field. Some wide-eyed dreamers have suggested that Langston Field technology could be brought to bear on these problems. But again, the scale necessary is many orders of magnitude beyond anything we have ever done. Suffice it to say, the terraforming challenges for Tier five worlds are beyond us for the foreseeable future and maybe forever."

Academician Sonders looked at the Emperor and smiled. "Majesty, you have made a very wise choice for your new Capital. The New Agamemnon System is unusual in that it contains three terraformable planets. It has a mineral-rich asteroid belt and three outer gas giants. A better home for us is hard to imagine." Then Sonders paused, looked around the war room and said in closing, "I know this has been a lot of information but are there any questions?"

The Emperor spoke up. "If we use virtually controlled robots, would that speed up the Tier two terraforming process here?"

"Yes, Your Majesty. Depending on how many are deployed, it could cut the time by a quarter to a third."

"Thank you, Academician Sonders."

Admiral Blaine was very uncomfortable with the Emperor's question. It worried him that the Emperor was considering technologies that the Saurons had used to quickly terraform their home planet. *If we did that, how do we avoid the path the Saurons went down? Once we start using robots like they did, the temptation would be great to make the linkage even closer, to eventually create cyborgs. He is the Emperor. I have pledged my allegiance to him. I will abide by his decision but I hope I can convince him not to pursue this dangerous course of action.*

November 2, 2798 A.D., New Sparta

The afternoon shadows were growing longer. Lord Blaine realized he had spent the entire day outside reminiscing. He looked up in the sky to where Ares was. It was still too bright out for him to see, but he knew it was there. An ominous foreboding came over Lord Blaine. *Ares. The God of War. Why did the Emperor have to name the planet that?*

2767 A.D., New Sparta

The next planet outward from New Sparta was similar to Haven. Unlike Haven, it orbited inside the outer edge of New Agamemnon's habitable zone. Its orbit took it near the system's asteroid belt. The circular patterns visible all over the planet's surface attested to the dangerous neighborhood it orbited within.

The planet had a surface gravity of point nine three gee and a weak magnetic field that protected its oxygen-nitrogen atmosphere somewhat from the solar wind; therefore, it hadn't suffered the same fate as Mars. At least not yet. The planet didn't have as many volcanos as Haven, but it had more than enough to replace atmospheric losses for the next few million years or so. The Tier two planet's oceans were filled with simple plants, like plankton, that made the atmosphere breathable. Although, just barely. Similar to Mars, some of the planet's oxygen was tied up in iron oxide rocks on the continents, so the land had a reddish tinge to it when viewed from space. As a result, the expedition's Imperial astronomers proposed the name Ares to the Emperor and he accepted it. Ares was seeded with Earth-stock life brought from Haven. The Haven life was well suited to Ares and thrived.

Reeducation hadn't been successful with the personnel that had been infected with the oxy-nanites; those crew brainwashed to be Sauron sympathizers. The Emperor knew there would eventually be political prisoners, there always were. He hadn't liked Admiral Blaine's original idea of setting up a penal colony on one of New Sparta's isolated islands, so he turned Ares into a prison planet instead. The Emperor had said: "What can eighty malcontents do on their own planet? Especially when the air has an oxygen content similar to the Tibetan Plateau on old Earth."

Unknown to the Emperor several of the prisoners, who had traveled to Haven just before the expedition Jumped to Andromeda, became infected with a local flu virus. The virus changed the prisoner's genetic structure slightly, adding genes that allowed them to pull more oxygen out of Ares' thin air.

Dmitry Ivanov was one of these prisoners. A man also infected with Sauron nanites that brainwashed him. That got him sent to the penal colony. Ivanov hated the Empire for taking him away from his love, Franciszka Soltyk. Originally, an Imperial biologist, Ivanov was now the little colony's chief biologist. A man, in all but name, his fellow prisoners knew as breedmaster.

November 2, 2798 A.D., New Sparta

Lord Blaine remembered that twenty years ago there had been a lot of resistance when he proposed sending terraforming packages to the near-by Tier one and Tier two worlds. The Emperor and many of his subjects didn't care about seeding the nearby planets with Earth-stock. They wanted to use the robotic industrial capacity to improve their standard of living. Now, not in the future. However, Pope Peter's support was the deciding factor. The Pope simply reminded his flock of God's message in Genesis. The Emperor was an astute politician, so he agreed. However, this was the last time Admiral Blaine and the Emperor disagreed on policy. The Admiral announced his retirement soon thereafter.

It was late afternoon and Lady Amanda had helped Lord Blaine into his dinner jacket. He waited outside on the terrace, sitting in his wheelchair while his guests arrived. He looked up and saw New Aphodrite hanging in the sky just above the horizon. New Aphrodite, a Tier three world just inside the habitable zone. This meant that the New Agamemnon System had the potential to contain three habitable worlds, though it might take a thousand years to make it happen. Prior to this, the Empire had found at most two habitable planets in a single star system. Together, the three planets had the potential to make the core of the new Empire richer and more powerful than Sparta had been.

Lady Blaine had invited all the children, grandchildren and great grandchildren. His children and grandchildren had all spent fifty years more than Lord Blaine in frozen sleep so they were much younger than him. They had spent the entire journey in frozen sleep while Lord Blaine had spent only half of his time in that ageless state. His Royal Highness Emperor Lysander VI and Fleet Admiral Fainchurch both attended the party in honor of Lord Blaine.

While very thoughtful of his wife, the press of everyone was very tiring. Finally, Lord Blaine had had enough. He commanded his chair to take him outside. He had modeled Blaine Manor after the one where he had spent the early days of his life. As he sat there under a tangerine tree, the stars came out as dusk turned to night. The stars, while not diamonds, looked brillant.

He looked up and saw New Sparta's large moon, almost the size of Luna back in Sol System. He imagined he could see the three widely separated Imperial Libraries whose construction he had commissioned when he became His Lordship, the Marquis of New Crucis. The libraries were just small outposts. Not much more than two buried modules attached to an airlock on the surface. One module containing life support machinery including the batteries charged during the lunar day by thermoelectric generators half-buried in the surrounding soil. The other module was divided into two sections. The first section contained four small workstation tables set against the module's walls and shelves holding blank data cubes. The second contained several bunks and a recycling station, a water closet and a food synthesizer.

Emergency supplies of air and other consumables were located inside the airlock on the surface. Engraved on the outside of all of the airlocks were two symbols. One was the symbol for the Imperial Library, the other a stylized oxygen tank. The airlock itself would open to anyone. Inside however, access to the buried Library compartments was secured by a puzzle lock. Reflectors installed on the top of the airlocks made the libraries stand out against the lunar background when illuminated by a laser.

The Libraries were insurance for the future of the human race if for some reason the colony fell back into barbarism. If that happened, when humans reached for the stars again, the knowledge would be there waiting for them. Knowledge such as how to build a Field. Something no one believed would be rediscovered if lost.

Lord Blaine wished he could see the *Cassie D* but knew it was orbiting at the Lagrange point on the opposite side of the planet. It had been orbiting there for many years now. It was originally stationed there as an emergency lifeboat but the colony hadn't needed it. Lord Blaine had read the reports on it. Maintenance hadn't been kept up. It was more a seldom visited museum now than anything else. It could never land on a planet's surface. If it tried, its engines would turn the surface beneath molten.

Lord Blaine cocked his head. *What is that?* He swore he heard wild geese honking. Out of reflex, he looked up but saw nothing. Then he remembered, it wasn't the right time of year for migrating geese.

It was darker now, and Lord Blaine looked up at the sky again. He looked to where the Milky Way galaxy would be visible. The furthest astronomical object that could be seen with the naked eye. He couldn't make it out. It still wasn't dark enough. Then he realized it didn't matter. It wasn't home anymore. This planet, this galaxy was home.

Lord Blaine's last thoughts were a coda to his life *I'm tired, so very tired. I have done my best. I have served God and done my duty to the Empire and my family. No matter what has happened back in the Milky Way, I have given mankind a beachhead here in Andromeda. Our Andromeda.*

Lagniappe

Oracle

On the marches of the Empire, in the mid-twentieth-sixth century, a new star system was discovered. Named New Utah, it was an unusual system. It wasn't the system's habitable planet that made it that way. No, while rare, habitable planets weren't unusual. It was the neutron star that orbited the yellow star system in an eccentric, twenty-one year cycle that made the system unique.

Neutron stars are common in the galaxy but neutron stars that can be reached by the Alderson Drive are not. Interstellar Jumps can only be made between stars undergoing nuclear fusion. Even then, many tramlines between stars don't exist. Neutron stars are long past creating self-sustaining fusion reactions. Matter impacting a neutron star will produce the Alderson force but not predictably. So, finding a neutron star that could be reliably reached without traveling far through normal space, and in a system with a habitable planet, was extraordinary. At least, the astrophysicists on Sigismund thought so.

After the astrophysicists at the Imperial University reviewed the Imperial Navy's Initial Assessment of the New Utah System, they proposed sending an expedition to study the neutron star. After all, no one had ever studied one up close for any length of time. What might they learn? They wanted to study gravity, subatomic particle physics and more. Much more. As with many grandiose research plans during a time of war, this one took a few decades to make happen.

2632 A.D., Imperial University, Sigismund

Academician Bhasin was angry. After supporting his research proving his interpretation of the Langston-Ward Grand Unified Field Theory, Admiral Blaine was now blocking any further investigation.

Couldn't the man understand the importance of what I am doing? I've proved my interpretation is correct. All I want to do is explore how it works in the real world, to see if intense gravity fields slow time at one end of a wormhole but not the other. If that isn't bad enough, he won't even let me publish what I have discovered so far. Something about waiting until the war is over. Damn, that man. I wonder if I can get space on the probe they're going to drop down into low orbit around that neutron star? A heavily shielded automated craft protected by a powerful Langston Field. I still have my test system. I'll talk to Chancellor Danvers.

3074 A.D., New Utah System

The Imperial Navy discovered the First Empire research station in the outer reaches of the New Utah System. One that appeared to be in periodic maser contact with an automated probe orbiting deep within the neutron star's gravity well. How the probe could have lasted over four hundred standard years in that environment was a mystery but they built well, back in the First Empire.

In the research station they found something called a Bhasin communications system. Or, they found half of it. Something no one in the Navy had ever heard of before. The station's computer claimed the system allowed instantaneous communication over any distance between two entangled Langston Fields. That is, through the wormhole connecting them.

The probe in orbit around the neutron star contained the other half of the Bhasin comm system; the other entangled Field. The computer claimed that the probe had been sent down for a short period; one standard year. But the war intervened. The station personnel had been recalled to Sigismund before the probe could be recovered.

The probe continued to orbit and collect data for over four hundred years before the Navy recovered it. The intense gravity field of the neutron star slowed time on the probe during that period. The time difference between the two wormhole openings grew to be a year. The Bhasin comm system became a kind of time machine. Not for material objects but for specially crafted photons that could carry information.

After bringing the probe back to the station, the Navy engineers removed the Bhasin comm system. They reinstalled it at the opposite end of the station from the part of the system they had originally found there. The station's computer warned in very explicit terms that the two small entangled black globes should not be brought near each other. Something about the possibility of an enormous temporal energy release, if they did. In any case, when the engineers finished the installation, they sent their first query through the comm system into the future.

The engineers nicknamed the comm system the Oracle. Over the course of the next year they were able to send and receive a few messages through time. However, the more the system was used, the more degraded the communication channel became. The static continued to build up until one final, cryptic message from a year in the future was received and the Oracle became useless.

They are coming!

The Alderson Drive

Theory and Practice – What it Means for Story Telling

Dan Alderson, the late Jet Propulsion Laboratory (JPL) scientist, designed both the Alderson Drive and the Langston Field for Jerry Pournelle to use in his CoDominium/Empire of Man science fiction stories. This paper summarizes the Alderson Drive parameters that have been published to date. The paper is intended as an aid to writers so that their new stories can be consistent with previously published material.

I want to thank David Sooby (aka Lensman), DJ Rout (aka Hippy) and Andrew E. Love, Jr. for their feedback, ideas, help and editing of this paper. It is a much better work because of their efforts.

Space Travel in the CoDominium/Empire of Man Universe

Space is vast and, as a result, in the CoDominium/Empire of Man universe there are two kinds of drives needed to travel between the stars. The Alderson Drive (aka the Drive) and reaction drives.

The Alderson Drive allows spaceships to travel from star to star instantaneously. However, there are limitations built into what the Drive can do. One of these limitations is that you must travel through interplanetary space to reach an Alderson point; a special place from which you can jump to another star. Reaction drives are used to reach these Alderson points.

Reaction drives can be fusion drives, thermal fission drives, ion drives, solar sails and even chemical rockets. Any type of reaction drive that can produce enough change in velocity (i.e., delta vee) to travel around a solar system. However, fusion drives[1] (or some variation) usually serve the purpose to propel spaceships through interplanetary space to, from, and between these Alderson points because they can do it faster and cheaper than other types of reaction drives. Even so, distances are so great, it takes a lot of time for them to do so (days, weeks or months).

Keywords (capitalization mostly from *The Mote in God's Eye*[2]):

Alderson Drive	Drive	Jump(s)
Alderson force	Field	Jump Lag
Alderson Jump(s)	fifth force	Jump Shock
Alderson point(s)	generator(s)	Jump point(s)
Alderson tramline(s)	hyperspace	Random Jump(s)
continuum universe	hyperspace wake(s)	tramline(s)

Summary (short form cheat sheet)

The Alderson Drive was designed so that spaceships cannot "sneak up" on inhabited planets (i.e., spaceships cannot Jump and materialize next to an inhabited planet). Therefore, this limitation (and others) will need to be taken into account when writing stories.

Alderson points (aka Jump points) are found outside the habitable zone in solar systems. For instance, a G2 star like the sun has Alderson

1 *Note: during the CoDominium period fusion drives are used to propel spaceships. Sometime during the First Empire period a new kind of reaction drive is invented. Fusion drives on warships are directed into their Langston Field which then creates an extremely efficient high intensity beam in the shape of a cone of light that is used for propulsion (The Mote in God's Eye, p. 42). The cone results from the beam being emitted from a small region of the spherical Field (i.e., the emitting region is a convex surface). The technique is utilized for propulsion by the Second Empire warships too. The Mote in God's Eye, p. 42, 57, 115, 124 suggests this and King David's Spaceship, p. 65 (in 3017 A.D.) confirms it. Therefore, only spaceships having a Langston Field can utilize this light pressure propulsion system, the rest use fusion drives directly for thrust. The drive cannot be used as a weapon because of the cone-shaped beam but it would be unhealthy for another ship without a Langston field to pass through the beam especially if it were at close passage.*

2 *The Mote in God's Eye.*

points between 1.5 and 39.5 AUs (astronomical units) from Sol (the distance from the sun to Mars and Pluto, respectively). This means that spaceships do not jump through interstellar space in our universe. Instead, they Jump from star to star through the continuum universe (aka hyperspace).

The distances at which Alderson points can be found around every main sequence stellar class has been modeled as part of this paper. Table B summarizes the output from the model.

A single star system can have anywhere from 1 to 6 Alderson points. As mentioned, Alderson points are places where entry to, and exit from, hyperspace can occur. Multiple star systems may (but usually don't) have more than 6 Alderson points. The number of additional Jump points in this case would still be small. Assuming the number of Alderson points around any given star are all equally probable, the average number of points in a system that the CoDominium or Empires control is likely higher than three.

The size of Alderson points can vary. The points can be as small as 500 kilometers across or as large as the distance from the Earth to the moon (about 385,000 kilometers). It's likely that Alderson points tend toward the smaller size (i.e., low single digit thousands of kilometers across).

Alderson points are fixed locations in space. That is, they remain a fixed distance from their star and do not move relative to the background stars. Planets move in orbits around their sun. Alderson points do not. Therefore, the distance between planets and Alderson points continually change in single star systems but in a repetitive manner. However, Alderson points can shift some under certain circumstances but they do not move far.

There are three exceptions to this rule. First, if an Alderson point is positioned directly above or below the poles of a star, the distance between an orbiting planet and the Alderson point will remain relatively constant. Second, multiple star system may have Alderson points that are in fixed locations in space or they may have Alderson points that shift position as the stars in the system orbit each other (or there may be some combination of fixed and shifting). Third, a star with a variable energy output can shift the location of the Alderson points nearer to, or further away from, the star.

Jumps take no measurable time. The travel is through the continuum universe. So, the Alderson Drive can be used to cross light-years instantaneously. But once you arrive at an Alderson point, interplanetary distances must be crossed using reaction drives to either reach the next Alderson point, a planet in that system or a refueling station. And this travel can take time. Depending on spaceship velocity, fuel levels and system geometries, it can take a long time (days, weeks or months). This is fundamental in determining what kind of interstellar political entities can form (i.e., the CoDominium and the Empires).

Each Alderson point connects to one Alderson point in another star system and only one; this is why the connections are called tramlines. It always connects to the same point in the same star system (i.e., they are point-to-point connections). If you draw a line between the two stars, the tramline would be on that line.

In the rare cases when a new Alderson tramline is formed, it does so instantaneously.

"Not all the tramlines are useful because, if flux densities aren't high enough, they won't carry anything big enough to have a drive aboard."[3] A 'subcritical' tramline counts toward the maximum of 6 Alderson points per star.

In general, Jumps are limited to tramlines connecting B8 through M5 main sequence stars. Main sequence stars more massive and hotter than B8 (O and B0 – B7) and less massive than M5 (M6 – M8) do not form useable tramlines.

The lengths of Jump distances vary. In the published literature, Jumps of anywhere from 1/3 to 35 light-years have been described. It is possible, in rare cases, for Jumps to be longer. However, most Jumps are between 5 and 20 light-years in length.

To travel from one star system with a habitable planet to another star system with a habitable planet, in most cases, takes multiple Jumps (i.e., a series of Jumps). Possibly a lot of Jumps. It is not unusual that making a lot of little Jumps between low mass stars is faster than making one long Jump to a more massive star. This is because the average normal space transit

3 *The Gripping Hand*, p. 118.

time through the M class star systems to reach their Alderson points can add up to less than the normal space transit time through a higher mass star system.

The typical speed (relative to the Alderson point) for a Jump is around 200 km/sec for a warship and 50 km/sec for a merchant ship. The typical speeds are related to the uncertainty associated with the Alderson point locations, the size of the Alderson points, how long the Alderson generators can remain on before burning out and the need to use mechanical Jump initiators (which are inherently slower and less precise than electronic initiators). Navy equipment is better than merchantman equipment and is therefore able to handle faster speeds for a Jump.

Just because stars are close together in physical space does not mean that they are close to each other via a series of Jumps. That is, it may take many Jumps to reach a nearby star, making for a long transit time.

Sectors are defined by Alderson point network connectivity (i.e., the fewest Jumps), not physical stellar proximity.

"The Drive's limits mean that uninteresting stellar systems won't be explored. There are too many of them. They may be used as crossing-points if the stars are conveniently placed, but stars not along a travel route may never be visited."[4]

There is a type of Jump called a Random Jump but its use is very rare and usually deadly. The mechanics of it are unknown. But whatever the mechanics of a Random Jump are, they cannot be such that the Moties could have used them to escape from their solar system over the million years they have existed as an intelligent species.

Making a Jump has a significant impact on human and Motie nervous systems as well as on computers. This is called Jump Shock (aka Jump Lag) and makes people feel very sick (i.e., nausea, weakness, disorientation, etc.). Jumps affect computers too. All computers are shut down for Jumps or they go haywire. Because of this, only simple mechanical devices are utilized during Jumps. Jump Shock in humans usually lasts five to twenty minutes. Motie Jump Shock is more severe and lasts longer than human Jump shock.

4 *Building The Mote in God's Eye.*

The Alderson Drive was perfected at CalTech in 2004 by a team of scientists lead by Dan Alderson. After that, its use for interstellar travel proceeded quickly. The first experimental spaceship using the Drive left the solar system in 2008. The first extrasolar habitable planets were discovered in 2010. The first extrasolar colonies were established in 2020.

Alderson Drive engines are large (relative to the ship they are on) and complex. This implies they are expensive.

Alderson engines accomplish four functions simultaneously. First, they transport a spaceship into the continuum universe. Second, they create correspondence particles of the ship and everything in it (i.e., a construct). Third, engines hold these correspondence particles together to prevent the construct from being disorganized into elementary particles. At this point, the Alderson force from the star you are Jumping from accelerates the construct to near infinite speeds. Spaceships then drop out of hyperspace naturally when they reach the gravitational well of the target star. When that happens, the engines take over again and accomplishes their fourth function. The construct is converted back to a real ship. All this takes place instantaneously.

The smallest Navy ship to carry a Drive is a longboat. In the Second Empire Period, the smallest civilian ship to carry a Drive is a racing yacht. Drive engine design allows them to be removed from a spaceship so they have some modularity.

Hyperspace wakes are created when a spaceship Jumps. A spaceship initially gains Alderson force kinetic energy but then must lose it before returning to normal space. This energy loss is instantaneous across the entire tramline and manifests itself in normal space as photons (electromagnetic radiation). This radiation can be detected and reveal not only that a spaceship has arrived at a Jump point but its mass (and therefore the probable class of ship).

Spaceships outfitted with a Langston Field can Jump with the Field turned on or off. Note that the Langston Field is only in use after the end of the CoDominium era (its first operational use was the protection of Aegis Station, in orbit around Sparta, during an attack by pirates in 2109).

There is no practical Faster-Than-Light (FTL) radio communication in the CoDominium/Empire of Man universe. Messages between the stars are sent by courier ships which Jump, carrying the messages with them. The only exception to this is when two Langston Fields are entangled (creating a wormhole between them) allowing for a very limited number of simple messages to be exchanged before decoherence fills the channel with static and the system becomes unusable.

Stars off the main sequence can have a different set of rules for Alderson point formation.

More Detail (main sequence stars except where noted)

Overview

The Alderson Drive allows spaceships to travel (Jump) from star to star instantaneously. Travel is from one Alderson point along a tramline to another Alderson point (so these are point-to-point connections). Tramlines are lines of equipotential Alderson force flux. The continuum universe (aka hyperspace) does not have a speed-of-light speed limit because there are no quantum effects there. The Jumps along the tramlines are made through the continuum universe. Therefore, spaceships do not travel through interstellar space in our universe. As Dr. Horvath said in the Prologue to *The Mote in God's Eye*, "Because of the Alderson Drive we need never consider the space between the stars. Because we can shunt between stellar systems in zero time, our ships and our ships' drives need only cover interplanetary distances."[5]

There are five forces of nature in the CoDominium/Empire of Man universe; gravitational, electromagnetic, strong, weak and the fifth force which is the Alderson force. The fifth force is the weakest and is produced by fusion reactions; that is by stars. The Alderson force is repulsive. It manifests itself in hyperspace. In hyperspace, it accelerates spaceships to almost infinite speeds (which make Jumps instantaneous).

---

5 *The Mote in God's Eye*, Prologue.

Alderson points (aka Jump points) are found outside the habitable zone of a solar system. There are a limited number of Alderson points in any solar system (in general a maximum of six) and there may even be none (i.e., not every star has Alderson points). Specific characteristics are listed and explained below.

Alderson Drive Design Philosophy

From the writer's point of view, the Alderson Drive was designed so that spaceships cannot "sneak up" on habitable planets. If spaceships could materialize next to an inhabited planet, an interstellar political organization like an Empire, CoDominium or Federation would not be able to protect planets from raiders. And, if such an organization can't protect a planet from raiders, why join it? Instead, raiders and pirates would dominate space.

Alderson Point Locations

The "endpoints of the *tramline* paths are far from the distortions in space caused by stars and large planetary masses."[6] In the CoDominium/ Empire of Man universe, there are several specific references to the distance of Jump points from their stars. In Sol System, one Alderson point seems to be just beyond the orbit of Jupiter (approximately 5 AU).[7] There could be another around Saturn's orbital distance.[8] There also appear to be at least two Alderson points outside the orbit of Neptune (minimum 30 AU).[9] This means that, based on the orbital position of Earth, the Jump points are somewhere between 4 and at least 31 AU from Earth. Note: Jump points do not have to reside in the orbital plane of the solar system (plane of the ecliptic) but could be anywhere at the proper distance, even directly above or below the sun. Also, the two Alderson points beyond Neptune must either be relatively close together or else they are much further out than the orbital distance of Neptune. It's the only way that a

6 *Ibid, p. 32.*

7 *Prince of Mercenaries*, p. 43-44.

8 *Building The Mote in God's Eye.*

9 *The Mote in God's Eye*, p. 169.

merchantman could use them and come no closer to Earth than the orbit of Neptune.

In *He Fell into a Dark Hole,*[10] the *CDSS Daniel Webster* materializes less than 1 AU from a black hole. A stellar black hole like this is between 5 and 30 times the mass of the sun (Sol).[11]

In *The Mote in God's Eye,* there is a reference to the home star of New Chicago being an F9 star.[12] It is called Beta Hortensis. New Chicago is 1.06 AU from Beta Hortensis.[13] In the short story *Reflex,* the New Chicago rebels are protecting a Jump point a half a billion kilometers (3.3 AU) from Beta Hortensis.[14] This means that, based on the planet's orbital position, this Jump point ranges from just over 2.2 AU to 4.4 AU from New Chicago. It appears there are at least three other Jump points in the system but we don't know what the parameters for them are. All we know is that Lady Sandra Fowler stopped on New Chicago on her way to a more distant planet and there are a series of Jumps that lead to the New Caledonia System. Since New Chicago was a center for its sector's interstellar trade, there may be more Jump points, possibly as many as six in total.

In *The Mote in God's Eye,* there is a reference to the home star of New Scotland and New Ireland being an F8 star named New Caledonia (aka New Cal).[15] The Alderson point that *MacArthur* arrived in the system at is about 1.5 billion kilometers from New Scotland.[16] This is about 10 AU. If we assume that New Scotland (which is further from New Cal than New Ireland) is in an orbit 1.5 AU from its primary, then this Jump point is somewhere between 8 AU and 11.5 AU from New Scotland.

Murcheson's Eye is a red supergiant star with a radius of approximately Saturn's orbit (9.5 AU).[17] It has two Alderson points. One outside the star and one inside the star;[18] say one is 9 AU and one 10 AU from the center

10 *He Fell into a Dark Hole.*
11 *Stellar black hole.* March 5, 2017 <https://en.wikipedia.org/wiki/Stellar_black_hole>.
12 *The Mote in God's Eye,* p. 3.
13 *Ibid.*
14 *Reflex.*
15 *The Mote in God's Eye,* p. 32.
16 *Ibid,* p. 36.
17 *Ibid,* p. 97.
18 *Ibid,* p. 95, 97.

of Murcheson's Eye. In *The Mote in God's Eye,* Murcheson's Eye is projected to explode into a supernova.[19] Per Wikipedia, a red supergiant that will explode into a supernova should be between 10 and 40 solar masses.[20]

The Mote is a G2 type star[21] but cooler (luminosity .78 Sol), smaller, less massive (.91 Sol) and less energetic than Sol (today a G2 type star). Back when *The Mote in God's Eye* was written, Sol was considered a G0 star. So, adjusting for the fact that Sol is now classified as a G2 type star, the Mote would now be considered a G5 star. The information in *The Mote in God's Eye*[22] (Mote Prime is .93 AU from the Mote) and the picture of the Mote System,[23] with its Alderson points, indicate the points are about 4.7 AU and 7.0 AU from the Mote.

See Table A for a summary of the previous six examples. Based on this information and other published references, we can model the distance Alderson points form in star systems. One observation from this information: the two outliers seem to be non-main sequence stellar objects (the black hole and Murcheson's Eye). We'll come back to them later.

Building The Mote in God's Eye lists several conditions that affect the location of Alderson points. First, you must have zero kinetic energy relative to a complex set of coordinates.[24] It is not clear what this means or what those coordinates are. Therefore, it is not specifically incorporated in the Alderson point model.

The second condition for a Jump is that you need to emerge from the continuum universe with precisely the same potential energy (measured in terms of the fifth force, not gravity) as you entered.[25] The way to think about this is that the intensity of the Alderson force at the point of exit must be the same as the intensity of the Alderson force at the point of entry into hyperspace. Since the Alderson force is produced by thermonuclear reactions (fusion), it is proportional to a star's fusion energy production.

19 *Ibid*, p. 278-279.

20 *Red supergiant star*. March 5, 2017 <https://en.wikipedia.org/wiki/Red_supergiant>.

21 *The Mote in God's Eye*, p. 243.

22 *Ibid.*

23 *The Gripping Hand*, p. viii, ix.

24 *Building The Mote in God's Eye.*

25 *Ibid.*

Fusion energy production is, in turn, proportional to the bolometric luminosity of a star. So, bolometric luminosity (hereafter called luminosity) can be used as a proxy for Alderson force intensity. Note: Alderson points can shift position some due to heavy sunspot activity or during a space battle using thermonuclear weapons.[26]

One of the results of all this is that the luminosity of the star, as seen from the Alderson point you Jump from, needs to be the same as the luminosity of the star you see at the Alderson point you arrive at. In *The Mote in God's Eye,* there is a description of *MacArthur's* arrival in the Mote System: "All systems look this way at breakout: a lot of stars, and one distant sun."[27] The only way this can happen (if the stars are of a different stellar classification) is if your arrival point is further away from, or closer to, the arrival star. As an example, if you Jumped from a G2 type star to a M0 type star, keeping the luminosity (and hence Alderson force) the same intensity means you would have to arrive at the M0 class star much closer to it than you were at in the G2 star system you Jumped from. In fact, your arrival point would be between .7 and 3.3 AU from the M0 star, compared to between 1.5 and 39.5 AU for the G2 star you Jumped from.

Third, sources of gravity influence the positions of Alderson points. The locations of the Alderson points are partially determined by how close to a gravity source they are.[28] [29] The gravitational influence is primarily determined by the mass of the star.

In summary, there are two factors we can use in determining the distance Alderson points can form from their stars; Alderson force intensity (which can be estimated by using a star's luminosity) and gravity (which depends on a star's mass). It seems that the distance Alderson points form from their stars scale proportionally to mass and luminosity. Therefore, based on the luminosity and mass of Sol and the location of the Jump points in Sol System, we can make a simple model predicting the range of distances Alderson points can form near other stars (Note: it is possible a more nuanced model might modify these distances).

26 *The Gripping Hand,* p. 165.
27 *The Mote in God's Eye,* p. 105.
28 *He Fell into a Dark Hole.*
29 *The Gripping Hand,* p. 184.

Alderson Point Model

The model is in the form of a spreadsheet. The model is based on information published in CoDominium/Empire of Man works. This information is what has been used to reverse-engineer elements of Dan Alderson's star drive. The Alderson point distances listed in Table B are the output from the model.

To begin the modeling, every main stellar class from B7 through M6 is listed in the first column on the left side of the spreadsheet. Next, from Internet sources (and in some cases interpolation of that data), the mass of every stellar class is listed in the second column. In the third column, the luminosity for each stellar class is calculated using the following relationship: stellar luminosity scales at the 3.5th power of mass (L ~ M^3.5).[30]

Note: all the masses and calculated luminosities are relative to Sol.

0	1	2	3	4	5
Type	Mass (Sun=1) (Note 1)	Stellar Luminosity Scaling Factor (Note 2)	Calculated Luminosity (bolometric) (Sun=1)	Alderson Point Mass Min. (AU)	Alderson Point Mass Max. (AU)

6	7	8	9	10
Alderson Point Bol. Lum. Min. (AU)	Alderson Point Bol. Lum. Max. (AU)	Maximum of Minimums (AU)	Minimum of Maximums (AU)	Alderson Points Range (AU)

30 *Luminosity*. September 10, 2020 <https://en.wikipedia.org/wiki/Luminosity>.

As mentioned, the distance Alderson points form from their stars scale proportionally to their mass and luminosity. Therefore, in column four, the mass for each type of star is multiplied by the minimum Alderson point distance published for Sol (5 AU). Then in column five, the mass for each type of star is multiplied by the maximum Alderson point distance for Sol (30 AU). In column six, the luminosity for each type of star is multiplied by the minimum Alderson point distance published for Sol (5 AU). In column seven, the luminosity for each type of star is multiplied by the maximum Alderson point distance for Sol (30 AU).

Then, for each type of star, the minimum values of mass and luminosity (columns four and six) are compared for overlap. The larger of the two values[31] is placed in column eight. For each type of star, the maximum values of mass and luminosity (columns five and seven) are compared for overlap. The smaller of the two values[32] is placed in column nine. This process results in a minimum range (column eight) and maximum range (column nine) between which an Alderson point can form for each type of star.

At this point, the model was tested to see if the published Alderson points for other main sequence stars fit within the model output. There was an Alderson point in New Chicago's System at 3.3 AU that did not. The model was adjusted by changing the inner Sol Alderson point distance from 5 AU to 1.5 AU and the outer Sol Alderson point distances from 30.0 AU to 39.5 AU. They are the average orbital distances from Sol to Mars and Pluto, respectively. With this change, all of the published main sequence star Alderson point distances fit within the model's predictions. The model's output (the range of Alderson point distances for each type of star) is summarized in Table B.

One item of note by looking at Table B, some stars with too little luminosity/mass or too much luminosity/mass will not form Alderson points. This is because star luminosity and star mass scale at different rates. Only when both luminosity and mass conditions are satisfied, can an Alderson point form.

31 This rule determines the innermost point where both bolometric luminosity and mass allow for the creation of an Alderson point.

32 This rule determines the outermost point where both bolometric luminosity and mass allow for the creation of an Alderson point.

Where specifically within the range of distances an Alderson point will form is beyond this model. This gives a science fiction author some flexibility, albeit they are still constrained by the other limitations identified in this paper.

As can be seen in Table B, Alderson points can be found .4 to 134.7 AU from stars. The points are always located outside their star's habitable zone. This is an extremely important point. It can take days, weeks or months to cross a solar system from an Alderson point to a habitable planet. The precise amount of time depends on the location of the Alderson point, a spaceship's speed, a spaceship's fuel and planetary geometries.[33] This crossing time gives a planet time to prepare itself for an attack. This in turn allows the possibility of an interstellar political organization like an Empire or a Federation to form. In turn, this leads to the military, social and astropolitical structure found in the CoDominium/Empire of Man stories.

One practical consideration. In general, the M class star Alderson points will be used more often than the points of a higher mass star. Higher mass star Alderson points, on average, are much further apart than low mass star Alderson points. This is where the travel time through interplanetary space enters into consideration. For a B8 star, the furthest Alderson points are three times the distance between Earth and Pluto. To travel between points located on opposite sides of such a star, requires reaching high speeds (i.e. up to 6% of the speed of light) in order to make the trip in a reasonable amount of time (about 7 weeks). But then, you arrive at the next Alderson point without any fuel. Reducing your speed increases the travel time but saves fuel. Naval spaceships have the option to use a lot of fuel. Merchant ships do not. Therefore, merchant ships will tend to use lower mass star Alderson points.

33 *The Gripping Hand*, p. 145.

Number of Alderson Points Allowed

Single star systems can have 0, 1, 2, 3, 4, 5 or 6 Jump points and no more. The reason for this limited number of Alderson points is that interstellar Alderson force interference patterns eliminate most tramlines.[34] A star with no Alderson points cannot be reached by using the Alderson Drive. It can only be reached through normal space (and that can take a long, long time). Interstellar travel through normal space was something the Moties did (i.e., 35 light-years in 190 years from the Mote to New Caledonia implies an average speed of 18.4% of the speed of light). Even the First Empire did not make any successful normal space interstellar voyages (at least no records of any exist). In general, you must be in an Alderson point to make a Jump (see Random Jumps below for the one extremely rare exception).

Multiple star systems (systems with 2 or more stars) may have more than the maximum number of 6 Alderson points. The number of additional Jump points in this case would still be small. An example of this is Sparta System where it is described as having a "score" of Jump points.[35] The star system contains two stars. Each star seems to have 6 Alderson points for a total of 12. In addition, it appears that taken together, the two stars can have another 6 Alderson points for a total system count of 18. It seems the use of the term "score" was poetic and meant to approximate the actual number of points. By the way, this is another reason Sparta is the Capital of the Empire of Man. The large number of Alderson points gives it trade and military advantages.

Alderson Point Size

There is a large variation in the size of an Alderson point. The points appear to be as small as 500 kilometers[36] or as large as the distance from

34 *The Mote in God's Eye,* p. 32.
35 *The Gripping Hand,* p. 60.
36 *Ibid,* p. 396.

the Earth to the moon (about 385,000 kilometers).[37] Given: 1) the surprise that characters in the stories show when the Moties hit a Jump point at 1,000 kilometers per second[38] 2) the surprise shown when the *Fomoria* accelerated at 9 gees and still hit its Jump point[39] and 3) the typical transit speed for a Jump, it is likely the points tend toward the smaller size (i.e., low single digit thousands of kilometers across). Think of Alderson points as roughly cylindrical regions.

Alderson Point Movement

In a single star system, Alderson points are fixed in space. Planets orbit around their star, Alderson points do not. This means that distances between a star and its Alderson points do not change. Distances between Alderson points and habitable planets/gas giant refueling stations change over time but in a repetitive manner (as the planets/stations orbit their star). The distance between Alderson points within a solar system do not change. Having said this, Alderson points can shift position slightly due to heavy sunspot activity or a battle.[40]

There are three corner case exceptions to this. First, if the Alderson point is located directly above or below a star, that is 90 degrees above or below the plane-of-the-ecliptic, there will be little relative distance change (there will be some because planetary orbits are ellipses and not circles). Second, in multiple star systems the Alderson points may shift as one star orbits another. Multiple star systems may have Alderson points that are fixed locations in space or they may have Alderson points that shift some as the stars in the system orbit each other (or they may have some combination of fixed and shifting). They may also have Alderson points that open and close as their host stars orbit each other. Third, if the star has a variable energy output (e.g., newly ignited stars or Cepheid variable stars), the location of the Alderson points can move closer to, or further away

37 *Ibid*, p. 185.

38 *The Mote in God's Eye*, p. 556.

39 *War World: The Battle of Sauron*, p. 290.

40 *The Gripping Hand*, p. 165.

from, the star.[41]

Interplanetary Travel

As mentioned earlier, Jumps between star systems are instantaneous (or as close as can be measured). However, the time it takes to travel within a star system can vary widely depending on the location of the Alderson points within that system. In some cases, it may be faster to Jump to another star, move around that system to another Alderson point and then Jump back to the first star.[42]

In *The Mote in God's Eye,* Second Empire warships could accelerate up to 6% of the speed of light and then decelerate back to zero. This uses all of their fuel. Unless it is an emergency, spaceships would not use all of their fuel in such a manner. No spaceship captain would want to be left with dry tanks unless there was a clear way to refuel.

The *MacArthur* accelerated at 4 gees for 125 hours to reach 6% of the speed of light. If it had had the time, it could have accelerated at, say 1 gee for 500 hours (~21 days), and reached the same speed while still having enough fuel to decelerate back to zero. So, the MacArthur carries enough fuel for 1,000 hours of acceleration at 1 gee. This gives us some idea of how many Jump points *MacArthur* could pass through accelerating/decelerating constantly without refueling.

How long would it take to travel from, let's say, Earth (1 AU from Sol) to an Alderson point located at the distance of Saturn (10 AU from Sol)? Let's assume that the Earth is in an optimal position (the same side of the sun as the Alderson point) and the ship had full tanks. The distance to traverse is 9 AU. Also, to simplify the calculations, let's assume that the beginning velocity and the ending velocity of the spaceship are the same. The travel time, accelerating at 1 gee the entire distance (accelerating ½ of the way, then decelerating ½ the way), would be about 8 ½ days (204 hours). FYI, merchant ships would need to travel at one quarter (¼) gee of continuous acceleration to make this same trip in 17 days (double the time of a warship). However, merchant ships usually accelerate for a period

41 *Ibid,* p. 188.

42 *The Mote in God's Eye*, p. 36, 37.

of time and then coast for long distances before decelerating.[43] Note: this changes the previous calculations. Merchantmen do this to save fuel which in turn improves their profit margins.

Alderson Tramlines are Point-to-Point Connections

"Not every pair of stars is joined by tramlines. Pathways are generated along lines of equipotential thermonuclear flux, and the presence of other stars in the geometric pattern can prevent pathways from existing at all. Of those links that do exist, not all have been mapped. They are difficult to find."[44]

Tramlines are point-to-point connections[45] between the Alderson points of two stars[46] (they are not point-to-multipoint connections). That is, Alderson points are found at each end of a tramline. This means that, a Jump from one Alderson point always takes you to one other star. And it always takes you to the same star. So, if a star system has five Alderson points, a ship can only reach five stars and they are always the same five stars. There is one rare exception to this and that is if a black hole happens to be between the two stars[47] in normal space. In this case, the tramline can shift a bit. Then you end up at the black hole and returning is a problem (see *He Fell into a Dark Hole* for details).

Graphically, a tramline looks like this:[48]

S1) A1———————————T———————————A2 (S2

43 *Ibid*, p. 25.
44 *Ibid*, p. 32.
45 *Building the Mote in God's Eye.*
46 *The Mote in God's Eye,* p. 32.
47 *He Fell into a Dark Hole.*
48 S1 and S2 are two stars, the "—T—" is the tramline between them and the "A1" and "A2" are the Alderson points at each end of the tramline. So, Alderson points are places at the end of a tramline where conditions are just right (assuming you have the correct equipment) to enter and leave the continuum universe (i.e., hyperspace). See the earlier section for determining where these locations are situated in a star system.

In order to Jump to another star system, different from the one you just Jumped from, you have to find, and travel to, another Alderson point in the star system you find yourself. In the case where there is only one Alderson point, you have to leave that system from the same Alderson point you came in through (think of a cul-de-sac). Only when there are two or more Alderson points do you have a choice to go somewhere else.

A network map of Alderson point linked stars can be drawn by knowing three things: 1) the stars that have Alderson points, 2) the number of Alderson points each star has (i.e., one to six) and 3) the point-to-point connections between Alderson points (i.e., the tramlines). Note: a star with zero connections isn't part of the network map at all. This has a number of story implications. A star with only one Alderson point won't be visited unless it has important resources. There is no reason to go there otherwise. A star with two or more Alderson points can be important for what is in the star system, or for what other systems connect to it. And finally, the galaxy could contain more than one network of Alderson tramline linked stars that the Empire won't find until it discovers a way to travel between stars in normal space.

Here's an analogy to describe the Alderson network map. Do you remember Tinkertoys? Alderson connections are like those. Assume the hub (star) has one to six holes (points). You can connect the hubs together using dowels. The dowels are like tramlines (connections are between two stars and only two stars). Some dowels (Jumps) are long and some are short. One difference is that Tinkertoys generally lie in a flat plane, while Jump points can be found anywhere on a sphere surrounding a star as long as they are far enough away from it. And remember, if the Jump points are out of the ecliptic (plane of the planets) it takes more energy to travel to them.

Formation of Alderson Tramlines

In rare cases when an Alderson tramline forms, it does so instantaneously.[49] In the case of one newborn star, the physical location of the

49 *The Gripping Hand*, 165.

Alderson point moved along a half million km arc. The movement was caused by the pulsation of the newly ignited star.[50] In a different case, the orbit of a neutron star around another star brought the neutron star into the outer system of the primary star. Solar wind and meteors rained down onto the neutron star. The resulting fusion created Alderson force, temporarily opening a Jump point.[51]

Tramlines and Alderson Force Flux Densities

"Not all the tramlines are useful, because if flux densities aren't high enough, they won't carry anything big enough to have a drive aboard." [52] Any Alderson points arising at the end of these 'subcritical' tramlines, count toward the maximum of 6 Alderson points per star.

An Additional Jump Consideration

An additional item of note: stars of the M through F type primarily produce energy using PP (proton-to-proton) fusion, while O, B and A stars primarily use the CNO (carbon-nitrogen-oxygen) fusion cycle. I don't know if that makes any difference in the amount of Alderson force produced. I assume not, since that's getting pretty far down into the weeds for a science-fiction framework.

Having said that, as fusion occurs between heavier and heavier elements, less and less energy is produced by the reaction. It might be that less Alderson force is produced too. We don't know. However, we do know that beginning with the element iron (atomic number 26) and extending upward in the Periodic Table, more energy is required to fuse the elements than is produced in the reaction. So, it is possible that the Alderson force is absorbed in the production of elements from iron upwards. But again, this is speculative and we don't have any indication of this from the published literature.

50 *Ibid*, p. 187.

51 *Ibid*, p. 50.

52 *Ibid*, 118.

The Alderson point model indicates that Jumps are limited to using tramlines connecting main sequence B8 through M5 class stars. Stars more massive and hotter than B8 (O0-9 and B0-7) form unusable tramlines. The exception to this is stars off the main sequence, such as the red giant Murcheson's Eye (see the section titled 'Stars off the Main Sequence' for more information). As mentioned earlier, for Alderson points to form at least two conditions must be met. First, the Alderson points must be created at points of equal Alderson force intensity (between the two stars). Second, there is a point of gravitational influence beyond where Alderson points form.

As an example, take an O6 class star and a G2 star. The O6 star has 40 times the mass of the G2 star but its luminosity is 400,000 times as much. Therefore, on just the luminosity equivalence alone, an Alderson point would need to form very, very close to the G2 star (at 1/100,000 of an AU). However, the gravity of the smaller G2 star would not allow an Alderson point to form closer than 1.5 AU from it. Therefore, no useable Alderson points would form.

Even if useable Alderson points could form around massive stars, they would form at such a long distance from their primary as to make travel to the other Alderson points in the system a very, very long slog. As an example, B7 stars form their Alderson points between 109.8 AU and 134.7 AU from the star. That makes treks between points time consuming and uses a lot of fuel.

Small stars have their own problems in forming useable Alderson points. M6 through M8 class stars (the smallest star that can maintain a fusion reaction) do not have any overlap between the Alderson force equivalence regions and the gravitational force regions. So, no useable Jump points will form for them either (see Table B).

Length of Jumps

Jumps can be short (1/3 of a light-year[53]) or long (at least 35 light-years[54]) or anywhere in between. It is likely that Jumps can exceed both of

53 *Building The Mote in God's Eye.*
54 *Ibid.*

these published limits. However, the lengths of Jumps are limited.[55] There is one reference that states in 2032 a roughly 60 light-year distance could be covered in two Jumps.[56] So, let's assume a maximum Jump length found of say, 42 light-years during the CoDominium period and longer ones of say, 53 light-years found by the time of the Second Empire period. It's a reasonable WAG, since four times the volume of space has been explored[57] by the time of the Second Empire and, as a result, longer Jumps are likely to have been discovered. In general, longer Jumps are rare because there is more opportunity for interstellar Alderson interference effects to disrupt them. Although, it is not clear what limits the length of Alderson tramlines other than interstellar interference patterns. It seems reasonable that Alderson force intensity might limit the length of tramlines. This is supported by, as previously mentioned, that subcritical tramlines can have flux densities too low to carry anything with a Drive. I think most tramlines tend to the shorter length of between 5 and 20 light-years.

Note: there is one reference[58] to a Jump from New Washington (over 300 hundred light-years from Earth) to New Chicago (over 600 light-years from Earth). This would imply a Jump of at least 300 light-years and maybe a lot longer, depending on the astronomical location of the two systems. However, this website[59] and I agree that the sentence should have been written "before the final series of Jumps," since no other reference to such a long Jump exists.

---

55 *Ibid.*

56 *War World I: The Burning Eye*, p. 2.

57 At the end of the CoDominium period humans had explored a distance of 100 parsecs from Earth (per *Falkenberg's Legion*, p. 432). The volume of a sphere centered on the Earth would be 4,190,000 cubic parsecs. *The Mote in God's Eye* Prologue states that the Second Empire of Man rules over 15,000,000 cubic parsecs. And the Empire of Man does not include the Outies. So, the volume of explored space in the Second Empire is at least 4 times the volume of that explored during the CoDominium period.

58 In *The Gripping Hand*, p. 366. New Washington is 100 parsecs (326 light-years) from Earth. The Coalsack Nebula is 600 light-years from Earth (January 15, 2017 <https://www.google.com/#q=coalsack>). New Chicago is beyond the Coalsack, let's say 20 light-years. Therefore, best case a direct Jump from New Washington to New Chicago would be about 300 light-years and depending on New Washington's location it could be much further.

59 *Jerry Pournelle's Future History*. March 5, 2017 <http://www.chronology.org/pournelle/>.

On the other hand, Niven and Pournelle may have needed this long Jump to describe how a system like New Chicago (> 600 light-years from Earth) could have been settled when it was.[60] Having said this, if a Jump of 300+ light-years were possible, then systems with such long Jump tramlines would be very valuable. They would be a nexus of interstellar trade/communication, making them extremely rich. This in turn would be another reason why the New Washington/Franklin System is so valuable to the Empire. It's at one end of a tramline that takes travelers to a new region of space without having to make many Jumps.

Average Number of Jumps between Stars with Habitable Planets

To get from one star system with an inhabited planet to another one in most cases takes multiple Jumps (i.e., a series of Jumps). Possibly a lot of them.

By the end of the CoDominium period, the closest any two stars with inhabited planets are, on average, over 100 light-years apart (given the most distant colonized system New Washington/Franklin is 100 parsecs from Earth and humans have colonized 200 planets). Therefore, if most Jumps are 5 and 20 light-years in length, multiple Jumps are necessary to travel from one inhabited planet to another.

As mentioned previously, there is a tradeoff between making a lot of little Jumps between low mass stars and one Jump to a bigger star. Also as mentioned, M class stars make up 80% of the stars in the galaxy. For the most part, habitable planets form around stellar class F, G and K stars. Not all of them will have habitable planets. This means that, to reach systems with habitable planets, travel will require a series of Jumps through M type star systems.

60 *The Gripping Hand*, p. 138.

Alderson Point Transit Speed

How fast can a spaceship be traveling and make a Jump? From the literature, it appears that some ships slow almost to a stop to Jump. Motie ships however have hit an Alderson point at high speed (1,000 km/sec [.33% of the speed of light]). Sauron ships have hit them at huge accelerations (9 gees for the *Fomoria* escaping from Sauron System). So, it would seem that the speed or acceleration is less important than how well the Alderson point's position is known (their position can shift slightly depending on certain circumstances and confirming their position is difficult), how large Alderson points are (which we don't know because they vary but ships have ended up between 500 km and 385,000 km apart), how long the Alderson generators can remain on before burning out (less than a minute during the time of the CoDominium[61] but probably longer during the Empire of Man periods) and how precisely a Jump can be initiated which is determined by the quality of the mechanical Jump initiators (Note: the mechanical initiator's pedigree reaches back to the fine Swiss mechanical watches of the twentieth century).

Early in the CoDominium period (just after the Alderson Drive was perfected), detecting and defining Alderson points in space was probably less well understood than it was in the First and Second Empire periods. Stories should have merchant spaceships (in any period) decelerating to low velocities (assumed to be 50 km/sec – 1/4 of what a warship typically does) to Jump (Note: this uses more fuel than if the velocity built up getting to the Alderson point could be retained). Warships can Jump at higher speeds (300 km/sec[62]) but usually Jump at slower velocities, say 200 km/sec, to ensure they hit the Alderson point and Jump. Missing a Jump burns a lot of fuel to come around and try it again – important for both a merchantman and a warship. Navy spaceship equipment is more capable than merchantman equipment and would explain the difference in approach speeds.

---

61 *He Fell into a Dark Hole.*

62 *The Gripping Hand,* p. 396.

Physical Closeness of Stars versus Alderson Jump Closeness

Just because stars are close in physical space, doesn't mean that they are close in Alderson point travel time. For instance, Sparta and New Washington are 20 light-years apart physically.[63] However, it takes 9 months to travel between them.[64] Another reference states that the travel time between them is 5 months,[65] but this is probably for a military courier which can travel twice as fast as merchant ships.[66] In the time of the CoDominium there does seem to be a faster route between Sparta and New Washington but how much faster is unknown.[67] Only that it is through unsettled systems with no refueling stations. This quicker route should be well established by the early part of the First Empire.

Sector Definition

Given that Alderson point travel time between star systems is more important than the physical proximity of stars, sectors are defined by Alderson point connectivity. In the CoDominium period, sectors include Crucis, Pleiades and Tanith. In the Second Empire of Man period, there is also a Trans-Coalsack sector. In both periods, there are likely more sectors.

Many Stars Will Never be Visited

"The Drive's limits mean that uninteresting stellar systems won't be explored. There are too many of them. They may be used as crossing-points if the stars are conveniently placed, but stars not along a travel route may never be visited."[68]

---

63 *Go Tell the Spartans*, p. 249.
64 *Prince of Sparta,* p. 166.
65 *Go Tell the Spartans*, p. 95.
66 *Prince of Sparta,* p. 166.
67 *Ibid*, p. 151.
68 *Building the Mote in God's Eye.*

One website states there are about 260,000 stars within 250 light-years of Earth.[69] Using the equation for the volume of a sphere, and assuming the same density of stars, gives us about 450,000 stars within 300 light-years of Earth (the maximum extent of colonization at the time of the CoDominium). That increases to about 2,080,000 stars within a 500 light-year sphere (about the size of the Second Empire in 3029). There are about 200 colonized planets at the end of the CoDominium period. So, 200 colonized planets out of 450,000 stars. If one assumes it takes on average 10 Jumps between nearby habitable planets, you can get a feel for why Pournelle made the observation he did.

As previously mentioned, 80% of the stars in the galaxy are M class red dwarfs. In general, they will not be of interest for human colonization. There are exceptions, though (see New Washington and Franklin). But the M class stars will be used as 'stepping stones' between one colonized system and another.

Random Jumps

There exists some form of Jump outside what has been described above. There is no definition and it is unknown what the exact mechanics of it are. In any case, it is extremely rare and dangerous. It is estimated that the chances of a ship surviving a *Random Jump* in spaceworthy condition are less than 12%. It is also estimated that the ship would have less than a .004% chance of surviving in a condition for further interstellar flight.[70] The Moties knew about the Alderson Drive. However, the local astrography prevented them from using it to escape their system. The Moties' only tramline in 3017 ended within Murcheson's Eye, a red supergiant star with a radius of 10+ AU. And the Moties didn't have the Langston Field to protect them from the star's photosphere. Whatever the mechanics of a Random Jump are, they cannot be such that the Moties could have used it to escape from their solar system over the one million years they have existed as an intelligent species.

69 *The Universe within 250 Light-years, The Solar Neighborhood.* March 5, 2017 <http://www.atlasoftheuniverse.com/250lys.html>.

70 *War World I: The Burning Eye,* p. 144.

It's possible that astronomical events are related to Random Jumps. Astronomers estimate that there is one supernova in our galaxy per century on average. A supernova should produce massive amounts of the Alderson force (100 billion times that of a normal star) and disrupt Alderson tramlines throughout the galaxy for a short period of time. This could be a source of the Random Jump. That is, temporary Jump points might form for minutes if a supernova were to occur somewhere in the galaxy. However, it's likely that all normal tramlines would be affected in some way too (probably scrambled). A nova might produce similar effects but not to the same extent as a supernova, since they are less energetic. The distance of the Alderson points from the astronomical event in question and the amount of Alderson force released by the event are the two factors that would determine the extent of any disruption.

The same argument goes for the black hole at the center of our galaxy. Periodically it should "eat" a stellar mass. Based on the earlier discussion, this must produce massive amounts of Alderson force and, similar to the supernova, simultaneously disrupt all the Alderson tramlines in the galaxy.

The occurrence of these astronomical events couldn't be predicted and would be random. And if the occurrence couldn't be predicted, neither would the location of the resulting Alderson points. However, in all three of these cases (supernova, nova and a black hole), a ship would not be damaged by the Jump any more than it would be by a normal Alderson Jump. Note: in *He Fell into a Dark Hole,* the damage to the spaceships was caused by gravity waves from the black hole, not the Jump into the black hole system. So, this mechanism wouldn't explain the Random Jump that the *Fomoria* made to escape Sauron System unless you postulated that the position of the Alderson point was moving rapidly because of the change in intensity of the astronomical event (and subsequent Alderson forces) which caused the spaceship to enter (and/or exit) hyperspace in a way that caused significant damage. Or, it is possible that a Random Jump affects the machinery that holds the continuum universe constructs together and this causes the spaceship damage.

Another possibility is that, as mentioned, "Not all the tramlines are useful because, if the flux densities aren't high enough, they won't carry anything big enough to have a drive aboard."[71] It might be possible for there to be quantum fluctuations in the intensity of tramlines. If that were to happen in one of these subcritical tramlines, it might be able to periodically carry a spaceship. Quantum fluctuations would be random. However, there is nothing mentioned in the published literature to support this. In addition, such subcritical tramlines would connect to specific solar systems. It would be easy to track a ship that made such a Random Jump. And we know from the War World stories that the *Fomoria* wasn't tracked when she made her Random Jump.

Lastly, why wouldn't this work in the Mote System? It may be that, as Renner suggests, the Alderson force from Murcheson's Eye overwhelms all but the one tramline from the Mote to the Eye.[72]

Jump Shock

Making a Jump has a disruptive impact on human and Motie nervous systems as well as on computers. This is called Jump Shock (aka Jump Lag) and is very uncomfortable (i.e., nausea, weakness, disorientation, etc.). Some people also come out of a Jump with the feeling of once having known everything there is to know about the universe but not being able to remember it.[73] Jumps affect computers, too, which is why all computers are shut down for Jumps (or else they go haywire). Only simple mechanical devices are utilized. The effects of Jump Shock on humans usually last between 5 and 20 minutes. However, they can last longer and in some rare cases they can drive people insane. Effects can be cumulative (i.e., the more Jumps you experience the more severe the effects can be). The effects on Moties are more severe and take longer to wear off.

71 *The Gripping Hand,* p. 118.
72 *Ibid,* p. 118.
73 *War World I: The Burning Eye,* p. 4.

Alderson Drive Development History

The Alderson Drive was perfected at CalTech in 2004 by a team of scientists lead by Dan Alderson. After that, its use for interstellar travel proceeded quickly. The first experimental spaceship using the Drive left the Sol System in 2008. The first extrasolar habitable planets were discovered in 2010. The first extrasolar colonies were established in 2020.

Alderson Engines

As with all technology, as engineers learn more, they are able to make improvements over time. The Alderson Drive engines are big and complex.[74] By the Second Empire of Man, the engines must be foolproof and highly automated since it doesn't take many people, and in some cases no specific person, to maintain or fix them.[75] [76] This makes sense since the Alderson Drive has been known for a thousand years. Even though there was a period of time similar to the Dark Ages between the First and Second Empire, because of its importance, the Alderson Drive technology was thoroughly archived by the Imperial Library on Sparta and elsewhere. So, no knowledge about it was lost.

Alderson Drive engines must accomplish four functions simultaneously.[77] First, they must transport a spaceship into the continuum universe (aka hyperspace). Second, they must create correspondence particles of the ship and everything in it (a construct). Third, they must hold these correspondence particles together to prevent the construct from being disorganized into elementary particles. At that point, the Alderson force,

---

74 *Building The Mote in God's Eye.*

75 *The Gripping Hand,* p. 178-179. The people on the spaceship were Kevin Renner (Commodore), Jacob Buckman (Astrophysicist), Horace Bury (Imperial Trader), Cynthia Anwar (Bury's body guard/doctor), two other women (unidentified but they could be ship's engineering personnel), Joyce Trujillo (Reporter), Nabil Khadurri (Bury's Valet and Personal Secretary) and Kevin (Chris) Blaine (Lieutenant). After at least 1,000 years of refinement it's not unreasonable for the designs to be well understood, highly automated and foolproof.

76 *The Gripping Hand,* p. 174.

77 *Building The Mote in God's Eye.*

from the star you are Jumping from, accelerates the construct to near infinite speeds in hyperspace. Dropping out of hyperspace occurs naturally when the ship's construct reaches a strong gravitational field at the end of a tramline.[78] At this point, the engine completes its fourth function. It converts the construct back into a real ship. All this happens in no measurable time.[79]

If you fire up the Alderson engines and you are not in an Alderson point, the engines get you into hyperspace but you immediately drop back out exactly where you were since there is no equipotential Alderson force to accelerate you.[80] Energy disappears but the process is not one hundred percent efficient and the engines begin to overload. During the CoDominium period, Jump engines can remain on for less than a minute in normal space before burning out.[81] The engines are designed to cut out after a Jump.

The energy required to make a Jump is much less than the energy required to travel through interplanetary space. As an example, it takes much more energy to travel from the New Caledonia Alderson point to New Scotland (roughly the distance from Saturn to Earth) than it does to make a Jump.[82] Still, the Jump engines use a significant amount of energy.

The engines must be mechanically initiated due to Jump Shock, which affects computers as well as people.[83] [84]

Alderson Drive engines can be put on spaceships as small as a racing yacht.[85] Longboats carry both the Field and the Drive.[86] Cutters designed for a crew of six carry neither Field nor Drive.[87] This seems to be the dividing line for the size of a spaceship that can carry them. The Moties sent simple frames with Alderson Drives attached to Murcheson's Eye to test whether the Alderson point had moved. We don't know how large these test

78 *He Fell into a Dark Hole.*
79 *Building The Mote in God's Eye.*
80 *Ibid.*
81 *He Fell into a Dark Hole.*
82 *The Mote in God's Eye*, p. 36.
83 *War World I: The Burning Eye,* p. 4.
84 *The Mote in God's Eye*, p. 34.
85 *The Gripping Hand,* p. 232.
86 *Ibid,* p. 233.
87 *The Mote in God's Eye*, p. 151.

vehicles were. All the description says is that they were a ship's frame with two tanks, a fusion engine and an Alderson Drive on it. [88] Given that Moties are masters of minimizing resources used, it's likely these are the smallest ship's possible that are capable of carrying a Drive and making a Jump.

Removing the Alderson Drive engines from a capital ship leaves room for significantly more weapons and fuel.[89] So the engines take up a large amount of space relative to the size of the ship they are installed on. Large, complex machinery is expensive. This also implies that they are designed as modules for removal, maintenance and re-installation.

Hyperspace Wake

Hyperspace wakes are created by Jumps.[90] When a construct enters the continuum universe, it is accelerated to almost infinite speeds. Therefore, it has acquired kinetic energy. This kinetic energy refers to Alderson force (fifth force) kinetic energy. The construct needs to lose this kinetic energy before it can drop out of hyperspace. During a Jump, a spaceship continually loses this kinetic energy, which shows up instantaneously across the entire tramline in normal space as photons (electromagnetic radiation). This is the wake. This energy wake can be detected and reveal not only that a ship has materialized in a Jump point but its mass; and therefore, its probable class. This is possible even if its Langston Field is engaged and it is not under acceleration (i.e., stealthed). Note this means that the Alderson force can be converted into electromagnetic radiation (important for a unified field theory).

Langston Field and Jumps

Jumps can be made with the Langston Field engaged or not. Note: the Langston Field is discovered at the end of the CoDominium period in 2092 and is found in use only after that time (i.e., in the First and

88 *The Gripping Hand*, p. 163.
89 *The Mote in God's Eye*, p. 556.
90 *Building The Mote in God's Eye.*

Second Empire periods). Its first use operationally was in 2109 protecting the Aegis station in orbit around Sparta.

There is No Faster-Than-Light (FTL) Radio

As Pournelle has said, "there's…no radio: the fastest message between star systems is one carried by a ship, but within star systems messages go much faster than the ships..."[91] So, courier ships carry messages between stars by making a Jump, then sending the message across the solar system by message laser/maser to the next ship/planet/station.

A repeater system can be established whereby a message is transmitted to a courier ship at a Jump point, the ship then Jumps with the message. The ship then transmits the message (by laser/maser) to another courier ship at the next Jump point in that star system. That ship then Jumps. This keeps happening until the message reaches its final destination. It will take time, probably days in the best case. So, there is no instantaneous two-way FTL communication in the CoDominium/Empire of Man universe.

Having said this, I'm not sure it is consistent. It has to do with 1) the assumptions that all science in our world is valid in the CoDominium/Empire of Man universe and 2) the Langston Field acts like an electromagnetic black hole.

A recent physics article suggests that two black holes could be entangled forming a wormhole connection between the two.[92] If the Langston Field is an electromagnetic black hole, two of them should be able to be entangled (in the quantum mechanical sense) forming a wormhole between them in an analogous manner. A specially crafted photonic quantum bit (aka qubit carrying information) then could be absorbed by one Field and radiated by the other, thereby transferring information. If the entangled Langston Fields are separated via a spaceship making an Alderson Jump, FTL communication would become possible.

---

91 *Ibid.*

92 Wormholes Reveal a Way to Manipulate Black Hole Information in the Lab. February 29, 2020 < https://www.quantamagazine.org/wormholes-reveal-a-way-to-manipulate-black-hole-information-in-the-lab-20200227/>.

It gets weirder. Another science article suggests that two entangled black holes can form a type of time machine.[93] This isn't new to science or science fiction; Stephen Baxter has used this idea in his Xeelee series as have other science fiction authors. Basically, you take one end of an entangled wormhole and either speed it up to a fraction of the speed of light or drop it into orbit around a neutron star/black hole. In either case (speeding one end up or dropping one end into an intense gravity well), time is slowed down for one end of the wormhole but not the other. When recovered, the two wormhole openings can be used to communicate backward and forward through time. Two caveats: First, the temporal difference between the two wormhole openings is fixed. Second, with Langston Fields, only electromagnetic energy is transferred. There is no physical or material transfer possible.

While I've used these ideas in stories, I have also limited their effectiveness. I have assumed that decoherence rapidly makes the communication channels unusable (they quickly fill with noise). Given what entangled wormholes would cost to create and deploy, and their limited lives, they wouldn't be practical for widespread use.

Stars off the Main Sequence

For stars that are off the main sequence, the rules may be different. Alderson point distance does not necessarily scale with luminosity. This can be seen in *The Mote in God's Eye*, where the Alderson points in the red supergiant star Murcheson's Eye are about 9.5 and 10.5 AU from the center of the star, and one Alderson point is within the star's photosphere. We know much more about red supergiant stars today than we did back when *The Mote in God's Eye* was written. This may account for the differences—for instance, Murcheson's Eye is projected to go supernova and

---

93 How to Time Travel with Wormholes. June 10, 2020 <https://www.businessinsider.com/how-to-time-travel-with-wormholes-2017-11?utm_source=facebook.com&utm_medium=social&utm_campaign=sf-bi-science>._

94 *The Mote in God's Eye*, p. 278, 279.

collapse into a black hole in 2,774,020 *A.D.*[94] Only red supergiants that are between 10 and 30 solar masses will do that.[95]

The enlarged surface area of the star means that the luminosity of a red supergiant star is many times what it would be for a main sequence star of the same mass. The core is burning helium or higher fusion reactions and it's not clear how much Alderson force is being created. But the take-away is that Alderson force is being produced. Also, the mass of the star is spread out through a larger volume of space. I'm not sure if I can recreate the specific logic for the location of the Alderson points in the Murcheson's Eye System but Niven and Pournelle put them where they are. This implies my reverse engineering of the Alderson Drive mechanics are not complete or else the astronomical data has changed since the early 1970s and we know some of the astronomical data has changed.

What Jerry Pournelle Wrote – from *Building The Mote in God's Eye*[96]

"The Alderson Drive is consistent with everything now known about physics. It merely assumes that additional discoveries will be made in about thirty years, at Caltech (as a tip o' the hat to Dan Alderson). The key event is the detection of a "fifth force."

"There are four known forces in modem physics: two sub-nuclear forces responsible respectively for alpha and beta decay; electromagnetism, which includes light; and gravity. The Alderson force, then, is the fifth, and it is generated by thermonuclear reactions.

"The force has little effect in our universe; in fact, it is barely detectable. Simultaneously with the discovery of the fifth force, however, we postulate the discovery of a second universe in point-to-point congruence with our own. The 'continuum universe' differs from the one we're used to in that there are no known quantum effects there.

---

95 *Red supergiant star*. March 5, 2017 <https://en.wikipedia.org/wiki/Red_supergiant>.

96 *Building The Mote in God's Eye.*

"Within that universe particles may travel as fast as they can be accelerated; and the fifth force exists to accelerate them."

There's a lot more, including a page or so of differential equations, but that's the general idea.

"You can get from one universe to another. For every construct in our universe there can be created a 'correspondence particle' in the continuum universe. In order for your construct to go into and emerge from the continuum universe without change you must have some complex machinery to hold everything together and prevent your ship—and crew—from being disorganized into elementary particles.

"Correspondence particles can be boosted to speeds faster than light: in fact, to speeds nearly infinite as we measure them. Of course they cannot emerge into our universe at such speeds: they have to lose their energy to emerge at all. More on that in a moment.

"There are severe conditions to entering and leaving the continuum universe. To emerge from the continuum universe you must exit with precisely the same potential energy (measured in terms of the fifth force, not gravity) as you entered. You must also have zero kinetic energy relative to a complex set of coordinates that we won't discuss here.

"The fifth force is created by thermonuclear reactions: generally, that is, in stars. You may travel by using it, but only along precisely defined lines of equipotential flux: tramways or tramlines.

"Imagine the universe as a thin rubber sheet, very flat. Now drop heavy rocks of different weights onto it. The rocks will distort the sheet, making little cone-shaped (more or less) dimples. Now put two rocks reasonably close together: the dimples will intersect in a valley. The intersection will have a "pass," a region higher than the low points where the rocks (stars) lie, but lower than the general level of the rubber sheet.

"The route from one star to another through that "pass" is the tramline. Possible tramlines lie between each two stars, but they don't always exist, because when you add third and fourth stars to the system they may interfere, so there is no unique gradient line. If this seems confusing, don't spend a lot of time worrying about it; we'll get to the effects of all this in a moment.

"You may also imagine stars to be like hills; move another star close and the hills will intersect. Again, from summit to summit there will be one and only one line that preserves the maximum potential energy for that level. Release a marble on one hill and it will roll down, across the saddle, and up the side of the other. That too is a tramline effect. It's generally easier to think of the system as valleys rather than hills, because to travel from star to star you have to get over that "hump" between the two. The fifth force provides the energy for that.

"You enter from the quantum universe. When you travel in the continuum universe you continually lose kinetic energy; it "leaks." This can be detected in our universe as photons. The effect can be important during a space battle. We cut such a space battle from The Mote in God's Eye, but it still exists, and we may yet publish it as a novella *(See the short story Reflex)*.

"To get from the quantum to the continuum universe you must supply power, and this is available only in quantum terms. When you do this you turn yourself into a correspondence particle; go across the tramline; and come out at the point on the other side where your potential energy is equal to what you entered with, plus zero kinetic energy (in terms of the fifth force and complex reference axes).

"For those bored by the last few paragraphs, take heart: we'll leave the technical details and get on with what it all means.

"Travel by Alderson Drive consists of getting to the proper Alderson Point and turning on the Drive. Energy is used. You vanish, to reappear in an immeasurably short time at the Alderson Point in another star system some several light-years away. If you haven't done everything right, or aren't at the Alderson Point, you turn on your Drive and a lot of energy vanishes. You don't move. (In fact you do move, but you instantaneously reappear in the spot where you started.)

"That's all there is to the Drive, but it dictates the structure of an interstellar civilization.

"To begin with, the Drive works only from point to point across interstellar distances. Once in a star system you must rely on reaction drives to get around. There's no magic way from, say, Saturn to Earth: you've got to slog across.

"Thus space battles are possible, and you can't escape battle by vanishing into hyperspace, as you could in future history series such as Beam Piper's and Gordon Dickson's. To reach a given planet you must travel across its stellar system, and you must enter that system at one of the Alderson Points. There won't be more than five or six possible points of entry, and there may only be one.

"Star systems and planets can be thought of as continents and islands, then, and Alderson Points as narrow sea gates such as Suez, Gibraltar, Panama, Malay Straits, etc. To carry the analogy further, there's telegraph but no radio: the fastest message between star systems is one carried by a ship, but within star systems messages go much faster than the ships....

"Hmm. This sounds a bit like the early days of steam. NOT sail; the ships require fuel and sophisticated repair facilities. They won't pull into some deserted star system and rebuild themselves unless they've carried the spare parts along. However, if you think of naval actions in the period between the Crimean War and World War One, you'll have a fair picture of conditions as implied by the Alderson Drive.

"The Drive's limits mean that uninteresting stellar systems won't be explored. There are too many of them. They may be used as crossing-points if the stars are conveniently placed, but stars not along a travel route may never be visited.

"Reaching the Mote, or leaving it, would be damned inconvenient. Its only tramline reaches to a star only a third of a light-year away—Murcheson's Eye, the red super giant—and ends deep inside the red-hot outer envelope. The aliens' only access to the Empire is across thirty-five light-years of interstellar space—which no Empire ship would ever see. The gaps between the stars are as mysterious to the Empire as they are to you. . . .

"If the Drive allowed ships to sneak up on planets, materializing without warning out of hyperspace, there could be no Empire even with the Field. There'd be no Empire because belonging to an Empire wouldn't protect you. Instead there might be populations of planet-bound serfs ruled at random by successive hordes of space pirates. Upward mobility in society would consist of getting your own ship and turning pirate."

Table A

What Has Been Written About Specific Systems' Alderson Points

(New Caledonia[97], Beta Hortensis [98])

Star Classification/Description	Mass (Sun=1.0)	Bolometric Luminosity (Sun=1.0)	Alderson Point Distances (AU)
Off Main Sequence Objects:			
Black Holes	5 - 30	Depends on Mass Falling Into It	1.0
Red Supergiant - Murcheson's Eye	10-40	10,000 - 500,000	9.0 - 10.0
Main Sequence Stars:			
F8V - New Caledonia	1.15	1.72	10.0
F9V - Beta Hortensis	1.10	1.45	3.3
G2V - Sol	1.00	1.00	5.0 - 30.0
G5V - Mote	0.91	0.78	4.7 - 7.0

Note: The luminosities of New Caledonia and Beta Hortensis were calculated from *Luminosity* March 5, 2017 <https://en.wikipedia.org/wiki/Luminosity>.

Table B
Alderson Point Distances (in AU) from Main Sequence Stars

Note: 1 AU = the distance from the Earth to the sun is about 93,000,000 miles or 150,000,000 km.

Type of Star	Mass (Sun = 1.0)	Calculated Luminosity (bolometric) (Sun=1.0)	Alderson Points Range (AU)
B7V	4.1	139.55	0
B8V	3.41	73.22	109.8 – 134.7
B9V	2.91	42.04	63.1 – 114.9
A0V	2.48	24.02	36.0 – 98.0
A1V	2.35	19.89	29.8 – 92.8
A2V	2.25	17.09	25.6 – 88.9
A3V	2.13	14.10	21.2 – 84.1
A4V	2.03	11.92	17.9 – 80.2
A5V	1.98	10.92	16.4 – 78.2
A6V	1.91	9.63	14.4 – 75.4
A7V	1.86	8.78	13.2 – 73.5
A8V	1.76	7.23	10.8 – 69.5
A9V	1.67	6.02	9.0 – 66.0
F0V	1.59	5.07	7.6 - 62.8
F1V	1.54	4.53	6.8 – 60.8
F2V	1.46	3.76	5.6 – 57.7
F3V	1.39	3.17	4.7 – 54.9
F4V	1.36	2.93	4.4 – 53.7
F5V	1.33	2.71	4.1 – 52.5
F6V	1.22	2.01	3.0 – 48.2
F7V	1.12	1.49	2.2 – 44.2
F8V	1.10	1.40	2.1 – 43.5
F9V	1.07	1.27	1.9 – 42.3
G0V	1.05	1.19	1.8 – 41.5
G1V	1.03	1.11	1.7 – 40.7
G2V	1.00	1.00	1.5 – 39.5
G3V	.97	.90	1.5 – 35.5
G4V	.93	.78	1.4 – 30.6
G5V	.91	.72	1.4 – 28.4
G6V	.87	.61	1.3 – 24.3
G7V	.84	.54	1.3 – 21.5
G8V	.82	.50	1.2 – 19.7
G9V	.81	.48	1.2 – 18.9
K0V	.76	.38	1.1 – 15.1
K1V	.72	.32	1.1 – 12.5
K2V	.70	.29	1.1 – 11.3
K3V	.67	.25	1.6 – 9.7
K4V	.61	.18	.9 – 7.0
K5V	.58	.15	.9 – 5.9
K6V	.55	.12	.8 – 4.9
K7V	.53	.11	.8 – 4.3
K8V	.51	.09	.8 – 3.7
K9V	.50	.09	.8 – 3.5
M0V	.49	.08	.7 – 3.3
M1V	.44	.06	.7 – 2.2
M2V	.38	.03	.6 – 1.3
M3V	.36	.03	.5 – 1.1
M4V	.34	.02	.5 - .9
M5V	.28	.01	.4 - .5
M6V	.22	.00	0

Note: 1 AU = the distance from the Earth to the sun is about 93,000,000 miles or 150,000,000 km.

Bibliography

Ball, Phillip. Wormholes Reveal a Way to Manipulate Black Hole Information in the Lab, *Quanta Magazine*. February 27, 2020. < https://www.quantamagazine.org/wormholes-reveal-a-way-to-manipulate-black-hole-information-in-the-lab-20200227/>.

Carr, John F. and Don Hawthorne. *War World: The Battle of Sauron.* Pequod Press, 2007.

Coalsack Nebula. January 15, 2017 <https://www.google.com/#q=coalsack>.

Green, Brian. *How to Time Travel with Wormholes. Business Insider.* June 10, 2020. <https://www.businessinsider.com/how-to-time-travel-with-wormholes-2017-11?utm_source=facebook.com&utm_medium=social&utm_campaign=sf-bi-science>.

Jerry Pournelle's Future History. March 5, 2017 <http://www.chronology.org/pournelle/>.

Luminosity. September 10, 2020 <https://en.wikipedia.org/wiki/Luminosity>.

Niven, Larry and Jerry Pournelle. *Building The Mote in God's Eye. Galaxy*, January 1976.

Niven, Larry and Jerry Pournelle. *The Gripping Hand.* Pocket Books, paperback edition, First printing January 1994.

Niven, Larry and Jerry Pournelle. *The Mote in God's Eye.* Pocket Books, paperback edition, First printing October 1974.

Pournelle, J.E. and John F. Carr. *There Will Be War.* Tom Doherty Associates, Inc., January 1983, *Reflex.*

Pournelle, Jerry. *Falkenberg's Legion.* Baen Publishing Enterprises, First printing October 1990.

Pournelle, Jerry. *He Fell into a Dark Hole. Analog*, March 1973.

Pournelle, Jerry. *Prince of Mercenaries.* Baen Books, First printing March 1989.

Pournelle, Jerry. *War World I: The Burning Eye.* Baen Books, First printing July 1988.

Pournelle, Jerry & S.M. Stirling. *Go Tell the Spartans.* Baen Books, First printing June 1991.

Pournelle, Jerry & S.M. Stirling. *Prince of Sparta.* Baen Books, First printing March 1993.

Red supergiant star. March 5, 2017 <https://en.wikipedia.org/wiki/Red_supergiant>.

Stellar black hole. March 5 2017 <https://en.wikipedia.org/wiki/Stellar_black_hole>.

Stellar Mass. September 10, 2020 <https://sites.uni.edu/morgans/astro/course/Notes/section2/spectralmasses.html>.

The Universe within 250 Light-years, The Solar Neighborhood. March 5, 2017 <http://www.atlasoftheuniverse.com/250lys.html>.

www.ingramcontent.com/pod-product-compliance
Lightning Source LLC
Chambersburg PA
CBHW060556310726
48982CB00008B/1147/J

* 9 7 8 0 9 3 7 9 1 2 7 7 5 *